# FORBIDDEN LOVE WITH A THUG

## SHVONNE LATRICE

# About the Author

**Other Works by Me:**

Good Girls Love Thugs 1-5
Falling for a Hood King 1-4
Married to a Distinguished Thug 1-3
She's Gotta Have It 1-2
Me & My Dope Boy 1-3
Yazir & Nina 1-3
Forbidden Love with a Thug 1-3
You Needed Me 1-3
Shorty is in Love with a Real One 1-4
I Got Your Back 1-2
My Baby Is a West Coast King 1-4
Our Love Is the Realest 1-3
She Got It Bad for a Heartless Gangsta 1-4
She Got It Bad for a Heartless Gangsta: An AK Christmas
Hood Boyz Fall In Love Too 1-3
Nobody Can Love You Like Them Roughnecks Do 1-4
She Gave Her All to the Hood's Finest 1-5

**Visit TheShvonneLatrice.com for paperbacks!**

$15.99
ISBN 978-1-966375-11-1

ONE

## Jersey Warren

---

*Shake that ass like ya tryna go viral. Move ya body like ya tryna go viral. Whine for me like ya tryna go viral. Viral, viral, viral, viral.*

"Viral" by Eric Bellinger blasted over the club as I wound my hips in the lap of one of my customers. This was gonna be the last dance of the night, because my body was tired and I had to be up early in the morning for class. Not only did I want to study for a couple upcoming exams I had, but it also wasn't safe to be out late as hell in Wilmington, Delaware.

Currently, I'm in the spring semester of my freshman year at Wilmington University. I'm majoring in business, and minoring in art, to hopefully get a job as a corporate art buyer. That was my dream job because I really loved art, but I was no painter or anything.

As of right now, things were rough as hell for me. Most nights I stripped at this club named Starzz, just to wake up and have to get ready for classes that lasted until 5:30 in the evening. This shit was wearing me out, but I knew summer wasn't too far away, and I would be able to have a little break from school. I couldn't wait though, because this summer I was gonna stack my fucking bread like no other, so I could move to a nicer neighborhood.

"Damn baby, you have a man?" the guy I was dancing on asked.

"Yes," I lied and moved his hands from pulling on my G-string.

"He don't have to know," he whispered onto my shoulder and almost gave my golden complexion a tan.

"Have a goodnight." I stood up and smiled as the song finished.

This shit happened every damn night, and boy was I tired of it. I hated being groped and breathed on by ugly ass random niggas who bitched and complained about having to pay thirty dollars for a fucking lap dance.

I collected my money from Joey who guarded the lap dance area, and then rushed to the locker room. I was waiting on my best friend Cheyla, and my brother's girlfriend Ivy so that we could all head home. We usually tried to leave together because it was too dangerous to be out alone.

Cheyla and I met when we were ten years old, because our brothers Portland and Sonny were best friends. Sonny and Portland were always together, and Cheyla and I would always tag along, so naturally, a friendship blossomed. I met Ivy through my brother Portland, when they got together about four years ago. They were super in love, even though my brother was a bit of a dog at times.

Currently, Sonny and Portland were in jail on some theft charges, but they would be out in some short months. I couldn't wait because I missed my big brother so much, and I know Cheyla missed hers. I just hoped that when they got out they would be ready to turn over a new leaf, quitting all that illegal shit.

"Shit!" Cheyla called out as she entered the back room sweating like a muthafucka.

"Damn bitch, what were you doing?" I frowned as I pulled my t-shirt dress over my head.

"I was out there getting that bread," she cocked her head and rubbed her fingertips against her thumb.

"Well I'm glad because you know that rent is coming up."

Our rent was $895 a month, and we went half on it. Sometimes I felt like I didn't even know what the fuck I was paying for, because the place was not up to par. But at least I had a place to eat, sleep, and wash my ass. I tried to be thankful for having the ability to sleep in a bed at night, instead of on the streets somewhere; especially where I lived.

I put my matted curly hair up into a bun, and shook my head as I thought about what I had to do to get it looking presentable again. I hated having to work with this shit, but getting it pressed was not something I liked to do too often. First of all, it cost too damn much, and secondly with my career, I always sweated the shit out within a week. Only positive was that it was low maintenance.

"I am so ready to go." Ivy walked into the back room.

Ivy was about 5'7, very slim, had honey blond hair, and smooth light skin. She was half black and half white, sporting pretty blue eyes. Although skinny, the niggas loved Ivy here at Starzz. I mean Cheyla and I were slim too, but we had more meat than Ivy.

I loved Ivy because she loved my brother. Most bitches can't wait to hop on the next dick in line when their man gets locked up, but not Ivy. She was holding my brother down, and shaking her ass every night to house their two-year-old Donovan. I smiled in her direction as I thought about it.

"Y'all wanna get some food?" I asked and plopped down on the bench to wait for Ivy and Cheyla to finish dressing.

"Yes, I'm hungry as hell. You think your mother will mind if I pick Donovan up tomorrow morning?" Ivy asked me as she wiped her body off.

"Nah, I think it's cool," I half smiled.

Portland would kill me *and* Ivy if he found out she was stripping and that I didn't tell him. She tried to make it work with him being locked up, but the little money he was able to get to her couldn't afford anything but food and clothes for the baby. She had to find a way to pay rent, so this was her only way; or so she felt. The highest paying job she was offered was $9.00 an hour, which wasn't shit for someone in Ivy's position.

"Alright," Cheyla slammed her locker closed, and then we went out to the parking lot.

Ivy was the only one of us who had a damn car at the moment, thanks to my brother. He offered me one, but I didn't want to take any food out of his son and girl's mouths. I would get my ass on that bus, or borrow my mom's car like I usually did. I did have my eye on this 2005 Nissan Maxima, but I needed about $600 more to get it.

We drove to IHOP after hopping on the 495 freeway, and none of us talked the whole way. It was obvious that we were thinking and just trying to clear our minds. Neither of us liked the way we lived, nor the way we had to make money, but there was no immediate way out. Self-respecting jobs just didn't pay as much when you had no degrees under your belt.

We got to IHOP in about fifteen minutes, and scoped the area before exiting the car. The last thing you wanted to do was hop out and get caught in the middle of two niggas having a gunfight. Once the coast was clear, we went into the fairly empty restaurant, sat down, and ordered right after.

"You have class tomorrow, Jersey?" Cheyla asked as she squeezed ketchup onto her hash browns.

"Yes, but only two from 12pm to 3:45pm," I replied slightly relieved.

"That's cool. You should work tomorrow night," Cheyla suggested.

"I was gonna take the night off, I'm exhausted, Cheyla."

"What about you, Ivy?" Cheyla turned her attention to Ivy.

"You know I'm down. I'm just hoping that during these last few months that Portland is away, no one in jail will tell him about how I've been getting my money."

"What have you been telling him?" I quizzed.

"Just that I work at the Nordstroms in Newark, and how good they pay," she shrugged. "You've been saying anything?" She raised a brow at me and I shook my head no.

"He only asks me about you keeping your legs closed," I grinned.

"Now, he knows he doesn't have to worry about that, but I guess my baby is paranoid. I can't wait to see his face," Ivy beamed and ate some eggs.

"I can't either. I'm excited to see Sonny, too." I tapped Cheyla who seemed to be in deep thought.

"Yeah, I miss my big brother and all the cash he used to front me," Cheyla smacked her lips.

"Lucky for you, he gets out one month earlier than Portland," I huffed and Cheyla nodded.

"Lucky I am," she replied.

After we finished eating, we sat in the parking lot and got high. Ivy then drove to our house, but she was too tired to go to her own apartment, so she slept on our couch. As soon as my head hit the pillow, I dozed off. Thank God no gunshots woke me up during the night like usual.

***

*M*y alarm woke me up at 8:15am, and I got dressed so I could go for a run. I always did that because it not only helped me wake up, but it helped me stay up. Whenever I would just get up and go, I would be tired again in a couple hours. It was best to do this early in the morning though, because the porch sitters and troublemakers were still knocked out sleep.

I finished my run around 9:10am, and then came home to shower. When I walked into my apartment, Ivy was making breakfast for us. I loved when she stayed over, because she always cooked for us. I hated having to purchase food because I was too lazy to cook, so being able to have home cooked meals in the morning was always a plus.

"Thanks, boo," I half smiled.

I went to the back to take a long hot shower, and wash my tattered mane, because I was in dire need of both. As I washed my face, I thought about my life and how shit was so crazy for me. My life had changed so much and I didn't think I was quite over it yet.

I grew up in a two-parent household and everything was perfect. Being the youngest of three kids, I always got my way and I loved it. Outside of my brother Portland, who is the oldest at twenty-five, I have an older sister named Raleigh who is twenty-three. My parents loved to travel, and they named their children after their favorite cities in the states of Oregon, North Carolina, and New Jersey. I'd never been to Jersey City, but since I was named after it, I definitely wanted to visit.

My dad Alvin Warren is a judge, and my mother was a perfect housewife. We lived in a one-million-dollar mansion in New Castle County, with maids, butlers, and the whole nine yards. That was until my father left the family three years ago for some twenty-one-year-old that he ran into. He claimed that he had fallen in love with someone else, and that we had thirty days to find somewhere else to live because she would be moving in. I have no idea how he came across her because he's a fucking judge! Anyway, he's now living with her ass, while my mom, siblings, and I are struggling.

Since my mom was a housewife, and depended solely on my father at his request, she works at Macy's. She does okay, but it's not enough to live the life we were used to, obviously. After being thrown out of the mansion, my mom was only able to afford a two-bedroom apartment in Browntown, which was more than cramped for the four of us. Portland started robbing niggas and stores for money in order to help out, which landed him in jail. Currently, my older sister Raleigh lives with my mom, helping out as much as she can with her call center paycheck. I hated to see my mom pinching pennies so I just moved out altogether to give her a break. She begged me not to, but I did it for her. I didn't want her worrying about me and how I got by. It was best if I wasn't in her face all the time, so she could have some peace of mind.

Strangely enough, my brother, sister, and I still communicate with my father, and he will give us a few hundred bucks whenever we see him, but nothing more. I want to hate my dad, but for most of my life he was great, so it's hard for me. Whenever I see my mother cry though, I want to murder him and that young hoe. And yes, my mother still cried herself to sleep some nights. I wasn't sure if it was because of the financial strain, or because she just loved my father so much.

I stepped out the shower, and then added my styling cream to my freshly washed hair. I put on my panties and then another t-shirt dress, before walking out to the kitchen to join Ivy and Cheyla. There was fruit, eggs, Canadian bacon, and waffles, and she'd already made our plates.

"About time, princess," Cheyla smiled.

I just chuckled and made a mental note to question her ass, because I heard her leave in the middle of the night.

TWO

## Cheyla Austin

_____________________

*A*fter eating breakfast with my friends, I went to my room to just chill. I was tired from being out half the night, and I wanted to be well rested for my shift later on. I hated going to work after having done a lot of shit, because that's when I gave lazy ass shows and lap dances. And them niggas barely came up out of their cash already.

As soon as I started scrolling on my phone, I heard a knock at the door.

"Yes?" I sat up and Jersey walked in. She was chewing what I assumed to be fruit, as she closed the door behind herself. She sat in front of my computer and stared at me. "What?" I chuckled.

"Where did you go last night?" she raised a brow. I sat up and smiled at her nosey ass.

"I went to see a new boo."

I really went to buy some pills from this cat I met at the strip club. Every night I needed to pop pills, because I had become addicted to them over time.

See, this all started about a year ago when I went to this party with an old friend of mine named Geraldine. Jersey didn't hang with her because she was bad news, and eventually I had to split my time between the two, because they always almost came to blows when in one another's presence. Anyway, I got a little drunk at the party and went to a room with one of the guys. I was just trying to get to know him, but me being drunk and free, I had no idea he was on some other shit. To make a long story short, he raped me and I became so depressed that I had to be put on antidepressants. That's back when my mother was clean for a couple months, and actually able to be a good mother to me and my older brother Sonny. The antidepressants led to harder drugs, and now I was a full-on pill popper.

I never told Jersey about that depression part, but I did let her know about the rape. After the party, I never talked to Geraldine again, but I heard she was a super cokehead now. I wasn't surprised because she was always into wild shit, even when we were back in the third damn grade.

"What new boo?" Jersey snapped me from my thoughts.

"This dude from Starzz."

"Now you know you shouldn't be meeting them niggas Cheyla, especially that late at night."

"I know but he was cute," we laughed in unison as she shook her head. "You should work tonight Jersey, I know you need the money," I changed the subject.

"I always need the money, but I'm gonna pass. My body is so sore, and for one night I want to not have my ass pinched or waist grabbed roughly. And I wanna watch Donovan for Ivy. You know she hates pushing him off on my mother."

Sabrina, Jersey's mother, was like my mother too. When my mom would go away for months at a time on drug binges, she would always take me in; she and Mr. Warren. I felt so bad when he left her because they seemed so happy and in love every time I came around. No one saw the signs, and everyone looked up to their relationship. I just hoped Sabrina found someone to make her happy soon, because I hated to see her so sad all the time.

"I feel you best friend, but I am gonna make that bread," I grinned and she laughed.

"Do what you have to do, but stop meeting niggas and going to meet up with them. You know niggas be shooting at that time of night."

"I know. That was the first and last time, I promise."

⸺

*I* walked out from the back room wearing a simple lime green G-string and matching pasties. I'd spread glitter all over my deep caramel complexion, and my hair was hanging down, sweeping my shoulders. I'd just popped a pill too, so I was really relaxed and ready to work.

"Damn," one guy commented and I turned to look at him.

"Hey, how are you?" I sat in his lap and he squeezed my ass.

He was fat and pale as fuck, with big eyes and crusty lips. His hair was braided up and you could tell it was time for them to be redone. He did smell really good though.

"Why don't you shake something?" He put a fifty in my panty line.

Shit, he looked broke as fuck but he clearly wasn't. He was giving me a nice amount of change for a lap dance. Thirty dollars was usually a lot, but fifty was unheard of up in here.

"Spoil Me" by Mya came on as one of the girls danced on stage, and I popped my ass in his lap. I felt his crusty hands grab my waist, but I just dealt with it since he was paying big money. The song couldn't go off quicker, and I hopped up. He placed another fifty in my G-string and I kissed his forehead. I wanted to make him a regular if he was gonna be dropping c-notes every time I gave him a dance. The wheels in my head were already turning, trying to calculate how many pills I could get with this new come up.

"What's your name?" he questioned.

"Caramel."

"Damn, what's your government?"

"Wouldn't you like to know," I winked.

I wasn't giving my shit to no damn body, not even this big money nigga! There was so much technology now, that people could find all your shit with just your name. I know one site that charges

$1.99 and they'll give you an address, phone number, and a couple family members, after only supplying them with the first name. Wilmington was already dangerous enough, and I didn't need shit extra in my life.

I sashayed through the tables some more, and I spotted a table of four guys. They were all cute as hell, but one in particular caught my eye. Shit, I would dance for him for free. I loved money but this nigga was just that got damn fine. I walked over by them, and into the area they were sitting in.

"You guys don't look like you're having a good time," I spoke to them all, but I was staring at one. Two of them looked like brothers, and the other two must've been their friends or something.

"Nah, we doing alright," the one I liked responded as he eyed me from head to toe. I sat down in his lap and felt his dick against my butt. *Mm, packing too?* I thought.

"What's your name?" I smiled down into his gorgeous face.

He had pecan colored skin, full lips, deep brown eyes, and long eyelashes. I could tell he was good and tall, and his body was probably one of a god. His brother, I'm assuming, had a mocha complexion, those same full lips, long eyelashes, a nose stud, and deep brown eyes. I knew he was tall too. The third one was light skinned with hazel eyes, and he seemed to be pretty tall like the brothers. There was another light skinned one with dreads, full lips, and a lot of facial hair. They were all hella good looking, so I'm sure they had plenty of bitches at their feet. The four of them were too damn fine to all be in the same group, making me wonder who was considered the ugly friend. I wish Jersey were here so she could witness all this shit I was seeing.

"I'm Kantwan," he responded.

"Kantwan? I've never heard that name before," I grinned.

"Well, I'm one of a kind, that's why."

He gripped my hip and I didn't bother to move him. "Picture Me Rollin" by Chris Brown came through, and I started to dance in his lap. I didn't care if he didn't pay, because he was that bomb. I shook my ass and looked back to see him smiling while sipping his drink. He placed a twenty in my G-string, and it was more than I expected, so I was cool.

Once the song went off, he said "I usually don't do this but what's your *real* name and *real* number."

I licked my lips and said "Cheyla," before reading off my number to him.

"Cool, I like that name. It fits."

I could look in his eyes and tell he had some good dick, and I had no business trying it out. He would have my head gone for sure, so I needed to tread lightly. I chilled with Kantwan until he and his people left, and then I went and bought some pills from my guy before heading home with a smile.

# THREE

# Ivy Horne

---

*L*ast night, I literally shook my ass until I couldn't anymore. My lower back was on fire, and so damn sore that I had to lie on my stomach the whole night. At least I came home with a lot of bread though.

It was a nice Thursday morning, and I wanted to spend it just relaxing with my baby, and letting my body recoup from last night's festivities. I could see the sun shining through my bedroom window, and I could already hear them loud ass corner boys making transactions, shooting the shit, and having freestyle battles.

I looked next to me and smiled at my two-year-old son sleeping soundly on his tummy. He was so cute and chunky, and was the spitting image of his father, Portland.

Portland and I met when I was seventeen, and he was twenty-one. He was so sexy and had his shit together which reeled me in. At first he wasn't too cool on fucking with me because I was underage, but over time that went right out the window. The first year of our relationship was so much fun, and it seemed like we fell in love instantly. After a while, the cheating, lying, and side chicks started to be the normal thing for us. I was young and stupid, and because I had no family, Portland seemed like a Godsend, despite all his wrongdoings. I wanted to stick by him because I knew he could be a great guy, and that he eventually would be. He shaped up a little before he went to jail, so I was hoping when he got out he would have a whole new mindset. I prayed he changed, because here we are four years later, and he's in jail while I'm home trying to make ends meet.

As I stated before, I have no family. My father was white and my mother was black, and they were killed while chilling in the car one night; that's all I know about them. My grandma raised me, but she died when I was fifteen. I've been on my own ever since until I met Portland.

I appreciated the money he did get to me though, because it really helped a lot. It mainly paid for food in the fridge, and diapers, clothes, and bottles for Donovan. As far as rent, utilities, and household necessities? Not at all. I found peace in the fact that my son was taken care of every month though, so that was the upside to the little money Portland got to me.

I kissed my son's head, and then put him in the middle of the bed after I climbed out. I placed pillows around him so he couldn't roll, and then went to use the bathroom. I turned on the shower, and then grabbed my toiletries so I could quickly get myself together before my baby woke up. I usually had to brush my teeth in the shower, because that's how much of my time he took up. Once he was up, it was all about him.

I finished washing my body and shit, and as soon as I stepped out I sniffed my hair. It smelled like strawberries, and I was happy that the smell of cigarettes, weed, money, and sweat was out of it. I found myself washing my hair more than usual these days, because nobody wanted to walk around with hair that smelled like a man. I put it in a French braid, and then slipped on a comfy dress. Just when I finished, my baby woke up crying with his little bottom lip poked out.

"Mommy's right here, baby." I scooped up his cute self, and kissed his fat face.

He stopped crying immediately, and I took him to the kitchen so that I could feed him breakfast. As I was putting a French toast stick into his mouth, my cell phone rang and I knew exactly who it was. I quickly answered it, and then put it speakerphone. Accepting the charges, I waited for my love's voice to come through.

"Hey pretty," he said and I blushed like I always did when he called me that.

"Hey daddy, how you holding up?" I quizzed and fed Donovan some more food.

"I'm as good as I can get. Do you need anything?"

"Umm, no, we're good."

"You still working at that clothing store or whatever?"

"Oh, yeah, and taking as many shifts as possible."

I hated to lie to him, but I had to for right now. It was just until I figured some shit out. If I could have it my way, Portland would never know about me stripping at all.

"I can't wait to get home so you can kick your feet up," he exhaled heavily.

"I can't wait until you get here either, but for other reasons," I laughed.

"Damn, it's been a minute, I know it's nice and tight for me." My clit throbbed from hearing those words.

"It is." I was a little bummed that it would be eight long months until I felt him again.

"Where is my little man?" he inquired.

"He's right here. Say hi to daddy," I smiled at Donovan, and he chuckled loudly making me laugh.

"There's my boy," Portland chuckled.

"Oh baby, I miss you and I cannot wait until you get here," I groaned.

"I know beautiful, me either. And I promise I'm never coming back here. I love you, Ivy."

"I love you too, Portland."

"I gotta go, but have a good day baby, and make sure you rest up, because when I come home you gon' need all of your energy."

"Sounds like a plan. See you sooner than later."

We disconnected, and I let out a deep sigh before continuing to feed my baby.

Once Donovan finished eating, I bathed him and decided to watch some TV with my feet in a foot soak. They were killing me, and I had to be right back on them by tomorrow night. Damn, I couldn't wait until my nigga got home.

*KNOCK! KNOCK!*

I picked Donovan up off of my lap, and then placed him in his playpen so that I could answer the door. I walked to the door slowly, and then peeked through the peephole to see Jersey and her sister Raleigh.

"Hurry up, girl!" Raleigh shouted and knocked again. "Damn!" she chuckled as I opened the door for she and Jersey.

"What are y'all doing here?" I questioned.

"Wanted to chill and see my nephew," Jersey responded.

"Oh alright, are y'all hungry? I was gonna make some submarine sandwiches," I said.

"Yes, I want one but with a lot of bell peppers please," Raleigh smiled and I smirked at her.

"I will take one too," Jersey said as she kissed Donovan.

After making the sandwiches, I brought them out to the sisters, and then sat down on the couch next to them.

"I talked to Portland just like an hour ago," I said before biting my sandwich.

"Really, what did he say? Did he sound okay? You know he doesn't call anyone as much as he calls you." Jersey shook her head.

"Yeah, he's fine, he sounds like he's doing okay in there. I'm just happy that he's gonna be back soon as hell."

"What are you gonna do about your job though, Ivy?" Raleigh frowned.

"I'm gonna have a new one by the time he comes home. I haven't found anything worth my while though, because they just don't pay enough for me to live."

"You should apply to my job at the call center."

"Raleigh, thank you, but I don't think that shit is for me."

"Yeah, I wouldn't wanna do that shit either. People talk shit to you and you can't even do anything about it because they're over the phone." Jersey bit her sandwich.

"It really ain't that bad, you just can't take it personal," Raleigh shrugged.

"Well, I think I'm just gonna keep looking, and if shit gets to a point where I can't find anything, I will hit you up, Raleigh."

"Fine with me," she responded.

We finished our sandwiches, and just watched movies. Cheyla joined us a couple hours later, and by 8pm, the girls headed home. We literally lived a couple blocks away from one another in Browntown, and I really liked that we were all so close.

FOUR

Jersey

———————

One Week Later...

"In Her Mouth" by Future blasted over the club as I shook my ass on stage. I had to make sure my feelings didn't spill out onto my face, because I was so over this shit. I needed to act like I loved it in order to make my bread. These niggas loved to see you love to seduce them. They could tell when you were not into it, and the money would stop coming. These niggas were so thirsty that you would think they'd never seen a woman's body before.

I swayed my hips from side to side as I went down into a dip. I paid no attention to the money that was starting to cover the stage, because I wanted to stay in my zone. I had sort of an alter ego to help me do my thing. Even though I'd been stripping for a while now, I still got nervous sometimes. And since we couldn't drink while on the clock, it was the only way I could somewhat loosen up.

I moved my bikini top to the side to expose my perfectly round 34 B's, and the thirsty niggas went wild. They were licking their crusty lips and throwing plenty of cash my way. I placed my thumbs into the sides of my G-string, and gave them a sensual smile that

18

made them hoot and holler. I slid onto my back, and then moved my panties down my smooth golden legs, and they all watched closely, waiting to see my pussy. I hated these niggas. A couple more twirls and sexual moves, and finally my turn was over. I was so happy when the song went off, and I saw the blue light flashing for me to get my ass out of there. Parrish came out to help me collect my money like he always did, and then we stuffed it into a baggie. I knew I had about $400 in there to keep, and I was happy as hell because that meant I could have some spending money since the rent was paid up for this month. I needed to hit the nail shop and get waxed, and it looked like I'd be able to do both.

Sometimes I admit the stripper life got to me. Some nights I wanted to be the best fucking stripper in Delaware. The wads of money, and the constant compliments got to my head on occasions. Other nights I wanted to just make my money and go home, because I felt disgusting and like a piece of meat. Plus, what upstanding guy wanted a bitch who took her clothes off for money?

I went to the back to wipe myself down, and kissed Ivy on the cheek as she walked out, since it was almost her turn to go up. Seeing her made me think about how she was gonna explain herself to Portland. Word was bound to get back to him when he was released from jail, that his girl was popping her pussy for cash. I just hoped he could move past that, because Ivy had forgiven him for plenty of things in the past. I lost count on how many times he'd cheated on her or humiliated her in front of other women. At times I wanted her to leave him, but when I would see them happy together I would change my mind.

Seeing Portland and Ivy's relationship let me know that I would never allow a man to treat me a certain way though. I refused to be cheated on and lied to constantly, or to cry myself to sleep at night while my man is out fucking some other girl. Maybe that's why I didn't have a man now. Plus, I was too focused on my goals to be out here with the drama.

I changed into another outfit that was barely there, because I wanted to get some lap dance money. I had one more payment to make on my classes, and I hoped tonight would help me pay that off. This little $400 wasn't gonna do anything, especially after I spent $100 for my nails, toiletries, and a wax. But I needed my classes to be paid off for this semester, because I wanted the rest of the money I made from now until August to be all mine to save up and spend a little. I hated that I worked so hard and barely had anything to show for it.

I walked out of the back, and bobbed my head to "Summer Sixteen" by Drake as I scoped the room. I was looking for niggas who looked like they had money to spend. I hated the ones who thought they had enough game to get free dances, or the ones who would try to just buy you some chicken strips in order for you to give them a free one. No amount of game or chicken strips would have me breaking a sweat for fucking free.

As I was passing a VIP booth, this one guy called out to me.

"Damn beautiful, come back over here," he said. I stopped and looked back at him and his friends chilling.

He was cute as hell. He had smooth light skin, hazel eyes, and he appeared to be nice and tall.

"What's your name?" I smiled as I walked into the booth.

"Tommy, what's yours, beautiful?"

"I'm Bliss, I know you just saw me up there," I grinned.

"Bliss, huh? Where you get that name from?"

"I'm sure you can figure that out for yourself, daddy," I licked my lips and he nodded with a smile.

I couldn't help but notice his friend watching me out the corner of his eye. He was sexy as hell too. He had a deep mocha complexion, facial hair, a low cut fade with deep waves in them, and I knew he was about 6'4. I could smell his expensive cologne from over here, and his demeanor told me he was somebody important, or that one day he was gonna be. He kind of made me nervous, because although quiet, you could tell he was a no nonsense type of nigga. He seemed like the type that demanded respect, and you felt obligated to give it to him. Right now he had me wanting to do all types of disrespectful things to him though. *Jersey, you need to calm down.*

"You wanna dance?" I turned my attention back to Tommy.

"I damn sure do," he said and leaned back.

"It's forty bucks even, and I don't have change," I stated sternly.

"That's fine Bliss, I can pay whatever you want."

I knew he wanted pussy, but I didn't get down like that. There were plenty of other girls who did though if he was really on that tip. If I didn't want you to have it for free, then you just weren't getting it.

I sat down in his lap, and wound my hips to the current song playing. I didn't know what it was, it just sounded like some husky nigga yelling over a beat.

I felt Tommy touch me, and I popped his hand back.

"No touching," I smiled at him and he threw his hands up in mock surrender.

After showing out in Tommy's lap, I stood up and he pressed two twenties into my hand.

"Let me get your digits Bliss," he said.

"I don't think so," I scoffed and glanced at his homie again.

I saw him laugh, and he had the deepest dimples with the most perfect set of teeth. They were so white that he must've had a dentist as a father or something, because I don't think ordinary brushing provided such luminosity.

"Oh what, you scared of a real nigga?" Tommy quizzed, pulling me from my obsession with his friend.

"I'm just not into mixing business with pleasure."

"So if I see you outside of here then I can get your number?" *Only if you're getting it for your friend,* I thought.

"I guess so. We will just have to see though. Nice talking to you Tommy," I winked and switched out of the booth.

"Damn, she's bad as hell," he commented to his friends, and I chuckled as I kept walking.

I floated around the club to give a few more dances, before feeling like I'd made a sufficient amount of money for the night.

*I*t was now 3am, and I was finally off and at home. The shower was calling me, and I'd just bought a new showerhead with a massager built in that I couldn't wait to put to use.

After cleaning myself with my Olay body wash, and brushing my teeth, I braided my curly hair and climbed into my bed. As soon as my body laid flat, muscle pains shot throughout it. This always happened after a long day. It seemed like my muscles were finally relaxing.

I said my prayers, asking God to please heal my mother's broken heart, and to melt the ice on my father's, before drifting off to sleep.

FIVE

## Cheyla

———————

Three Nights Later...

*I*t was 2am, so I finally decided to take my ass home. I wanted to hit up old boy for some pills, but I was way too tired. Yeah, I couldn't believe it either, that I was too tired to get high. I was usually always down to score some pills, but tonight I had overworked my body and needed rest more than anything.

As I was walking out, I saw that Kantwan guy and flashed him a faint smile. He had yet to hit me up, but I wasn't tripping like that. He was cute as hell, but there was no point in me chasing him when I knew we wouldn't go far.

Not that anything was wrong with him, it's just I didn't do relationships. How is getting close to someone to the point where you would cry if they left you a good thing? I never wanted to be that attached or in love with a person to where I'm just miserable without them. I don't even see why people got into relationships. I never wanted to end up like Jersey's mother, no offense.

"Aye, Cheyla!" he called after me. I stopped walking and rolled my eyes before turning around. *Why the fuck did he call out my fucking government*, I thought.

"Hey boo," I smiled once he neared me.

"Come hang out with me at the crib."

He was looking so damn good, that I didn't want to keep staring at him. I inhaled sharply, and looked to my left to give myself a break from seeing such impeccable features.

"Look, just because I'm a stripper does not mean I sell pussy aight? And if that's why you asked for my number you can delete it nigga!" I barked and turned around.

He laughed loudly as hell, and then grabbed my arm.

"I'm not trying to pay to fuck so chill out. I don't need to pay for pussy ever ma, trust me. It's just late and nothing is open, so I offered for you to come to the crib," he shrugged. I felt so stupid, but I was gonna play it off.

"Bye Kant!" his brother yelled and he put his hand up in response.

"Marsh is open," I folded my arms.

"Where is that at?"

"It's on Marsh Road, right by Marvi Cleaners."

"All the way over there?" He furrowed his brows.

"Nigga what? It's only ten minutes if you hop on the 495."

"Anywhere that you have to take the freeway is far." We laughed in unison, then stared at one another for a little bit. "Alright but only because you're pretty." He bit his lip and eyed me from head to toe before speaking again. "Do you wanna follow me or what?" He inquired as he looked behind me for my car.

"Yeah, I could do that."

"Alright, cool," he said and then jogged to his car.

When I got in mine, I saw he was waiting for me to follow him. He had an all-black Ford Mustang with shiny rims, and black tint that was sure to get his sexy ass pulled over.

I trailed him all the way to Marsh Diner, and then we parked right next to one another. He got out wearing the cutest fucking smile on his face, and my panties got a little wet. I just wanted to jump in his strong ass tatted arms, and press my lips against his. I kind of wondered to myself why he was after me, because I was just a typical chick from the hood. The way he looked, I knew he could have any girl he laid his eyes on. Shit he probably had a damn girlfriend.

We both flashed each other flirty smiles, and then went inside the breakfast spot. No one was there except for a sprinkle of people, so we were seated right away.

"Tell me about yourself, Cheyla," he stared into my eyes as he rubbed his fresh fade.

"Why you wanna know about me?"

Damn he was super fine, and he was making me a little bit nervous. No guy had ever made me nervous before, because there was no reason to be. However, his sexy demeanor and looks made me a bit uneasy. I think it was because I felt like he could make me do anything he wanted without even trying, and that was not a good thing. If he did have a girlfriend, I'm sure she was stuck on stupid for this nigga and wouldn't leave even if he told her to.

"Because you're mysterious. You seem kind of sneaky but that shit is sexy," he smiled flashing his perfect choppers.

"Well, my name is Cheyla Austin, I'm nineteen, I'm a stripper, and I have an older brother named Sonny."

"Word, what about your parents?"

*Damn, nigga, why?*

"I don't know my dad, and my mom is a streetwalker," I replied very quickly.

"Like a prostitute?" he cocked his head and I nodded.

"Now your turn," I said, wanting to stop talking about my mother.

She wasn't my mother anymore. All she did was sell pussy to get high, and get arrested for prostitution. She'd been arrested for prostitution so many times that it was ridiculous. But just like a disobedient child, she keeps doing it over and over again. I needed to start disowning her ass like I've done to my pimp ass father. He had long ago let my mother free from his ring of hoes, but by that time she was a broke junkie, and needed the money that opening her legs got her.

"Well, my name is Kantwan Camren, I'm twenty-one, I work at Costco right now, and I have two older brothers named Kill and Ka'shea."

Costco? He definitely looked like a straight up drug dealer, so I was caught off guard. It was kind of a turn on to know that he had his mind right, yet had that thug appeal.

"Kantwan Camren, that's a tongue twister," I laughed and so did he.

"Yeah I know. I don't know what my mother was thinking, but she was obsessed with creating names for her kids."

"It's cute though, I like it."

"Thank you."

"What about your parents?" I asked.

"My mother died in a car accident, and my father is still alive but he is pretty ill."

"Oh wow, sorry to hear that, Kantwan," I tucked my lips in.

"Nah, it's been this way for a while now. I've learned to live with it, and to enjoy my life while I still can. I just wished he'd allow us to visit him."

"Damn, I hear that."

We continued to get to know each other just a little, and then had some good ass pancakes. Afterward I was dead tired. I was already exhausted from work, but now I felt like a zombie.

"We should do this again, but not at this time," he said as he stood in the doorway of my car.

"Yeah, I think that would be cool."

"See you around, Cheyla," he kissed my cheek and then jogged to his car. My nipples hardened at the feeling of his full lips on my cheek.

I hadn't had any personal male attention in the longest, so the littlest things had me on one. If we got anywhere, which wouldn't be far, I'm sure he would not like my pill popping.

# SIX

## Kantwan Camren

---

The Next Morning...

*I* woke up and sucked my teeth when I saw my dick was rock hard. I'd dreamt about Cheyla, and it was some super nasty shit. Ever since the first day I spotted her ass sauntering by, I'd been wanting to smash. The funny thing about it though, was that I liked her ass too. For the first time in a long fucking time, I wanted more than a wet dick.

I grew up in the house I still live in now, in Hilltop, with my two brothers, my cousin, and my parents. My mother was a maid, and my father fixed cars for a living. We weren't rich growing up at all, but there was never a night where my mom didn't have dinner on the table. There was never a Christmas morning that we went without gifts either. I was beyond content growing up; I was very happy.

When I was fourteen, my mother died, and it seemed like my whole word fell apart. Her car crash set the tone for the next couple of years to come, because our family just crumbled in the worst way. My dad got injured on the job three years after her death, and could no longer work and bring home the bacon like before, which defi-nitely put a strain on the five of us.

About a year after that, things were okay again because my oldest brother Ka'shea was selling drugs, and making a nice amount of money hugging the corners from sun up to sun down. But he slipped up and sold some product to an undercover cop and got arrested, leaving us to have to struggle again a couple months later. He got sentenced to four years, only because his lawyer really harped on the fact that this was his first offense. Ka'shea was smart as fuck, so showing how well he did in school when my mother was alive, helped sway the judge's decision.

As of now, my brother Ka'shea had one year left, my dad was in a home at only 53 years old, I worked at Costco living check to check damn near, and my brother Kilexis sold yayo. The only bill I had was the house note, and by now it was only $600. But that didn't include utilities and all the shit that was going wrong with the house that I had to pay out of pocket for. I didn't mind though, because this house was my parents' and had sentimental value.

I got up because the sound of some hood rats arguing with some niggas outside of my house was annoying as fuck. This shit always happened when a girl didn't wanna come up out of her digits. In my opinion, if I have to curse a girl out for her number, I don't want the shit.

I walked to the bathroom, and as I wet my toothbrush, I saw my best friend Tommy was calling me.

"What's up with you?" I answered.

"Nigga, what's up with you? What you getting into today?"

"I'm just going to the carwash, and then I have to go to work."

"Nigga you should call out, I got some bad bitches that's willing to do any and every fucking thing son."

"Ain't nobody interested in them herpes infested jawns you be fucking with my nigga." I turned my lip up at the thought of them trashy hoes Tommy liked. "And what about Sasha my nigga?"

"Man, ain't nobody worried about no fucking Sasha. She always tripping and shit. Maybe if she shut her fucking mouth every now and then, a nigga wouldn't be trying to run up in other bitches."

Sasha had been with Tommy for a cool four years now, and I swear he was only with her because she spent major bread on his ass. When Tommy met her, she wasn't shit to him but some pussy, but after his mama put his ass out for selling her expensive electronics, Sasha somehow became *wifey*. I think it was just because he needed somewhere to stay, and because he knew Sasha was willing to do anything for his ass. I wasn't about to let his ass come stay at my crib, because if he tried selling anything in this house, he'd be a dead muthafucka.

"Well nigga, you need to break up with her ass then. That shit is nasty, especially because you love raw dogging these bitches," I replied.

"Nigga, condoms are a form of fucking slavery! How come they didn't need them muthafuckas back in the day? That's because fucking raw is the normal thing, y'all condom wearing niggas are weird," he said and we both laughed loudly.

"Nigga, shut yo' ass up. I'll be weird all day before I go around sticking my dick inside every bitch with no cap. And back in the day, muthafuckas were dying from syphilis and shit because they were like yo' ass."

"Well they went out happy and not backed up like you."

"I ain't backed up at all son, I'm good. But look, I gotta start my day so I can get to work on time and shit."

"I guess I will take these hoes down all alone. But you up for hitting Starzz tomorrow night or what?"

"Yeah, I'm off, so I can do that."

"I know you wanna see that little bitch you had dancing in your lap all night, so I knew you were gonna say yes."

"Why does she have to be a bitch, nigga?"

"That hoe shows her pussy for coins, a bitch is an understatement."

"Bye, Tommy."

I quickly hung up because he was starting to irritate me. Not just because I liked Cheyla, but also because he was so disrespectful sometimes. I had no problems calling a chick a bitch if she was one, or a nigga for that matter, but to call a girl a hoe or a bitch just because she stripped, was fucked up.

I brushed my teeth and then hopped in the shower so I could go on about my business. On my way out of the door, I decided to send shorty a text.

**Me:** *What's good?*

**Cheyla:** *Chilling, you?*

SEVEN

## Ivy

------

*I* was excited about today because I was gonna be able to see Portland. This visit was planned long ago, and I'd been preparing for it for a while now.

He was locked up in Delaware County Prison in Philadelphia. It wasn't too far away, only thirty minutes, but I still couldn't just pop up whenever.

"Look at my handsome baby," I cooed to Donovan.

I kissed his plump cheeks, and then scooped him up into my arms. I loved my baby so much, and I would do anything to make sure he was good. I grabbed my purse and then went outside my apartment so we could leave.

"Damn baby, can I come with you?" some ugly ass nigga with a dirty du-rag called out to me.

"I'm fine, thank you."

I usually would've ignored him, but these niggas in Browntown were crazy as fuck. You could get popped any minute, and nobody would even fucking care.

"Oh alright. Drive safe," he said and shoved some potato chips into his mouth.

After buckling in my baby, I climbed into the driver side and smiled widely. I hadn't seen Portland in three weeks, and I couldn't wait to lay my eyes on him. I could already imagine the feeling of his big strong hands holding my small ones as we sat across the visiting table.

We got to the jail in about an hour due to traffic, and thankfully Donovan slept the whole way. I was scared that he may have become fussy and I would have to pull over, but I guess he was too tired for all that. He'd stayed up half of the night being a little bad ass, and it must've worn his little butt out. I was thankful in hindsight.

After waiting a while, we were finally able to see Portland. When he walked out, I swear I fell in love all over again. I stood up with Donovan on my hip, and as soon as he got close to us, he hugged us both tightly. He took Donovan from me and kissed his fat cheeks before handing him back over. God I missed him so much, I just hoped he got his shit together upon being released. I wasn't doing another bid with him.

"You look beautiful, Ivy," he said to me and I blushed.

"Thank you, daddy." I bit my lip and adjusted DJ in my lap.

"So that means everything is going good with you?"

Portland was so handsome. He had smooth golden skin, brown eyes, and perfectly lined facial hair. He looked just like a younger version of the singer Tank. Him being so fine was the reason he had so many thirsty bitches after him. I just wished that he hadn't entertained so many of them.

"No, everything won't be good until you come home to us. Isn't that right Donovan?" I looked down at my baby.

"Baby girl, I know. Soon enough I will be there, and I cannot wait. I'm just as anxious as you."

He grabbed my hand and kissed the back of it.

I was happy for my man to come home, but I was worried about him finding out about me stripping. I planned to quit a little bit before he got home, but I knew it was nothing for a nigga to recognize me and point me out. I didn't know how Portland would feel because he was very possessive of me. The thought of other men having seen my body may be a breaking point for him, even though a nice amount of girls had sampled his dick during the course of our relationship.

If he did break things off with me, I would be miserable. I loved him with every inch of me, and I wanted us to grow old together, despite our history.

"What you thinking about?" he smiled.

"Umm, just how good things are gonna be when you come home."

"They're gonna be great, what you talking about?" he grinned.

"I know, and that's what I'm thinking about."

While we talked, I noticed some girl kept glancing over at us. She was sitting with another inmate, but her eyes were focused on Portland and me. She looked at my son in my lap, and then bit down on the left side of her lip like she was thinking. She seemed a little on edge like she wanted to say something, but she just turned back to the prisoner in front of her and began speaking.

"What's her problem?" I scoffed.

"Who?" Portland questioned.

"Old girl over there. She's looking over here like she has a problem."

"Aye, you not even supposed to be worried about her, you need to be focused on your man right in front you."

"I am, I am."

I spent more time with Portland, and then headed home. Before I got to my apartment, I treated myself to Dunkin Donuts, and also bought my baby some new outfits and toys, since last night was really good to me. I then stopped at Italiano Pizzeria on Fourth Street, and got me a cheese pizza with some hot wings.

Once I got home, I started to eat my food but I saw Jersey was calling me.

"Hello?" I answered.

"Hey, how was my brother?" she questioned. "I'm gonna see him next week."

"He's good. He looked even better though," I chuckled.

"Eww," she giggled. "So I'm guessing you didn't mention Starzz to him."

"No, I couldn't. I'm trying to think of the right time, Jersey. You know how your brother is. If he finds out I'm showing my body for money, he's gonna blow a fuse. Shit, if he finds out *you're* showing your body for money he's gonna flip."

Donovan made a sound, and I rubbed his back so he could fall back asleep.

"Yeah, I know. He's my brother though so he will forgive me. As for you, I just hope he understands why you had to do it."

"Yeah, me too. I was thinking about just quitting and keeping it a secret, but I know some ignorant nigga is gonna run their mouth to him which would be way worse."

"Yeah, at least if he knows ahead of time, he won't feel too bad about someone mentioning it or recognizing you," she agreed.

"Right, so are you working tonight?"

"Unfortunately, yeah. I need a little more to pay off my classes, so I just wanna get it out of the way," she responded. "What about you?"

"No, I'm gonna let my body recoup. I'm gonna take a nice hot bath in this Epsom salt I just bought."

"I hear you on that. You have to let your body recharge. Well, see you tomorrow then, babe."

"Alrighty, and make enough for the both of us tonight."

"You know I always try," she laughed and we disconnected.

"Let's hope daddy is understanding," I said to a sleeping Donovan as I lifted him to take him to his crib.

EIGHT

Jersey

———————

June 20th, Three Years Ago...

"*D*ad, what is this about?" I asked.

"*Just sit down, Jersey,*" he responded. He was wearing his usual get up of Banana Republic from head to toe. My father was a well-dressed guy, and always looked like money.

As I sat down, I looked at my sister and brother with worried expressions. The only time he called house meetings like this was when we were in some sort of trouble.

"Alvin, what is this about?" My mother finally entered the study wearing her favorite apron, and then sat down on the couch.

"First of all, Portland, Raleigh, Jersey, I want you guys to know that I love you very much. I've been dealing with something for a while now, and I've come to the conclusion that I need to be happy and live my life. I'm tired of lying and being miserable in my own home."

"What are you talking about Pop?" Portland frowned.

"Honey," my dad looked over his shoulder, and out walked some bitch who looked like she was Raleigh's age. She wore short ass shorts, a tube top, and some *stiletto heels. Her brown skin was beautiful, and her short bob was perfectly trimmed. "This is Trixie, my girlfriend."*

*"What!" my mother shot up off the couch.*

*"Your girlfriend!" Raleigh joined my mother by standing up.*

*"Settle down. Now Trixie and I have been together for about a year now and—"*

*"A year! Wow Alvin! Are you serious!" my mother screamed as tears fell out of all of our eyes.*

*"Yes, a year. The four of you have thirty days to move out, and I will pay for any movers that you may need. Trixie will be coming to live here in a month."*

*"How old are you?" I questioned.*

*"I'll be twenty-one in four months," she giggled and held up four fingers.*

*"So just like that? You're kicking us to the curb for her?" Portland furrowed his brows at my father.*

*"You guys are grown damn near. I mean, it's time you get out on your own don't you think?" my dad responded.*

*"Jersey is sixteen, Alvin, she is not grown!" my mother yelled and wiped her tears with the back of her hand.*

*"Close enough. Now like I said, you have thirty days," he smiled and Trixie leaned down to kiss his lips.*

*I got up to leave because I couldn't believe what I'd just heard and seen. As I ascended the stairs, I heard my whole family screaming and shouting at one another. This was officially the worst day of my life.*

I was going to see my dad today, because I hadn't talked to him in two months. It's not like he reached out to me either though. If Portland, Raleigh, or I wanted to see him, we had to do the legwork. I really missed the days where my dad cared more about his kids than getting his dick sucked by some young hoe.

I couldn't get that horrible day out of my head, and whenever June 20 came around, I always felt depressed. Everyone in our family tried to talk my dad back to his senses, but it never worked. Trixie was what he wanted, and Trixie was what he was gonna have. He wouldn't even come to Christmas or Thanksgiving dinners; it was like we didn't exist anymore. He did have the nerve to send a Christmas card to his mother though, and it was a family photo of he and Trixie. My poor grandmother almost had a heart attack when she opened it.

I walked up the big ass incline, and once I reached his huge brown double doors, I knocked repeatedly. My dad lived on a quiet street named Pheasants Ridge, with huge mansions everywhere. I missed this house and all the good memories we made here as a family.

A few moments after knocking, our old maid Hannah came to answer the door.

"Oh Jersey, is Mr. Warren expecting you?" she frowned.

"No, is he busy?" I asked and adjusted my book bag strap.

"No, but let me see if it's okay for you to come in," she smiled and slammed the door in my face.

How ridiculous was this? If I didn't need two hundred bucks to pay off my classes, I wouldn't be here. I'd had enough, but I spent it on that 2005 Nissan Maxima, since the guy said he couldn't hold it for me any longer. I could easily get the money for school by working tonight, but I really needed to study for my Geology test. I hated that subject so I wasn't too good in it, and needed all the practice I could get.

"Okay Jersey, come in," Hannah smiled and opened the door for me. I walked into my old house, and stood in the foyer until Hannah closed the front door.

"Where is he?" I asked.

"In the library."

Hannah was a very frail Asian woman, with short dark hair just past her ears. She'd worked for the family for years, just helping out my mom, and we all grew to love her. But when my dad kicked us out, it seemed that Hannah had forgotten all the times we'd spent together. She never held conversations with me, it was always hi and bye these days. I had bigger problems than trying to keep up a relationship with an old housekeeper though.

I walked to the library, admiring my father's new renovations to the house on the way. I'd been here plenty of times since he damn near had it torn to shreds on the inside, but every time I came, something new had been done to it. The newest and most disgusting additions were big pictures of he and Trixie. There were no photos of my siblings and myself which kind of hurt. You would think I would be used to this shit by now, but I wasn't. I guess a teensy part of me hoped that he would wake the fuck up and get his shit together. It'd been three years though, and it seemed like he was never returning.

I entered the library and there my father was with Trixie sitting in his lap. The sight alone disgusted me. She was giggling and planting kisses all over his face and lips. Why couldn't my dad see that she was nothing more than a cheap ass gold digger? Maybe today he would finally tell me how he met her, because a girl like her should never be rubbing shoulders with a prestigious judge like my father.

"Hey," I said hoping to break up the nasty sight.

"Jersey, hey baby girl," my dad smiled as if he and I had a good relationship.

He was a very nice looking guy. He looked like a slightly older version of Idris Elba. My mother said he was always a ladies' man, but he'd put that behind him to marry her. I guess he was lying when he told her that.

Thank God he was in a good mood though, because he always flipped when we needed more than one hundred dollars. For some reason he thought that was a lot of money, even though it wasn't shit to someone like me who had bills.

"Trixie," I nodded my head towards her.

"Hey Jersey, how are you, sweetie?" she smiled and stood up.

She was wearing the shortest shorts I'd ever seen, and keep in mind I'm a stripper. Her top was really tight, accentuating her DD cups. She had blemish free mocha skin, and a short bob in black. Trixie was a beautiful girl, but she had the wrong intentions with my father and I knew it.

"Jersey, Trixie asked you a question," my dad snapped me from my thoughts of her.

"Oh, I-I'm good Trixie, thank you," I said. "Could you give my dad and me a moment?" I gave her a fake smile.

"Oh sure, I will be back honey," she grinned at my father and started to switch out. Once my dad had enough of watching her ass, he turned his attention towards me.

"Daddy, where did you meet her?" I frowned.

"Jersey, don't start that. If you came here to insult the woman I love, you can leave."

"Dad, I need some cash, two hundred dollars."

"Again, Jersey? What the hell are you doing with your fucking money!" he yelled.

I wanted to say, *maybe if you didn't leave your family to struggle, I wouldn't have rent and utilities to pay, you bitch ass nigga!*

"Dad, I have expenses," was all I said.

"This is it for this month Jersey," he sighed and reached for his wallet. Wow, you haven't seen or spoken to your child for two months and that's what you say? If I didn't need this cash, I would curse his ass out. "Here," he stuck his hand out angrily, with two one hundred dollar bills and a fifty hanging between his fingertips.

"What's the fifty for?"

"Get you some food or something, you look frail," he spat and reached for his glass of bourbon. "What the hell is your mother feeding you? Ice chips?"

"No dad, I don't live with mom anymore, remember? And I eat all day," I responded dryly and he just mumbled to himself. He didn't even care to ask why I lived alone. He didn't care to ask this time or the initial time I'd told him that I'd moved out. "Well, I guess I will see you later," I said.

"And try to visit your father without your hand out for once, Jersey."

"Will do, Dad."

I walked over to get my bag and then left.

As soon as I didn't need his ass anymore, I was gonna let him have it. It always took so much out of me not to curse his bitch ass out, but I knew my classes being paid for, or whatever I needed at the time, came before my feelings.

I drove myself to Maryland Avenue Sub Shop, because I was craving a small turkey sub and they had the best ones. Not only that, but they were walking distance from my apartment.

After placing my order, I stood to the side and sipped my soda. So many thoughts were traveling through my mind. I needed to find a way to get on my feet and stop living stripper tips to stripper tips. Once I paid this last little two hundred dollars for school, my money was only going on bills and nothing else. I needed to be on some super save shit.

As I was drinking my soda, the clerk called me to get my sandwich, and a familiar cologne traveled up my nose. I looked to my right and it was the Tommy guy standing next to me.

"Hey beautiful," he smirked. I laughed because he found me, and I could see in his face how happy he was.

"Hey Tommy," I shook my head with a smile.

"Oh, so you remember me! Yes!"

"Calm down, aight?"

With the bright lights in the restaurant, he looked so much cuter.

"So what's up, can I have your number?" he touched my arm. I wasn't wearing a bra, so I jumped when I thought he was trying to touch my breasts. "Damn, you good?" he frowned.

"Yes."

When you worked at a gentlemen's club, you were always paranoid that someone was trying to feel you up. It kind of had me on edge whenever I was around guys, because people thought that when you were a stripper, you enjoyed being violated by niggas even when not at work. The truth was that some of us hated it just as much as the average woman.

"Yes to giving me your number, or yes to you being good?" he questioned. I pushed the sleeves of my thermal up, and twisted my mouth like I was thinking.

"I guess since you're so determined."

"Fasho." He retrieved his phone from his pocket. I read off my number to him, and he shot me a text so I could store him. "Well look beautiful, I have to go, but be on the lookout for my call," he smirked.

"I will," I responded and he rushed out.

I hadn't had a boyfriend since my junior year of high school when I was sixteen. That went absolutely nowhere, and I hadn't had a man or suitor since. Now that I was nineteen, maybe it was good I got someone to keep my mind off of all the bad shit surrounding me.

Once Tommy left, I went and got my sandwich before heading home to eat in front of the television.

# NINE

# Tommy Brownson

---

After getting Bliss' number, I headed home so I could get some home cooked food. Come to think of it, she never even told me her real name, but to be honest, I didn't really care. I was only interested in smashing, so her name didn't make a difference to me. Yeah she was sexy and she was beautiful, but she was a stripper, which meant hoe. I would never wife a stripper ever, and she was no different. I didn't care how pretty a bitch was, if she was a hoe she would get treated like one.

I pulled into the driveway of the home I shared with my girlfriend Sasha on Oak Street. Sasha paid all the bills and shit, so I was free to do whatever with my money. We were deep in the hood, but it was what I grew up around so I wouldn't want to live anywhere else. I would feel weird not hearing gunshots ring out at least once a week.

I hoped Sasha had me a plate ready, because if not, we were gonna have a fucking problem. A nigga like me needed to be treated like a king, and if she wouldn't do it, another bitch would.

I hopped out of my Lexus, which Sasha paid the note on, and strolled to the front door while taking in my surroundings. I nodded my head at a couple niggas who were sitting on their porch steps, and laughed as I saw some dude make a transaction at the corner of Warner Street.

Entering the house, the smell of baked chicken hit my nose like a ton of tasty bricks, making me lick my lips. Although only the middle of the day, I expected home cooked meals at any time that I requested them. If Sasha was at work, then I got them from one of my other hoes.

"Thanks, baby," I squeezed her ass as she finished making my plate. She turned around and threw her arms over my shoulders to kiss my lips.

"Sit down," she smiled. I did as she asked and prepared to feast on my plate. She set it in front of me, and then she sat across the table with her own food. "Where have you been all day?"

"Why?" I frowned.

"Because I was just wondering if you were working or something," she shrugged with her passive aggressive ass.

"Yeah, I was working, fuck you asking me about work for?"

"Because I needed some help with the bills this month. I'm not able to do as much overtime at the Save-A-Lot," she complained like always.

"How much you need?"

I wasn't sure if I was gonna give her anything, but I wanted to make her think that I was, so that she wouldn't run her mouth.

"I need $200." She stuffed some food into her mouth.

My girl was beautiful as fuck. She had smooth brown skin, hazel eyes like me, nice big breasts, and a fat ass with thick thighs. Yeah, Jersey had a nice body too, but I was a titty man, and she didn't have nearly enough to make me want more with her. Anything under a C cup never got more than one night with me.

"Alright, I got you," I half lied.

I may give it to her and I may not. Shit, I needed to make sure my money was spent on the things I needed first before I started giving handouts and shit. What the fuck I look like breaking her off if my own shit wasn't together. Yeah, I didn't have bills but shit, I liked nice clothes and things.

We finished our food, and she stood up to collect the plates off the table. While she was standing at the sink, the sight of her massive ass had my dick hard as hell. I walked up behind her and bent her over, not bothering to let her cut the running water off. I pulled her thong down, and then slipped my dick inside her.

"Shit, Tommy," she moaned.

She gripped the counter as I rammed into her sopping wet pussy from behind. I reached under her to pull one of her D cups out of her bra, and then fondled her nipples as I went ham.

"Oh fuck, shit, shit," I called out as my dick got harder. I slipped out once I reached my peak, and blasted her with my nut. "Good girl," I commented, then smacked and squeezed her ass.

I walked to the back making sure to keep my pants up, and then wiped my dick off with a hot soapy towel. I saw a wet spot at the tip of my shirt, and blew out hot air because that meant I had to change it before I left. I switched my white t-shirt and then headed towards the door.

"Tommy, you just got here," Sasha whined as she grabbed her underwear from the floor, and started towards me.

"Look, you want this $200 or not?"

"I do."

"Aight then, I got to go make it," I said and pushed the screen door open hard as fuck.

Damn, and that's exactly why I never brought my ass home. She bugged me too fucking much, always needing money, quality time, and all kinds of shit.

I drove over to my best friend Kantwan's house since he was off today. I just wanted to get high and play some video games, then maybe pull up on some hoes later.

"What's up with you?" Kantwan greeted me as he opened the door.

"Doing me, son, what's good with you?" I dapped him up and then walked inside of his house.

When I got all the way in, I low key rolled my eyes when I saw Kantwan's brother Kill, and *his* cousin and best friend Elijah. I couldn't stand Kill, because he thought he was the shit and he wasn't. He pushed weight and he had a lot of respect in the streets from everyone except me. I mean who the fuck was he for me to be respecting? Yeah, he'd laid a couple niggas down but so what? Muthafuckas acted like he was some god or some shit. And the hoes acted like his dick was made of gold. Hoe ass nigga. As for Elijah, he was a stuck up ass nigga too, just like his fucking cousin.

Now their boss Axel was *that* nigga, and I respected him in hopes of him putting me on like he'd done Kill and Elijah.

"What's up?" I said dryly and plopped down on the couch.

Kill and Elijah pretended not to hear me, and just continued smoking on the blunt they had. See what I meant? Treating me like I was beneath them. Just watch, when I became the king of these streets, that nigga would be begging me to look his way.

TEN

## Kilexis "Kill" Camren

──────────────

The Next Afternoon...

"Kill, please man," this little bitch ass nigga named Jerrell begged.

"Nigga, I told you that you needed to have my fucking money, and you thought I was playing!" I held one of his fingers in between pliers.

I'd cracked eight fingers so far, and I was about to do the rest. My cousin Elijah sat and watched with a smile on his face. My boss Axel had me in charge of a couple traps on Broom Street where Jerrell worked. And whenever money or product was funny, I had free will to do as I pleased in getting rid of the problem.

"No man, I just needed more- ah! I needed more time!" he cried out as I cracked the ninth finger.

"I don't give extensions when it comes to my bread," I said and cracked the last finger.

He howled so damn loud I thought he was about to transform into a fucking werewolf. I paced the room as he panted and whimpered over his sore and broken fingers. I pulled my gun from my waist and shot him six times, three to the face.

"Call Stone in here so he can clean this bitch up," I told Elijah.

Elijah went outside to get my man Stone, and then we watched he and his crew clean the basement I had Jerrell in. I turned my nose up, because he had shit all over himself, and clearly that nigga had something dead inside his body because the smell was beyond foul.

"You ready?" Elijah asked me and I nodded.

We treaded outside and the sun felt good on my back. It wasn't too hot today in Wilmington, it was just right.

I was born and raised in Delaware, and all of my life I lived in the hood. There was always somebody getting shot or robbed, to the point where it wasn't even news anymore. It was actually more surprising if you didn't get shot at, jumped, or robbed out here. Niggas were dying every damn day and it hadn't slowed up yet. If I sat and wrote down all the homies I'd lost to gun violence, I'd need a damn scroll.

I remember shooting dice one day with my homeboy Mickey, and all of a sudden bullets started flying everywhere. It was broad daylight, but niggas didn't even care. A bullet hit me in my knee, but thank God I got away before it pierced anything else. As for my boy Mickey though, rest in peace.

I grew up in a two-parent household until my mother died tragically as fuck. She died in a car accident coming home from cleaning one of those white folk's houses. It was simple; some dumb drunk nigga was switching lanes without looking, and caused my mom to spin out into a busy intersection. A big ass truck was coming through, and rammed my mom's car into a pole. It was the worst day of my life, and it happened January 29, two days after my fifteenth birthday.

After that, times just seemed to get worst. My dad worked as a well-known mechanic, but when he fell and injured his back, he could no longer do what he loved. Living off of his disability checks were like living with no money at all. Then we began depending on my older brother Ka'Shea, and all the wads of money he was bringing home from selling dope. But because of our luck, he was arrested just months later for possession and distributing. That's when I became determined to find a way out on my fucking own. I kept my ear to streets in order to find out who I needed to speak to in order to sell here and there, and that guy was Axel. Once I met him and he saw how hungry I was, it was a no brainer to put me on.

I made sure to move smoother and smarter than my brother, making sure to never have product just sitting in my pockets, and not just selling to any nigga that approached me. I had to ask about you before selling. It may sound like I was doing too much, but here I am years later, and 'bout the only nigga who ain't been knocked for pushing, other than my cousin and best friend Elijah.

I wasn't in the same corner boy position that I was given six years ago; now I managed traps for Axel, and had much better ends coming my way. I wasn't no rich ass nigga but I was good, and niggas knew to show respect when I entered the room.

Parking my car on the street, Elijah and I hopped out and took a seat on my porch. I lived in an apartment on Franklin Street in Hilltop. Hilltop was the hood, but it was my hood. Niggas knew me 'round here, and would never try and take me out if they knew what was good for them.

"Hey Kill," this chick named Amelia walked by in some tights that were super see through.

Her ass was fat, but she had a face only a mother could love. She'd been jocking me since we were in tenth grade, and she hadn't let up since.

"What's up, ma?" I responded.

She and her friend walked closer to Elijah and I, then stopped to stare at us lustfully.

"Kill, Eli, this is my friend Sophie," Amelia pointed to her light skinned friend with slanted eyes. She looked mixed with Asian or some shit.

"Nice to meet you, ma," Elijah responded and I just nodded.

"You should come see me tonight Kill, if you're not busy or anything. But even if you are, I don't go to bed until real late," Amelia licked her lips.

"I may hit you up and see what you talking about later."

Just in case I wanted some pussy tonight, I didn't wanna write her off. I'd fucked Amelia a couple times, but so have many niggas, so she wasn't shit to me. I can't understand for the life of me how she thought I was gonna be with her, when she'd been ran through by so many niggas.

"You better," she winked.

"And what about you, baby?" Amelia's friend Sophie looked at Elijah. I'd never seen her pretty ass before, so I knew she wasn't from 'round here.

"Where you live at, ma? You ain't from Hilltop," Elijah squinted his eyes, seemingly reading my mind.

"I'm not from Wilmington, I live in Elsmere," she replied.

"With the white folks, huh? What you doing down here, ma?" I frowned.

"Came to see my girl Amelia, and the type of niggas I like don't live where I live."

"Word, well you gon' be with her?" Elijah pointed to Amelia, and Sophie nodded. "I may come through with him then, don't be on no bullshit, shorty."

I laughed at his ass. I didn't have to say that to Amelia because she knew what was up. If there was ever a nigga that was trying to chill with Amelia and not fuck, his ass would get clowned from here to Rhode Island.

"Oh, I ain't never on no bullshit," Sophie sucked her teeth.

"We may see y'all later then," I said, hoping they got the hint to keep it pushing.

They both nodded, and then headed towards Conrad Street before hitting the corner. I just shook my head at how easy them hoes were.

"You gon' get some head from that Blasian jawn too?" Elijah smirked.

"Now why the fuck would I let her suck my dick after she sucked yours? I may get some head before you though."

"Nah the fuck you not."

"Don't tempt me, Eli," I said before pointing to the blunt in his hand.

"So what *are* we doing tonight?" Elijah asked as he lit a blunt. "I know we ain't gon' spend all of it with them."

"I was just gonna chill, but what you thinking?" I asked him as I nodded my head to a guy walking by.

"Wanna go to Starzz?"

I'd been hitting Starzz more than usual lately because of this stripper named Bliss. She was so fucking fine, but I wasn't a relationship type of nigga, so I just preferred to look and not touch. I didn't wanna get her number and go through all those hoops just to waste her time, but damn was it hard. She seemed like a good girl despite her occupation, and fucking with a nigga like myself would fuck her up.

I didn't even like girls that stripped, but something about her made me want her. She was the only stripper in history to make my dick hard just by moving on stage. Sometimes I would have to occupy myself, because if I kept watching I would get blue balls. She was that fucking bad. She had long, wild, curly hair, smooth golden skin, a small but shapely frame, and pouty lips. She had a bull nose piercing, a tattoo down her right rib cage, one on her collarbone, and another one on her left hip. I paid attention to every detail of her body. She had some pretty ass feet too, made a nigga have a foot fetish low key.

"Nigga, do you wanna go?" Elijah shouted, snapping me back to reality.

"Yeah, that's cool." I adjusted myself, because thinking about Bliss had my dick hard as a missile.

After getting good and high, we waited for Kantwan to come over so we could all hit up Starzz. He liked some little cutie named Cheyla, and had been salivating over her every time we went. I was happy when he'd finally gotten her number because I was tired of hearing about her ass.

We walked into Starzz after paying the $10 fee, and it was popping as usual. I refused to sit with the thirsty niggas though, which is why I always paid to get into VIP. Thankfully tonight, whack ass Tommy wouldn't be with us. He was a bottom feeder ass nigga, and it made my skin itch every time he tried to holla at Bliss. Speaking of Bliss, I saw her waiting in the cut so that meant I was just in time to watch her pretty ass do her thing.

The beat of "B.L.O.W." by Tory Lanez dropped, and she sauntered on stage in a hot pink G-string, and a bra that only covered her dime sized nipples. I licked my lips and kept my eyes on her as I sat at the VIP table. I didn't want to miss shit in the process of sitting down. The way she moved her body made me hot all over, and I could only imagine planting my dick deep in them guts, and groping all over her little sexy ass body.

Once her set was over, I waited for her to start walking through the tables, looking for patrons to give lap dances to. I cringed every time she shook her ass on a nigga, but she wasn't my bitch and she never would be. She got closer to our area, and Elijah commented.

"Damn," he said.

"Hey," she waved and her beautiful face lit up. We made awkward eye contact like always, until she walked off.

"Damn nigga, you like her?" Elijah nudged me. I hated that he knew me so well.

"Fuck make you think that?"

"Cause you watching her like she's a full course meal," he chuckled and so did Kantwan.

"Nigga, worry about yourself," I laughed, wanting to change the subject.

For the rest of the night I watched sexy Bliss, and when she left, so did we since there was nothing more to see. The bitches started getting thirsty for dollars too, so I wanted to get out of there.

"Why don't you talk to her?" Elijah asked me as he, Kantwan, and I got into my car.

"Ain't shit to talk about."

"So you just gon' watch her pretty ass from afar like some creepy ass nigga?" Kantwan quizzed.

"She's a fucking stripper my nigga, we're supposed to look. But anyway, Kant, you coming with us or am I taking you home?"

"Where y'all headed?" he inquired.

"Going to Amelia's," Elijah answered. He didn't have to say much, because niggas only went to her crib for one thing.

"Fuck nah, take me home," Kantwan scoffed and we laughed.

We pulled up to Amelia's apartment on Harrison, and parked right in front. I scoped the scene, and then Elijah and I got out the car. We jogged up her porch steps, and I knocked lightly because I didn't want to cause too much ruckus.

"Kill, man, what's up!" this guy named Ernie hollered from across the way.

"What's good with you?" I hollered back.

"I need that shit, you got me?"

"When I come back out. Be right there in forty-five minutes," I pointed to the corner and he nodded.

"I was thinking you weren't coming," Amelia answered the door.

I declined to respond, as Elijah and I walked into her house. She closed her front door, locked it, and then led us to her living room. I spotted Sophie, and she was smiling at me all lustfully while sipping on some clear.

"We got some Smirnoff, want some?" Sophie asked.

"You got a fresh bottle?" Elijah quizzed.

Ain't no way we were gonna let these bitches serve us some fucking drinks. If I couldn't pop that shit open myself, then I wasn't drinking it.

"Yeah, but it's vanilla," Amelia responded.

"Nah, never mind," I shook my head and waved it off.

"Come talk with me for a little bit, Kill," Sophie said, surprising me. She looked to Amelia, who shrugged before going to sit in Elijah's lap.

"Come on," I waved Sophie over to me, and then led her to the bedroom upstairs.

Entering the bedroom, I closed the door behind me making a smile spread across her pretty face.

"You got a boyfriend?" I asked before I sat down on the bed. I knew she had one; she was way too bad.

"Yeah, but so what? You don't fuck with girls who got boyfriends?"

"I don't give a fuck about your boyfriend. And if he has any sense he won't say shit to me about you."

"He's a square, he won't even try nothing."

"Ain't nothing wrong with a square, at least he getting money the legit way."

"I don't like them type of niggas."

"What type do you like?" I bit my lip. Sophie was beautiful, and she reminded me of a slightly lighter version of Omarion's baby mama.

"I like the thug type, like you, Kill."

"You ain't acting like you like me."

"How so? I asked you to come back here with me," she giggled.

"Because if you liked me you would've been on your knees sucking my dick as soon as we got up in here, ma."

She stared into my eyes, and then peeled her jean jacket off. She wore no bra, and her nipples were showing out. Dropping to her knees, she reached her small hands up my pants and undid my jeans.

"You're nothing like my boyfriend," she said referring to my dick length.

"Less talking, more slobbing," I said. "Shit," I mumbled as she began to suck on the tip of my dick.

She moved her mouth up and down, and her lips were super soft. I gripped her hair, and guided her up and down at the pace that I wanted. A tear slid out of her eye since I was bumping her tonsils, and that shit made my dick harder.

"Damn girl, your boyfriend would be hot knowing you sucking my dick like you love me," I moaned.

Pulling her off, I reached up under her skirt and yanked her panties down. She held onto my shoulders for leverage as she stepped out of them, and then I got a condom from my wallet.

"You don't eat pussy?" she frowned.

"Love it."

"So what's up then?"

"You can sit on this dick, or I can leave. What you want?" I furrowed my brows as I rolled the condom down. She sucked her teeth, and then climbed into my lap. "That's what I thought."

"Oh fuck," she called out and bit down on her lip.

Her pussy was nice and tight, which made me wonder if she was even this hoe that she pretended to be. I bounced her up and down, and when her pussy relaxed I began to slam into her.

"Aaah, aaah, uuuh, aaah, uuuh!" she screamed with every thrust I delivered, and it was low-key annoying. Don't get me wrong, I loved to hear some moaning, but she sounded like them over the top bitches in pornos. "Oh, oh my gosh!" she called out and shook violently in my lap as she gushed.

"You good?" I grabbed her waist and squinted my eyes.

"Shit!' she hollered. "Yes, yeah I'm good."

"Get on all fours."

She got on all fours, but I had to push her face into the pillow. I grabbed her waist and made her ass toot up some more, then slipped back inside her. I closed my eyes and pounded her ferociously as I tried to drown out her annoying moans.

"Mmmm," I grumbled as I filled the condom up. I slowly slid out of her, and then carefully pulled the condom off.

"Oh my gosh, Kill," she panted and rubbed her hair back.

I said nothing as I stood up and fixed my pants. I walked towards the door, and I heard her sit up.

"Take my number!" she called after me. I heard Amelia getting fucked by Elijah downstairs, so I needed to kill time anyway.

I closed the door, and then pulled my phone out so that she could put her shit in. I would never hit her up for some pussy because it was beyond mediocre, and her moans were extra. But I would damn sure hit her up for some head.

Once Amelia's moans subsided, I said goodbye to Sophie, met up with Elijah, and then we left. As soon as I got to my crib, I showered and knocked the fuck out. Today had been a long ass day.

## ELEVEN

## Jersey

---

One Week Later...

It was my last class of the day and the damn week, and boy was I happy. I wanted to rush home and get a good nap in before having to get ready for work. I'd been feeling like I was about to doze off onstage these past few days.

As I stood up to walk out of class, my teacher stopped me.

"Jersey, I just wanted to let you know that your work was really great," my professor handed me back my paper.

"Thank you, Dr. West," I grinned and took my paper.

"Yes, I finished grading it last night so I thought I'd give it to you now. Keep up the good work, Jersey."

"Will do," I cheesed and then left the class.

Seeing this A plus on my paper made me feel really good, and almost gave me somewhat a burst of energy. It's crazy because I was hoping to at least get a C on it, and didn't even think I'd get an A.

I left school and stopped at this Chinese food place around the corner from my house, and then took my ass home. Once I got there, I heard "Loose Rap" by Aaliyah blasting from Cheyla's room.

I shook my head because she was never turned down as people say. Cheyla could party all fucking night, even if she was dead tired.

I walked into my room, grabbed my earplugs, and then shoved them into my ear for some peace and quiet. I changed into some boxer shorts, and then collapsed onto my bed to eat and then knock out for a couple hours. My body was so pleased with me right now.

---

*I* woke up around 7pm to my alarm going crazy. I hopped up so quick that I got light headed, so I fell back down. Once I gained my composure, I picked up my shower caddy, and then went to the bathroom to shower for tonight. I couldn't believe that some strippers thought showering in the morning was enough.

"You wanna ride together?" I asked Cheyla who was dancing in her room while putting on makeup.

"Yeah, that's cool. I don't like driving anyway, and Ivy isn't working tonight," she responded as she continued to sway her body. This bitch just got a car, and was already talking about she didn't like driving.

"How can you dance right now knowing we're gonna be dancing all night," I chuckled.

"Because I just love to dance." She flashed me her pretty smile and then started brushing her fresh press.

I went to my room to put on some jeans and a top, and then I packed everything I would need for the night. As I was getting ready to walk out of my room, my phone buzzed and I saw it was that Tommy guy. I'd been ignoring his texts that were sent prior, but he still hadn't given up. I didn't know if he was just thirsty, or if he really liked me.

**T:** *You working tonight?*
**Me:** *Yes.*
**T:** *Finally, a response. Maybe we can chill after.*
**Me:** *Maybe, maybe not.*

I shook my head and threw my phone back into my bag. Not that Tommy wasn't cute, I just didn't feel like dating right now, well tonight. Some days I wanted someone to hold me and talk to me, and others I just wanted to be alone and stack my bread. Tonight was one of those nights where I wanted to be lonely and at the top.

"Come on!" I shouted to Cheyla.

"Alright!" She came rushing out in a t-shirt dress, and we were on our way out the door.

When I pulled into the stubbly parking lot of Starzz, there were barely any places to park, so I knew I was gonna make a whole lot of money tonight. I always judged my tips by how many free parking spots were available. Because it was Thursday night, that meant tomorrow was gonna be even better. I smiled to myself as I spotted a park to swing my Maxima into.

"Girl, tonight we gon' make enough money to pay our rent up for three months!" Cheyla half joked.

"Maybe not three, but definitely two," I chuckled.

"Good enough!"

Cheyla and I hopped out quickly, and as we walked towards the entrance, I saw an all-black 2012 Yukon Denali pull into the parking lot. Everyone outside was in awe, because even though the car wasn't new, you could tell it was well taken care of. We watched it swoop into a park, and then waited for the passengers to reveal themselves. The dark tinted windows rolled down, and I spotted that sexy chocolate nigga in the driver seat. He fired up a blunt and took a long hard pull before blowing out a cloud of smoke so large, I felt like everyone in the parking lot could get a hit from it. He glanced over at me, and we made our usual awkward eye contact before he looked to someone in the backseat to pass the blunt to. Damn, that nigga was the shit.

"Who is that nigga?" I asked Cheyla as we both watched him.

I tried to sound like I was annoyed, when really I was intrigued like a muthafucka. I was tired of not knowing anything about his fine ass.

"Girl, I'm pretty sure that's Kantwan's brother," she shook her head.

"The guy you been chilling with?"

"Yeah girl, his brother is a for real thug, and sexy runs in the family as you can see."

"He's weird as fuck," I turned my lip up.

"How so? You don't even know him, Jersey."

"I know. It's the way he's always looking at me. I don't know. He's kind of scary," I laughed.

The way he looked at me in the club, I knew he had some dirty thoughts. Unlike with the rest of these niggas, I didn't mind him imagining things about me. I just wished his ass would ask me for a fucking dance, since I was too chicken to offer.

"He's intimidating, that's for sure. That's a nigga that demands respect right there," she smacked her lips and started towards the entrance of the club.

"Yeah."

I stood there for a little longer, and watched him as he laughed and showed his beautiful smile again. His dimples were deeply embedded in his smooth mocha cheeks, just above his beard. His full lips fit perfectly between his beard and perfectly lined mustache. The watch on his wrist that held the blunt was blinding, and so were the small studs in his ear and nose. This nigga was about to have me standing out here all night if I kept dissecting every sexy thing about him.

I shook my head and then went inside the club so I could change. I slipped into a pink-netted dress, with a pink thong under, and put pasties over my nipples. I'd just done my hair this morning, so my curls were popping and juicy. I knew it was almost my turn, so I went to the side of the stage to wait, hoping that sexy ass nigga was already inside and waiting for me.

The beat to Rihanna's "Yeah, I Said It" dropped, and I sauntered up the stage in my fit. I scanned the crowd as I caressed myself, looking for the guy in the Yukon Denali. He came every night and always watched me dance. I was used to him being here, and I felt like he made me dance better. However, no matter how many times I walked by his section, he never asked me for a lap dance or a private one. He would also leave whenever he saw me walking through the club in my regular clothes, so I knew he was here for me.

I swung around the pole, and then kicked my legs up in the air so I could be upside down. As I was about to twirl again, I spotted him swagging in with two other guys. He looked sexy as usual in a crisp white polo, under a gray crew neck, with light blue jeans, and some fresh white Nike Roshes. He wore the same thing every damn day, just in different colors and with different shoes. He was like a cartoon character.

"Aye baby, move something," a patron called out to me as he leaned on the bar connected to the stage.

I hadn't realized I was stuck upside down watching Mr. Chocolate, until my head began to throb from letting the blood rush to it. I moved down the pole, and took my netted dress off, causing plenty of dollars to fly onto the stage as if a fan were in the room. Once Mr. Chocolate was seated in the VIP area, I stared him down as I slid down to the floor. I flipped onto all fours, with my ass facing the crowd, and began slowly popping as Rihanna sang in a seductive tone.

*Yeah, I said it, boy, get up inside it. I want you to homicide it. Going slow and I want you to pop it.*

I closed my eyes after making eye contact with him again, and imagined his strong hands caressing my body. I flipped back over, and then removed my panties in which the fellas began screaming. However, right now the only person in the room was Mr. Chocolate. He watched me closely, and folded his arms across his strong chest as I continued to dance seductively just for him. I refused to take my eyes off of him, because I wanted him to know this was the dance that he refused to ask me for. He scanned my body with his eyes, and I saw him adjust himself, which made me smile on the inside. The fact that I could get a cocky nigga like him hard, without even touching him, had me feeling myself.

Once the song went off, I was still lost in my fantasy, until the blue light telling me to scram brought me back to reality. When I looked down, there was more cash than I had ever made before.

Parrish helped me collect it like always, and then I grabbed my thong and dress before running to the back.

"Damn bitch, you did a bomb ass job!" this girl named Gretchen said to me, and put her hand up for a hi-five.

"Thanks," I chuckled nervously.

"You are welcome. You had everyone's eyes glued to you, girl!" she said and then left the back room.

I quickly changed into some blue latex booty shorts, and the matching bandeau top, along with some clear slide in heels. I checked my appearance in the mirror, and then sashayed out onto the floor as another girl swung around the pole like a tetherball. I made sure to walk towards Mr. Chocolate's section, and then I slowed down upon reaching it.

We both smiled at each other, and he bit his lip making his dimples show. He was so fucking bomb that it made no damn sense. I could tell he knew I was just up there showing out for him.

As I was about to speak, I felt someone grab me from behind.

"Bliss," the voice whispered into my ear. I turned around to see Tommy, and gave him a faint smile.

"Hey Tommy," I said. This nigga just ruined my whole damn plan, kind of.

"What's up baby girl, looks like I missed your set," he said as he held onto my hands.

"Yeah, shame on you."

Tommy looked sexy tonight in a blue sweater, white jeans, and blue Vans. I could tell he'd just gotten a haircut, and his hazel eyes were so beautiful. He smelled really good too.

"So what's up? Can we hang out after?" he asked me.

"Not tonight, we can hang out on my off day."

He seemed to really be into me, so why not give him a chance? Mr. Chocolate gave me no play anyway.

"Okay cool, how about a dance though," he held up a one-hundred-dollar bill, so you know I was with it.

"Sure, where are you sitting?"

"Oh, these are my people," he pointed towards Mr. Chocolate and the two people he came with.

"Cool," I nodded and walked up the two steps to give the dance.

As I wound my hips in Tommy's lap, Mr. Chocolate kept glancing at me out the corner of his eye. I would happily give him a dance, but clearly he thought he was too good.

"So when is your next off day?" Tommy asked.

"Monday."

"Cool, how about dinner?"

"Sounds good."

If Mr. Chocolate didn't wanna get at me, then someone else would. Plus, I ain't want no cocky ass, sexy ass, fresh to death ass nigga anyway... right?

# TWELVE

## Cheyla

_____________

I hadn't had any pills in a while, and damn was I having withdrawals. I didn't even wanna finish working because I wanted to hit up the guy that always had the good shit. I felt like he only came here to recruit customers though, because after the first night I met him here, he hasn't been back. But damn, I would only need to take one and I would be on cloud nine for hours and hours. The shit I used to get would only last one hour, so you know I was on this new cat.

Omarion's "I'm Up" finally went off, so I got up out of the lap of one of the guys I was dancing for.

"Damn baby girl, let me get a private one," he smiled.

"No, I have to go."

"I got $200 with your name on it," he said and waved the money in front of me.

I didn't wanna stay because I wanted to go get high, but I knew I could get high _and_ have some spending money if I had that $200 in my life. I needed to get my damn hair done, and this money would help me do so.

"Come on," I said as I folded up the forty dollars he'd just given me for the initial lap dance.

He stood up happily and followed me to the private dance area. He handed the money off to Joey, who was the guard in a way, for the private dance area. Joey made sure that niggas paid up before we danced, and didn't try to slip up out of here with a five-fingered discount. He also made sure that these niggas didn't try to violate us, because believe or not, some dudes thought a private dance came with pussy and head too.

I moved the velvet curtain back, and then allowed this guy to walk in for the dance. He wasn't ugly at all, but he was annoying as hell. He was about 5'10, skinny as fuck, with curly hair, brown eyes, and the most perfect set of teeth I'd ever seen. If you had have seen his teeth, you would've thought they were dentures, because that's how perfect they were.

He wore no jewelry though, and his clothes didn't seem to be of any name brands that they talked about in the rap songs. He may have been the non-flashy type though, because the way he was spending money tonight showed that he obviously was no broke nigga. And if this $200 was a part of his bill money, that wasn't my problem nor concern.

Ginuwine's "Pony" came on, and I low key rolled my eyes. I was not looking forward to dancing to such a sensual song for him. I was praying that Juvenile or Master P came on, so I could pop my ass quickly, collect my bread, and be out.

"What's your name, babe?" I asked him as I made sure the curtain was pulled all the way.

"Monty, what's yours?"

"Caramel, I thought you knew?"

"What's the name your mama gave you?"

"I ain't got a mama, so I named myself Caramel. Don't you think it fits?" I licked my lips and a big ass smile spread across his face.

"Oh, it definitely fits."

I walked over to him, and as soon as I started to caress my body and sway my hips, his already huge smile widened. I gave him a half one because I didn't want to let on how ready to go I was. I straddled his lap, and began moving my body slowly in a snake motion. He brought his long skinny hands up to rub my back.

"No, don't touch," I whispered and he nodded before dropping his hands.

I continued to dance on him, and it seemed like "Pony" was six damn minutes long. Before Ginuwine could even say his last words, I was out of his lap and at the curtain, holding it open for him to leave out.

"Thanks beautiful, I will be back to see you... tomorrow?" he questioned and I nodded.

I felt kind of bad about all my thoughts of him, now that I knew he might become a regular. Having a regular that would spend that kind of money is exactly what I needed.

"Bye, babe!" I called after him, just to feel better about how I'd acted towards him. He threw up the peace sign to me, along with a smile.

As he walked off, I spotted Kantwan staring at me. I waved to him, and he just nodded his head to say what's up. He seemed to be bothered by the fact that I was in the room with old boy, but what the fuck did he expect? I'm a stripper, and plus he was nowhere near being my man. We text here and there, and had a couple cool phone conversations, but other than that he was just another nigga. He was fine as hell though. I sometimes entertained the idea of him becoming my man, but I knew that wasn't what I wanted. Guys that aren't as fine as him break hearts, so I could only imagine the damage he'd do to a bitch.

Grabbing my cut from Joey, I walked to the back so I could quickly change into the jean shorts, t-shirt, and Keds I had waiting in my locker. I also made sure to clean myself between the legs with a wipe, and change into some different panties. I always took a shower whenever I got off work, but since I was making a little pit stop, I needed something to tide me over until that happened.

I rushed out of the strip club, and as soon as I made it to my car, I dialed my drug man Loren. He gave me the location to meet him at, and I couldn't get out of that parking lot fast enough. I just wanted to shower, pop one, and chill until I dozed off.

I parked a little ways down from where he told me he'd be at, and then climbed out of my Corolla. I spotted him leaning against a liquor store on Broom Street, just past Chestnut. He was wearing a hoodie, and his right foot was flat against the brick wall, making him lie diagonal.

"Hey," I said and placed my hands into my pockets.

"What's up?" he huffed.

He was really dark, and had even darker eyes. He wasn't cute nor was he ugly, he was just there. He was kind of weird, but shit, I didn't give a fuck.

"Hey, I need like ten," I chuckled nervously.

"You know you still ain't paid me for the ten I loaned you last Monday."

"Okay, so add it all together right now." I had money to spend tonight, thanks to Monty.

"That's gone be $100 even," he said surprising me. I planned to spend about $50, but he was tripping right now.

"Are you serious? You think I'm a fool?"

"It's $100 or nothing."

"I guess nothing," I smacked my lips and turned to leave.

Before I even took a step, he grabbed me by my hair and threw me into this little window gate with a Bud Light poster on it. I saw my blood drip down the picture of the beer, as he gripped my hair tighter into his strong hands.

"You still owe me money bitch, and I want that shit right now," he gritted in my ear.

"I-"

*WHAM!*

He slapped the shit out of me, and it was so hard that I flew from the curb onto the street a little. I was dazed as hell as I walked back onto the sidewalk. I quickly dug into my pockets so I could pay him, but he backhanded me again.

"Stop, I'm gonna pay!" I screamed and tapped my bloody nose with the back of my hand.

He grabbed me up by my neck and said, "I should make you

pay with that pussy." An evil smile made its way across his face as he choked me.

"Aye nigga, put her down!" a familiar voice yelled.

Loren dropped me to the ground, and turned his attention towards Kantwan.

"No, it's okay!" I pleaded to Kantwan, fearing he was about to get shot or stabbed.

I knew Kantwan could beat Loren's ass, but Loren had to be armed. I wouldn't be able to live with myself if Kantwan died trying to defend my drug addict ass.

As soon as they made it to each other, they began tussling.

"Oh my gosh! Stop!" I hollered and rushed over to them.

To my surprise, Loren hadn't pulled out any sort of weapon, despite Kantwan fucking him up pretty badly. Kantwan finally snapped from his trance, and stood up off the bleeding guy. *Damn that was sexy as hell*, I thought.

"Go get in your car and follow me," Kantwan ordered and I nodded to say okay.

We both got into our cars, and then pulled from the curb, making a U-turn towards Lancaster Avenue. Just then, the sound of police sirens were heard, making my heart damn near beat out of my chest. I was tempted to go to the home Jersey and I shared, but I didn't want her questioning me about my fucked up face.

After about ten minutes, we made it to this little house down on Franklin. He hopped out and gestured for me to park behind him, which I did. As soon as I parked, he walked to my door, opened it, and then grabbed my hand into his. I followed him into the house, and he looked at my face as soon as the front door closed.

"Who was that nigga?" He furrowed his brows as he towered over me.

It was unfair to other humans for him to have such perfect features. His cologne permeated the air, and his strong jawline twitched as he waited for my answer. I stared up at him for a little bit, as his long eyelashes moved like fans every time he blinked. His small chin hair and mustache looked so perfect against his pecan complexion. Lord, where did such a sexy ass nigga come from?

"He was an ex-boyfriend," I lied.

"Nah, try again," he shook his head. "He was fucking you up like you owed him some money."

Tears started to race down my cheeks, and he pulled me into a hug. My bloody face had messed up the front of the jacket that he was wearing.

"It's just pills! Nothing else!" I sobbed. He finally pulled away, and held my face in his hands.

"You have to quit that shit, Cheyla, ain't no telling what that nigga was about to do to you. Stay here with me tonight," he looked me up and down. "Oh, do you wanna take a shower?"

"Kantwan, I don't know you—"

"I mean by yourself, Cheyla," he laughed at me and his beautiful smile made me smile.

"Oh, well yes, I would like to take a shower," I said and we both laughed some more.

"Okay. The towels are in the cabinet in the hallway, and I can bring you a t-shirt to sleep in."

I went to take a nice hot shower, and was a little upset that all he had was Irish Spring for soap. It smelled good, but it was manly as hell. I was kind of happy that I didn't see any female soap in here, because honestly I would've been more than a little jealous.

I came out of the shower wrapped in a towel, and went in search of Kantwan. I found him in his bedroom, changing into something more comfortable.

"Now I can see your pretty face without all that blood," he chuckled when he saw me.

"I know," I half smiled and took the shirt he handed to me. I went to the bathroom to put it on, and then came back to his bedroom.

"You hungry?" he asked.

"A little."

He just nodded and left the room. He came back a few minutes later, with some sandwiches that appeared to have all the fixings. We scarfed down the sandwiches and the little bags of chips. We drank some water, and then he cut the lamp off. The only light in the room was coming from the television by now.

We faced each other as we laid down, and just smiled. He pushed my shoulder length hair behind my ears, and then leaned forward to kiss me gently. Before I knew it, we were tongue kissing and he was getting on top of me, touching between my legs.

I didn't have any panties on because I didn't have an extra pair. I shivered at the feeling of his fingers toying with my clit. He then removed his hand, and moved it up the big t-shirt to play with my nipples as we kissed harder. He pressed his erection against my pussy, and damn he was packing. I was happy to know what I felt at the club was the real deal. I wanted to feel him inside of me so badly, but I knew it would lead to more, which I didn't need. I could already tell that he would have me acting a damn fool. I wouldn't be able to function, because I would be thinking about him all day.

"Kantwan, wait."

"Right, I still need to take you out first, huh?" he smirked. I just nodded in agreement.

He pecked me once more, sending shock waves through my body, and then climbed off of me.

"Goodnight," I whispered.

"Goodnight," he responded and cut the TV off with the remote.

I turned my back to him and closed my eyes. Suddenly, I felt his strong arm pull me close. His six-pack was damn near stabbing me in the back, and his dick was prodding me in the ass. He hugged me tightly from behind, and kissed my neck before plopping his head against the pillow. Smiling to myself, I drifted off to sleep.

# THIRTEEN

# Ivy

———

*I* was able to talk to Portland this morning, so the rest of my day went pretty great. I chilled with my son all day, and looked at some schools online. I wanted to look into some majors and see if any of them piqued my interest. I had no idea what I wanted to do, nor did I know what I liked, but I knew shaking my ass for random niggas definitely wasn't it.

Now it was about 7pm, so I wanted to take a nice hot shower before work tonight. I wanted to have enough time to get in there and really take my time before having to drop Donovan off with his aunt Raleigh.

Raleigh was like a sister to me, too. I loved her and how she was very headstrong. She was always about her money, and she never let a nigga play or mistreat her. I think because of what her father did to her mother, she refused to lie down and be a man's doormat. I wished I were more like her, because then maybe Portland would've had some act right during our relationship. As the old saying goes, a man will only do what you allow, and I allowed Portland to do me however. That would be no more though. When he gets out of jail, I hope he's prepared for the new Ivy. The don't take no shit Ivy, and the drop your ass like a whore's panties Ivy.

I had to learn that being a ride or die was not turning a blind eye to your man's wrongdoings, but sticking by him when he was struggling or in need. For years I had the two mixed up, thinking that me allowing Portland to come home after sleeping around, was me being a ride or die. Me holding him down while he served a two-year bid was being a ride or die, not all that other shit.

I turned the shower on after placing Donovan in his little playpen, and then let the hot water run all over me. My hair was getting dry due to the constant washes, but I had to because the owner was forever allowing people to smoke cigarettes and weed in the establishment. I always walked out smelling like perfume and a human ashtray. And we all know that is not a good look, male or female.

I scrubbed my scalp good, and then rinsed the soap out of my hair as my mind drifted. I was really worried about Portland coming home. He would be here in just a couple months, and I'd made no progress in finding another income. I wasn't sure what I was gonna do. And even when I did find a new job, who's to say that someone won't tell him what I'd been doing while he was gone? It was by the grace of God that he hadn't found out while being behind bars. I snapped myself from my thoughts once I saw my hands started to look nasty.

I scrubbed my body down from head to toe twice, and then climbed out to brush my teeth. Your breath could never be too fresh when you had to dance for these niggas. How would that look? Me losing out on a tip because my breath was on hum. I laughed to myself at the thought.

I walked out of the bathroom, and found a simple casual dress to throw on. I didn't like wearing my good shit to the club, because I felt like it would get ruined, or them grimy bitches would try and steal it while I was dancing. One time I accidentally left some expensive tights that Portland purchased me in the bathroom, and as soon as I came back they were gone. No one would admit to the shit either. Them hoes were smart enough not to wear them at the club too.

I gathered all of the things Donovan would need to get through the night, so that he wouldn't be too much trouble to Raleigh, and then we headed out.

I pulled up to Raleigh and Sabrina's house, then put my jacket on since it was pretty cold out by now. It was the end of March, but the sun wasn't showing its face in the daytime as much, like it should've been.

"Come on, baby," I said to Donovan as I grabbed his carrier and diaper bag out of the car.

He grinned and cooed, making a smile appear on my face. I kissed his fat cheeks as I sauntered up the walkway.

Before I reached the door, Sabrina yanked it open wearing a wide smile.

"Is that my grandbaby?" she beamed.

She reached for his carrier and I handed it over right away.

"Mrs. Warren, I thought Raleigh was gonna watch him," I frowned as I closed the front door behind me.

"Oh she is. She's just in the bathroom right now," she responded as she leaned down to kiss my baby.

"So how are you feeling, Ivy?"

"I'm doing okay. I can't wait until your son comes back though," I half smiled and sat down.

"Same here," she sighed and sat down next to me.

I felt so bad when I looked at her, because you could tell that she was still broken up from Mr. Warren leaving her. It may have happened years ago, but they'd been together since she was seventeen. I couldn't imagine being with someone for the majority of my life, just for them to leave me for no reason at all. She refused to sign the divorce papers, Jersey told me, so Mr. Warren had given up on divorcing her.

"I'm sorry you guys have to lie to him," I exhaled, referring to Portland.

"It's okay baby, we all understand. It's just not a good idea to upset him this close to a release. If he acts out in there, his stay could be extended."

"Yeah, that's true. I have to go, tell Raleigh I tried to stay and speak." I stood to my feet.

"I will let her know. Be safe, Ivy."

I nodded and then left to go to work.

When I walked into Starzz, I saw Jersey dancing for some guy, and I felt bad because he was ugly as fuck. But I guess in this business it didn't matter, because it's not like we were fucking them. If a nigga was paying top dollar he could be as ugly as he wanted to be, just as long as he kept his hands to himself.

I went to the back to change, and since I saw I wouldn't be gracing the stage for about an hour, I decided to go out on the floor and make some petty cash. I wore a black one-piece body suit, which was only made up of about three pieces of fabric. It was a thong in the back, and only covered my nipples and pussy in the front. I wore black heels that were clear on the bottom, and then let my golden blond hair hang down.

One thing you had to have while being a stripper was confidence. So what if you knew how to move like Ciara, if you weren't comfortable wearing little to nothing, then it wasn't the occupation for you. Plus, niggas could smell when your self-esteem was low, and that shit was not sexy at all. A bitch could have a body like a bag of steel cut oats, but if she had that arrogance, niggas wouldn't even notice. She'd make way more money than the self-loathing bitch with a body like Amber Rose.

I walked out onto the floor, and bobbed my head to the music this girl Pound Cake was dancing to. Her name fit because she had plenty of cake. She made a bitch want to get ass implants sometimes. I had a small nice ass too, but her shit was literally able to carry a cup on it; we tried it.

I danced a little as I walked by, and I felt someone staring at me. I looked over, and there was this light-skinned guy with dreads. He wasn't dressed too flashy, but he definitely didn't look lowball. He was super cute from what I could see, but then again it was dark. I made my way over to him, and once I got close, he pulled the cup away from his face.

"You don't appear to be having a good time," I smirked.

"Oh, I'm just chilling," he squinted his sexy brown eyes.

Yeah, he was definitely cute. Scratch that, this nigga was fine as fuck, and I could tell by his calm demeanor that he wasn't one of those thirsty niggas that usually frequented Starzz. He had the head of a snake tatted on his neck, with the tongue stretching all the way to the bottom of his chin. His cologne was invigorating and alluring at the same time. I hadn't been attracted to anybody really, especially here at work, but he definitely had my interest. It was just something about him that screamed boss nigga. It was something Portland didn't have anymore.

"Well, would you like a dance while you're chilling?" I questioned and waited. "It's usually $35, but I will do it for $25 for you," I smiled.

I wanted to hopefully turn him into a loyal customer by giving him a discount. I wanted him to visit me all the time, because I could make more money that way, and because he was extremely easy on the eyes. *I wonder if he has a bitch... It shouldn't matter Ivy.*

"Nah, I don't want no discount, but I will take the dance. If you give me a discount, you may not put in the same work and I don't want that. I wanna see everything that little sexy ass body can do," he responded seriously and set his cup on the table. Forward much?

He kind of scared me but in a good way. He had me feeling like I needed to deliver the best lap dance I'd ever given to anybody. I kind of wanted to offer him a private dance, but I didn't want him thinking that I was just interested in his money. I should've only been interested in his money, but I wasn't.

I turned around to sit in his lap, and worked my ass as "Jimmy Choo" by Fetty Wap played loudly. He didn't touch me at all, but I did see him reach for his drink a few times. For the first time in the history of me being a stripper, I wanted the person to touch me. I wanted to feel his tattooed hands on my body.

Once I was done, I was about to get up but he locked his strong arm around my waist. My sense of touch kicked in majorly, sending all kinds of messages to my pussy. I wanted his strong arm to stay wrapped around my waist forever.

His crew neck sleeve rose up, and I saw a pretty ass watch around his wrist.

"What's your name and not your stripper name?" He looked up

at me and sipped his drink. I knew he meant business, and I was scared to play games with him. Damn.

"If I tell you, you have to keep it a secret," I giggled nervously.

He licked his full lips, and looked my body over before responding. His facial hair scratched my arm, and for some reason my clit throbbed when it happened.

"Secret is safe with me."

I never told guys my name, in fear that it would get back to Portland in jail, but he didn't seem like the type of nigga to go home running his mouth. This was a real nigga right here, not a bragging ass dude.

"It's Ivy," I stuck my hand up to him to shake his.

He put his drink back down, and then shook my hand. His other arm was still wrapped around my waist, locking me in his lap. I could sort of feel his dick through his jeans, and from the feeling alone, I knew he had an anaconda. *Fuck, I ain't had dick in forever*, I thought.

"Ivy, that's a pretty name. Like Poison Ivy."

The way he said my name in his raspy tone had me on one. He smiled at me, and the top row of his teeth were whiter than cocaine, and the bottom was covered with a diamond grill. A grill was not cute, but on him the shit was boss as fuck.

"What's yours?" I bit my lip, hoping I wasn't making a wet spot on his jeans.

Just then, Jersey walked by and gave me a strange look. I guess because he and I looked super cozy. I couldn't get up just yet though; I had to know this nigga's name. I wouldn't be able to sleep at night if I didn't get his name. I may have to pull out my toy when I get home.

"Elijah, but everyone calls me Eli," he said.

"Nice to meet you, Elijah," I said and moved his hand from around my waist abruptly.

Jersey had reminded me that I was with Portland, and being way too flirty with Elijah. Niggas knew Portland all around Delaware, and it would be nothing for them to run back and tell that not only did they see me stripping, but that they saw me flirting with some nigga the way that I was.

"Damn, what, you don't like that name?" He frowned and chuckled because of how quickly I got up.

"No it's cute, umm, I have to go get ready so…" I stuck my hand out for the money.

"My bad." He placed two twenties into my hand.

"I don't have change ye—"

He put his hand up to say it was cool.

I nodded and rushed off towards the bar for some water. When I got there, I looked over my shoulder at him, and he was on his phone talking to someone. *Ivy, you need to be careful*, I told myself.

## FOURTEEN

## Jersey

---

A Couple Days Later...

Tonight was my date with Tommy. He'd been real patient with me, and I was starting to like him a little. He was cute and appeared to have his shit together, so I saw no reason not to give him a chance. And unlike most niggas, he wasn't begging me to come to the crib and chill, he wanted to take me on a real damn date.

I hadn't hung out with a guy alone in a while, and I was a bit nervous even though we would be in public at dinner. What was I supposed to talk about? How much was I supposed to divulge on a first date? What was I supposed to even ask him? It was way more stressful than the little dates I used to go on with my high school boyfriend.

I chose to wear a long sleeved blue dress, which was open in the back, and stopped a few inches above my knees. It was just the right amount of sexy, and perfect for a first date in my opinion. It felt good to be able to be sexy without having to be in a G-string and pasties. I almost forgot that wearing clothes that covered more than your nipples and vagina could be sexy too.

After tousling my hair in different directions, I finally settled on a position, and then slipped into some blue sandal stilettos. I gave myself the once over in my full-length mirror, then went and sat down in the living room with my black clutch.

I guess Tommy would let me know when he arrived, since he'd already text me to let me know he was on his way. I hoped that by the time he'd gotten here, my nervousness would have calmed down a bit.

"Ooh, you look pretty," Cheyla smiled as she emerged from her bedroom.

"Thank you," I cheesed.

"You're welcome. I hope you and Tommy become a thing, because maybe Kantwan and I could become a thing, and that'd be dope if we were dating best friends."

"Wait, I thought you said Kantwan was a no go."

"Yeah, but the more I talk to him, the harder it is for me to deny the attraction. Plus, have you seen him, he's so fucking sexy," she sighed and walked to the kitchen.

The way our apartment was set up, you could see clearly into the kitchen from the living room. The only thing separating the two was an island.

"And you still haven't let him take you out on an official date?" I quizzed.

"No, but I will. I just need to get some shit together."

Cheyla and this Kantwan guy were weird. A week ago she spent like four days over his house, before she finally came home. She didn't come to work either, and if she hadn't been texting me faithfully, I would've thought she was dead. I didn't know what they were doing, but if they liked it I loved it. I could tell Cheyla was denying her feelings for him though, because that's how she was. She treated relationships like they were the plague.

His brother, whom Cheyla confirmed for me was named Kill, crossed my mind every now and then still. He hadn't been by the club in weeks, but he was way too gorgeous for me to forget about. I remember everything about him, right down to the tattoo on the side of his hand that read *Trust no one*. I could still smell his Gucci cologne, and I could picture his beautiful smile and deep dimples with ease.

I knew he was from Hilltop because he had it tattooed on the side of his neck, but that was all I knew about him outside of his nickname. He was so mysterious, and he never talked when I was around him. The less I knew, the more I wanted to know. Even his name was sexy, despite its violent meaning.

I found myself asking Tommy little things about him, but I didn't want to be too obvious and upset him. I was really starting to like Tommy, so I didn't wanna ruin what we were somewhat building, over a guy whose voice I'd never even heard.

I could tell, however, that Tommy was not a fan of Kill. He made him sound like some bitch nigga who thought he was better than everybody. I didn't get that vibe from him, but then again, Tommy actually knew him. I got the impression that he was very sure of himself, and that he demanded respect. Maybe that came off as stuck up behavior to some, but not to me.

"What are you thinking about?" Cheyla snapped me from my thoughts.

"Oh, nothing," I responded just as my phone started ringing. I saw Tommy's name, and a smiled formed on my face. "Hello?" I answered.

"I'm here, beautiful," he said and I could hear him smiling as well.

"Okay," I quickly hit the circular end button on my iPhone. "Well, that's my date." I stood up as Cheyla flipped through channels while holding a bag of chips.

"Have fun and don't give the pussy up too soon," she taunted.

"Weren't you just busting it open for Kantwan a week ago?"

"Actually, no. He's a gentleman and didn't pressure me at all. We just chilled."

"Bye," I waved her off and locked the front door behind me.

I saw Tommy's Lexus sitting in the middle of the street with the hazards blinking, and I strutted over there. I hoped he was watching, because I was putting a little extra switch in my hips for him. I reached the door, and I heard the locks click, so I pulled on the handle.

"Hi," I said as I slid into his leather seats.

They were heated, which felt so good against my somewhat sore back. I'd worked until 3am the night before, and took damn near no breaks.

"Damn, you look good and you smell good," he licked his lips.

"You do too."

He wore a blue polo, with dark blue jeans, and he had a nice chain and watch on. His hazel eyes looked beautiful even in the dark car, and his full lips made my mouth water. I usually didn't go for light-skinned guys, but Tommy was good looking as hell.

"Thanks," he rubbed his fade.

He looked over his shoulder, and then pulled off towards Oak Street, making a left on Maryland Avenue so we could hop on the 95. We arrived at this Malaysian restaurant on Concord Pike named Rasa Sayang, located inside the Independence Mall.

Since it was a Wednesday night, there was a really short wait. I'd never been here, so I allowed Tommy to order for us based on what I told him I liked.

"The food will be out shortly," the waitress nodded.

"Great," Tommy smiled at her before turning his attention to me. "So damn, I finally got Jersey out," he stroked his chin hairs. "It's hard not to call you Bliss since you took so long to give me your name," he chuckled and so did I.

"Please don't call me that outside of work," I half joked and sipped my water.

"So why were you brushing me off?"

"I don't know. I guess guys just aren't my main focus. And I'm not used to someone being so interested," I said and pushed my curly hair to the other side.

"Really? You're beautiful as fuck though."

"Thank you. And no, I meant that usually when I brush a guy off, he doesn't keep coming for me like you did."

"Oh, well I'm a persistent guy," he shrugged and smiled. His smile was so warm, and you could tell he was a really nice guy.

"I like persistence," I said and he bit his lip.

"So what you in school for?" He quizzed.

"For business and art. I want to become a corporate art buyer."

"Oh, alright."

"What do you do? I see you got a Lexus, nice jewelry and clothes, so it must be something that pays well," I chuckled.

"I do what I can, you know. I mainly do little odd jobs."

"Odd jobs like what?"

"You know, all kinds of shit."

What kind of answer was that? I didn't wanna push it too much since it was just the first date though. Maybe he was embarrassed, or maybe it was some illegal shit that he didn't feel comfortable spilling to me yet.

"Well, do you have any siblings Tommy?" I inquired.

"Yeah, I got an older brother named Andre, but he's in jail right now."

"Wow, really? I have a brother in jail too."

"Word? I hate that shit. I miss my brother like crazy."

"Yeah, me too," I sighed. "But he will be out in about seven months, so I'm just waiting for his release day."

"Lucky you. My brother murdered somebody so he got life."

"Damn, I'm sure he was just defending himself."

"I don't know. He killed his girlfriend when he found out she cheated on him. I guess that's self-defense," he shrugged.

*No the fuck that ain't!* I thought. I hoped that kind of crazy did not run in the family, because that was not some shit I wanted to endure.

"Oh, dang," was all I could think to say in response.

We talked about a lot of stuff over dinner, and the food was really good, especially their curry red snapper. We ate dessert, and then Tommy paid the bill. As we walked out of the mall and to his car, he grabbed my hand in his, making me smile. I was really feeling him, but for some reason I found myself thinking of Kill and not him when my mind became idle.

"So, should we go chill at your crib?" he smiled as he backed out the parking space.

"I don't think that's a good idea, Tommy."

"Oh, aight," he pursed his lips and then started towards the exit of the shopping center.

We listened to music the whole way, until he finally made it to my home. He pulled over into an empty spot, and then we both removed our seatbelts from our bodies. We looked at one another, and then he leaned over to kiss me. His lips were so nice, and felt great. I caressed the side of his face as we indulged in one another. He rubbed his hand up my dress, which caused me to pull away. I was not feeling the idea of having sex with him this early.

"Thanks for the dinner, Tommy," I said and pulled on the lever to get out.

"Jersey—"

I slammed the door before he could finish. I really enjoyed my time with Tommy, but he was trying to move way too fast. Hopefully we could take things slower, and allow our relationship to develop. I hoped he was okay with that, because I could really see us becoming something.

"How was it, sweet thang?" Cheyla asked, standing in the doorway of her room.

"It was really nice."

"Nice? Did he make your pussy wet with just eye contact?"

I burst into laughter and she joined me.

"No, he did not make my pussy wet with just eye contact. Give it time, Cheyla."

"Fuck that shit, Kantwan had me ready to suck his dick in the back of Starzz the first night I met him. If that nigga doesn't have you struggling to tone down your inner hoe, then it ain't gon' work," she smacked her lips.

"Inner hoe? I don't have that." I removed my heels from my feet and walked into my room, which she followed.

"Oh yes, every woman has a little hoe in them, it's just that some of us choose to suppress it, and some of us choose to act on it."

"Not me."

"So you've never met a guy that made you wanna fuck right then and there?"

Kill immediately came to my mind. The first night I saw him, everything in my body tingled, and he hadn't even touched me. He was the first guy in years to have me thinking about nasty shit, and wanting to know what the dick was like. I couldn't tell Cheyla that though, because she would be determined to hook us up. Maybe that wouldn't be such a bad thing though...

"Yeah you have, bitch!" Cheyla interrupted my thoughts with her cackling and clapping, because she knew she was right.

"Look, get out, I have class in the morning," I chuckled, and shoved her lightly out of my room before closing the door.

I changed into a nightshirt, and then crawled into bed. As I listened to the faint voices of people out on the street, my mind drifted to Kill. Lying on my side, I rubbed my thighs together at the thought of him sexing me. I shut my eyes tightly, trying to fantasize about Tommy instead, before falling asleep.

# FIFTEEN

# Tommy

___________

Outside in the Car...

*I* watched Jersey walk her ass into the house, after turning down this dick I was trying to offer her. I was hot as hell. She went from being some hoe I was trying to fuck, to me actually spending money on her ass. I had no plans to ever take her ass out, but she was yapping about how niggas didn't take chicks out any more. I knew right then if I invited her over to the crib, while Sasha was at work of course, she would stop talking to me.

Now it'd been three damn weeks since I'd been trying to get her to suck my dick at the least, and all I'd gotten was a measly ass kiss. She didn't even use tongue.

I usually would've given up by now, but my ego was involved. I usually always got the pussy, no matter how stuck up or hard to get the bitch was. I was determined to fuck Jersey and I was going to. I just hoped that her ass didn't get sprung after I ran up in her pretty ass, because if so, that number was getting blocked!

I sped off towards my crib that I shared with Sasha, and prepared to hear her going off in my ear about where the hell I'd been all damn night. I pulled into our driveway, and parked behind her Jeep Cherokee. It was so crazy how we literally lived less than five minutes from Jersey. I wasn't tripping though, because I had cheated on Sasha with hoes that lived next door, across the street, and even some of her co-workers.

I shut the engine off, and then swagged into the crib. I walked into the living room and smiled when I saw it was spotless. I could tell she had sprayed some Febreze or some shit, because it smelled like fruity flowers. That was one thing about Sasha, a nigga never had to chill in a pig sty or go hungry.

I went into the kitchen and opened a cabinet to get one of my two ounce bottles of Jack Daniels. I downed it in damn near one gulp, and then tossed it into the sink. I needed a little something to calm me down, because I was furious about tonight. I just knew that I was gonna be knee deep in Jersey's guts. I sucked my teeth as I headed to the back.

I entered the bedroom, and Sasha was lying there pretending to be sleep. I knew she was wide-awake, but I was gonna go along with her bullshit. She could never go to sleep if I was out late, and the shit was annoying.

I stripped down to nothing, and as soon as my head hit the pillow, she turned to face me. What the fuck, son!

"Where have you been all night, Tommy?" she asked. I could tell she was frowning even though my eyes were closed. I was lying on my back with my face pointed towards the ceiling.

"Handling my business," I replied nonchalantly.

I didn't give a fuck about how she felt right now. I was horny as hell, and angry as fuck. She couldn't fix either one, because I was horny for Jersey and not her. Her pussy was the same old pussy I'd been getting for years, and I was bored of it. I only fucked Sasha when I just needed to bust a nut and nothing else. Most times I just bent her over so I wouldn't have to look into her face, and I could imagine someone else. Sasha was beautiful and had a banging body like I said before, but after a while, fucking the same pussy becomes a chore. She would sometimes walk around naked to entice me, but my dick just wouldn't be into it. Right now my dick was not in the mood for her, it wanted Jersey and not the same old same.

"Handling business? Tamara said she saw you in the parking lot of the Independence Mall with some bitch!" she hollered, and the bed moved letting me know she was sitting up.

I sat up calmly, and then rapidly grabbed her by the neck as if she was a rag doll.

"Look, I'm tired as fuck and I want some pussy. I don't feel like dealing with you and your bullshit aight? Yes, I was out with another bitch, but I'm sure you'll be happy to know I didn't fuck yet. I will though, so don't get your hopes up," I growled and let go of her neck.

Her best friend Tamara had some fucking nerve running her mouth to Sasha, when she was just sucking my dick, and letting me raw dog her two days ago. I think she was still mad because I made her ass get an abortion, but shit, I didn't want no fucking kids.

Sasha stared at me with her eyes bucked, and then just laid back down without uttering another word. I heard her sniffle a little, but I really didn't care at all. Unless she could convince Jersey to come over and let me beat it up, we had nothing to talk about.

▭

*I* woke up the next morning, and frowned because my mouth felt dry as fuck. This always happened whenever I drank alcohol right before bed. My stomach was in need of food, so I walked into the kitchen to see Sasha sitting at the table sipping coffee.

"Why don't you make a nigga some pancakes or something," I said and rubbed my six-pack.

"Sure," she replied dryly and stood up.

I thought about the way I'd came her at the night before, and realized that I needed some money, so I had to make up with her ass.

"Aye look, I ain't mean to choke you and shit. And I wasn't with no other girl, okay?" I hugged her from behind and kissed her ear.

"Okay," she sniffled.

I let her go and then went to shower and brush my teeth. When I got out it was a bowl of grits, next to a plate of pancakes, turkey bacon, and eggs. That's what the fuck I'm talking about. Sasha knew how to treat a king.

"Thanks, baby. And maybe we can go out this week," I sold her some wolf tickets.

She grinned and then said, "Okay."

"Yeah, but you got me?"

"Got you? What do you mean?"

"I need to hold $80 babe."

"For what, Tommy? I just gave you cash last night! I'm barely covering the bills, which you said you would help me out with!"

"I can't do this shit!" I shot up out of my seat to leave.

"Okay, wait!" She reached for her purse and retrieved her wallet. I tried to contain my smile as I saw her count out eighty dollars. "Here."

"Thanks, baby." I sat back down, and resumed eating after pocketing the money. She would flip if she knew she paid for Jersey and I to have dinner last night.

After eating my food, I kissed Sasha goodbye and dipped out to Kantwan's crib. I wanted to turn around and go home when I saw his brother's Denali in the driveway. I got out anyway, and when Kantwan let me in, neither Kill nor Elijah spoke to me. I chuckled at them and then popped a squat in the empty La-Z-Boy.

"So what you been getting into?" Kantwan quizzed.

"Robbed these two bitches on Connell and Elm," I laughed.

"Still robbing niggas to get by," Kill shook his head.

"Yeah, I am, you got a problem with that?" I frowned at him.

"Just not a cool way to get money," Elijah chimed in.

"Oh and y'all think pushing white on the corner is? Fuck out of here!" I waved them off.

"At least I'm working for my shit and not just taking what someone else has worked for," Kill mugged me. "Only bitch ass niggas do shit like that."

I had to take a deep breath, because this nigga was making my blood boil.

"Chill out Kill," Kantwan told his brother.

"Anyway *Kant*, I also been getting into that jawn from Starzz, Bliss," I licked my lips.

I couldn't help but notice that Kill looked my way upon mentioning her. He looked like he wanted to say something, which made me smile on the inside.

"Oh word? You hit?" Kantwan inquired, as Kill fired up a blunt and took a pull.

"Nah man but I been trying," I scoffed.

'

"Ain't you got a bitch at home?" Kill scowled.

"So, ain't like I'm looking to marry her. I just want the pussy and then she can be on about her way," I laughed as Kantwan shook his head at me.

"Dumb ass nigga," Kill mumbled.

"What nigga?" I stood up.

"I said you's a dumb ass nigga," he hopped up as well and glared at me.

"What, you wanted that hoe?" I laughed and clapped my hands.

"If I wanted her I would have her," he looked into my eyes.

"Stop calling every damn girl you know a hoe, T," Kantwan shook his head like he was tired of me. This was not the time for him to be reprimanding me.

"Nigga please," I said to Kill and sat back down. He paused but then sat down as well.

"I hope you never fuck," Elijah joked and that was it.

I was pissed. I think because I was feeling like I would never get the pussy, and the fact that they were laughing at me about it angered me. In addition, I think Kill was kind of interested in Jersey, and I didn't want him chasing her too. Bitches acted like this nigga Kill was the greatest thing since sliced bread, and a part of me felt like if he wanted her he could have her.

In the past, I'd tried to smash a plenty of bitches that had given it up to Kill on the first night, and they acted like I was some dirty ass roach or something. I don't know what it was about him, but he was just a regular ass fuck nigga in my eyes.

"Aight, what's up?" I stood up and pulled off my crew neck. I was ready to take on Kill or Elijah—shit, both at the same time if they wanted to.

"Sit down boy, before I have to put you over my knee," Kill said, and took a pull on the blunt.

"Aye y'all, calm the fuck down," Kantwan stood between his brother and I, even though Kill hadn't moved from his sitting position.

"Nah, I'm tired of this nigga thinking he better than every damn body!" I screamed and charged Kill.

He hopped up with the quickness, and we started going at it. He got me twice in my nose and jaw, infuriating me further. I swung and hit the side of his head, which seemed to turn him into a fucking monster. He started pounding on me to the point where I just put my arms up to defend myself as I fell to the floor.

"I told you to stop fucking with me!" he yelled as he pummeled me.

"Aye Kilexis, man, stop!" Kantwan yelled his brother's government name as he pulled him off of me.

I stood up off the ground, and my face was on fire. I knew I looked a mess and I was pissed.

"That's it Kantwan, pick!" I shouted.

"What?" he frowned.

"It's me or this nigga! I can't play friends no more!"

"Man, I ain't about to pick. That's some dumb shit!" Kantwan twisted his face up.

"Enough said." I threw my hands up, snatched my sweater, and stormed out.

"Bye bitch," Elijah called after me.

I turned to charge him, but Kantwan stopped me.

"Fuck off me, man!" I pushed him back and went to my car.

I was done with all of them niggas, and I couldn't wait until the day that they all needed me.

SIXTEEN

# Kantwan

_______________

$\mathcal{I}$ was tired as hell right now, but thanking God I was off work. I really hated my job at Costco, but right now it paid the bills. When I first got hired I was only making $13/hour, but a couple raises later and now it was $17/hour. I made just enough to pay the house note, buy food, and splurge very minimally here and there. However, this was not something I wanted to do forever. On top of that, I worked for the one in Glenn Mills, Pennsylvania, so it was a cool thirty minutes away; not ideal.

After dragging my ass to the back to clock out, I gathered my things so I could leave. It was around 6pm, and the sun was completely gone by now. I couldn't wait until summer when the sun stayed out a little longer. It seemed like when the sun went down, niggas thought it was their cue to act a fucking fool.

Although ready to just knock out, I couldn't contain the excitement I felt about tonight. Cheyla's little sexy ass was finally gonna let me take her out. I wasn't the type of nigga that chased women, nor was I the type to be into strippers, but it was something about Cheyla that I really liked. I could also see that under that hard ass exterior, she was a really nice and cool chick.

Her occupation as a stripper had nothing to do with her personality, because she didn't let me smash once during her little vacation at my crib, and trust me I wanted to. She only stayed with me until her face healed, so that Jersey and her other friend Ivy wouldn't ask about her wounds. She also made me promise to keep her secret, and of course, I agreed. Plus, I didn't know her friends like that for me to be dropping news on them about her.

I got home in about thirty minutes, and got my ass into the shower right away. As soon as I got in, I let the water run over my waves, and closed my eyes so I could calm down. I was way too excited to go on this date, and it was low key embarrassing. My dick was already hardening at the thought of her.

I really don't know what it was about Cheyla, but I just had to have her. There were plenty of bitches in Wilmington for me to bang out, but I wanted her. On top of that, I was never the type of nigga to just be smashing hoes left and right. Yeah I had my fair share, because I love pussy, but these hoes 'round here had them sick pussies, and I'll be damned if one of them burned me.

Muthafuckas like Tommy didn't care though. There were women that he knew had STDs prior, and he would still fuck raw. He was one of those 'it can't happen to me' type of niggas. Me on the other hand, I'd witnessed niggas get burned and it was not pretty.

My homeboy Trey, rest in peace, got burned by some bitch in high school once. I just remember him screaming in pain at the top of his lungs, as he stood over the toilet with a dripping dick. We had to call 911 for that nigga. I knew right then that my dick had to be picky.

Once I was cleaned to my liking, I brushed my teeth as Young Jeezy blared through my portable speaker in the bathroom. For some reason, I always played his shit when I was getting ready. It didn't matter if it was for work or what, one of his albums stayed in rotation.

About an hour later, I was fully dressed and smelling good, so I texted Cheyla and asked her if she was ready since I was on my way. Soon as I got the word that she was ready and waiting, I dipped out.

On my way there, I was thinking about all kinds of shit

regarding my life. I couldn't do this Costco shit forever, and I felt like there was no time for me to go to school if I wanted to pay bills. I would definitely have to cut back on my hours at work if I wanted to take classes, and right now that wasn't in the budget. I was frustrated because I felt stuck. I knew in order to do better for myself, I needed an education or some kind of certified training in something, but there was no room in my life for it.

How can I cut back at work, when that would result in less bread? Then how would I enroll in school when that would require more money on top of the shit I already had to pay now? It was just a mess, and I was hoping I figured something out soon. I was tired of staying up until one and two in the fucking morning, worried about being a Costco team member for the rest of my fucking life. That wasn't an option, but all I could do right now is pray for God to show me the way.

I was so lost in my thoughts, that I'd passed up Cheyla's apartment and had to make a fucking U-turn. I luckily found a park on this otherwise packed street, and then headed up to her door. I heard her talking to another girl, who I assumed was her roommate and best friend Jersey that she'd told me about during our time together at my house. The same girl that I knew Tommy wanted to fuck, and my brother Kill wanted to fucking marry. I laughed because Kill would never admit that shit. I ain't never seen him eye a girl with so much passion in my fucking life.

I knocked and then looked at my surroundings as I waited. I saw a homeless man walking down the street looking into people's cars and just shook my head. *I better not catch his ass peeping in my shit*, I said to myself. I nodded my head to say what's up to a couple hustlers who were chilling on their porch steps, and then turned my attention back to the door.

Finally, the door came open, and I saw the girl Jersey that Tommy and Kill had fought over. If she only knew she was such a hot commodity 'round here.

She smiled when she saw me and said, "Kantwan, right?"

"That's me," I grinned and then she gestured for me to come inside.

"Cheyla is ready, she's just getting her car charger," she said and then sat down.

I felt kind of fucked up because I knew Tommy was just trying to fuck her, and I hadn't said anything. Then again, maybe she and Tommy had a fucking agreement. I don't know, but I just hoped me knowing didn't come back to bite me in the ass.

I mean yeah, Tommy and I hadn't spoken since he and Kill almost came to blows, but he was still my nigga. I couldn't throw him under the bus just to make Cheyla and her home girl happy, even if he and I weren't on speaking terms.

Tommy and I had been cool for years, and I hoped that little tiff back at my crib wasn't the end of our friendship. But I wasn't one to chase anybody, especially a grown ass man, so if he wanted to have his boxers in a bunch then that was him. I just hoped he wasn't expecting a call from me, because he'd be waiting forever. If I was gonna pursue anything with great zeal, it was gonna be Cheyla and my bread.

"Hi," Cheyla walked out wearing a red strapless dress.

It was short but not too short, and she had on red heels to match. Her dark caramel complexion was beautiful, and had not a dull area in sight. Her dark hair was hanging down, sweeping just under her shoulders. This girl was fine as fuck, and it made me wonder why in the hell no one had tried to bag her pretty ass already. *God, please don't make her turn out to be one of those sick hoes*, I prayed silently.

"Damn Cheyla, you look good as fuck," I stood up.

I was wearing a gray button up, with light blue jeans, and all white leather Givenchy sneakers. No, I didn't buy them, my oldest brother Ka'shea got them for me when he was out of jail and pushing major weight in the streets. It was a birthday gift, and damn was I grateful.

"You look nice too, and you smell good," Cheyla licked her lips, even though she had some tan gloss on them.

She tapped her nose ring, I guess to make sure it was in place, and then walked over to me for a hug. As soon as I slipped my hands around her waist, I pulled her in and lightly kissed her neck.

She giggled and then asked, "You ready?"

"Born."

I took her hand, and then led her out to my car after saying bye to Jersey.

"I got my nails done just for you," Cheyla said as she buckled her seat belt.

"You ain't have to do that, you know you're bad regardless."

"I'm glad you think so, but I was due for a fill anyway," she chuckled as I looked over my shoulder, and then pulled from the curb.

We ended up at Mrs. Robino's on Union Street, which was a well-priced Italian restaurant. I liked this placed because they had a thing where you could create your own pasta dish. Try pasta with crab, it's so damn good. After placing our appetizer, drink, and entree order, the waiter pranced away to put it in for us.

"Damn, so you're finally out with a nigga," I smiled and so did Cheyla.

"Yeah, I haven't been on a date since... Does prom count?" she chuckled.

"Nah, prom doesn't count whatsoever."

"Well then this is my first date, I guess," she shrugged.

"You've honestly never been on a real date? Why?"

"I've just never been interested in going. I mean people have asked me, but I always turned them down."

"Well, I must say that I am happy to be able to take you out," I smiled and so did she. "Is there a reason why you were never interested in going out with other guys?"

"I guess I just didn't like them as much as I like you."

"That's the perfect answer," I grinned and we laughed in unison.

Our dishes arrived to the table about forty minutes later, and Cheyla's eyes lit up.

"I'm guessing you're hungry?" I laughed.

"Yes, very. Did I look that desperate?"

"Yeah, I can tell you ain't ate in a while."

"Shut up!" she giggled. She was so fucking pretty, especially when she laughed like that. I adjusted my hard on before digging in.

We polished off the dishes, and decided to share cannoli for dessert. As we exited the restaurant, I saw her shivering, so I threw my coat over her shoulders. She looked up at me as I did it, and a faint smile spread across her face.

"Thank you," she chuckled nervously.

On the way back to her home, we just rode in silence, listening to my playlist of music, with the heat on. We glanced at each other every now and then, giving half smiles and shit. Every time I got a glimpse of her legs, my dick bricked up, so I had to stop looking. I pulled up to her apartment building, and stopped with my car still running.

"This was fun, Kantwan," she bit her lip and stared into my eyes like she was thinking.

"Yeah, it was. I'm hoping we can do it again and very soon."

"I don't think that's a good idea," she said and then opened the door abruptly.

"Cheyla!" She slammed the door before I could finish.

What the fuck just happened?

The next day...

The way Cheyla ended our date had been heavy on my mind all last night and this morning. I kept trying to see if I'd said something to make her switch like that. I thought maybe she saw my dick was hard and got scared, but she'd seen that plenty of times when she stayed with me.

"Nigga, snap out of it," my brother Kill snapped his fingers in my face.

"I'm just trying to figure out what I did."

"Instead of going crazy and making up reasons, just hit her and ask her ass."

"Aight."

I grabbed my phone, and scrolled in my texts until I saw Cheyla's and my conversation. I clicked it, and then paused for a second to figure out what I wanted to say.

***Me:*** *Good afternoon, beautiful. I'm just a little confused about your reaction last night. Did I do something to offend you?*

My phone vibrated shortly after, and I was surprised to see that she'd text back so fast.

***Cheyla:*** *No, I started my period and had to get out of the car before it ruined my dress and your seats. Lol*

That didn't explain why she declined my second date offer, but okay.

***Me:*** *Oh, alright. So we're good?*

***Cheyla:*** *Yeah we're good, and I can't wait to see you again.*

I knew her ass was lying like fuck, and it made her appear to be a bit off kilter. That shit was kind of sexy though, so for now I would let her slide. But if she kept acting like a weirdo, I would have to keep it pushing unfortunately.

"What she say?" Kill questioned.

"That she started her period." I gave him a look to let him know I didn't believe it.

"Damn, she sounds crazy and weird," he chuckled.

"Yeah, but I like them crazy."

"Until they bite your dick off one night," he said and we both started laughing.

# SEVENTEEN

## Jersey

One Week Later...

*I* was so happy to be off tonight, but even happier that my friends weren't going in either. I was looking up some movie times, because I wanted us to all go out and chill and shit. It'd been a while since we'd all had the night off together, so I was excited to hang with my friends.

As I was scrolling on my phone looking at the current films in theaters, I walked into Cheyla's room.

"Hey, I was thinking you, Ivy, and I could go see a movie tonight," I leaned in her doorway.

"I was thinking we could go hang out with Kantwan," she countered, brushing her hair in the mirror.

"What? I thought you said you were gonna stop talking to him."

"I changed my mind."

Cheyla always did this shit. She would meet a guy, and as soon as he started trying to get close, she would back off, change her mind, back off, and then keep it going until the guy got fed up. I thought with Kantwan she'd be different since she actually let the nigga take her on a date, but I guess not. I knew he would soon get tired of her and bounce like all the others.

"You need to stop being so indecisive Cheyla, that's why you haven't been on a date until Kantwan," I sighed and sat on the edge of her bed, admiring her new comforter.

"I know, and that's why when he texted me asking what was wrong, I changed my mind and decided to try him out some more," she smiled at me and then switched to her closet. "So are you going?"

"I really wanted to hang with you and Ivy alone."

"Ivy is coming with me. It's gonna be us two, Kantwan, his brother, and his cousin Elijah."

"So Ivy is going," I said more so to myself. "I wouldn't have told Tommy I couldn't see him tonight if I knew I couldn't hang with y'all."

"Where are you going?" she asked when she saw me leaving.

"I'm gonna tell Tommy that we can hang out."

"Just come with us, please!"

"Cheyla, no! And how would Tommy feel, knowing I'm hanging out with his people and he's not around. And why isn't he gonna be there anyway?"

"Girl, hell if I know. I'm just worried about Kantwan. Just come with us and chill Jersey, ain't like Tommy is your man. Plus, he couldn't even get your pussy throbbing when y'all went out!"

"Fine, what are you wearing?"

"I'm just gonna wear jeans and a t-shirt. We're just chilling, it ain't nothing special. But hurry up because we have to pick up Ivy in ten minutes."

I plodded to my room, and then pulled out some cuffed jean shorts, a quarter sleeve crop top, and some red chucks. I combed my fresh press down, and smiled in the mirror. I had a love hate relationship with getting my hair pressed, because it was pricey but easy to handle. My naturally curly hair was too much damn work, but it was cheaper. I knew this press would be gone after I went to work tomorrow night, but I was gonna enjoy it while it was thriving.

I grabbed my purse, phone, and charging port before following

Cheyla out the door. After getting Ivy, we pulled up to these condos in Hilltop, on Franklin and Third. It was deep in the hood, but the places were still kind of nice.

Cheyla pulled up to a car that she saw was leaving, and waited for them to pull from the curb so she could take their parking space. She pulled in, making sure the side facing the street wasn't sticking out, and then shut the engine off. She checked her appearance in the visor mirror, and Ivy checked hers in some little mirror she had in her purse. I wanted to pretend I didn't care, so I opted out of the mirror check.

We got out the car and walked down a couple houses, until Cheyla pointed to the one we were here to visit. I nodded my head as we stepped onto the porch, because these little homes were really clean, despite the location.

"Whose house is this?" I asked Cheyla.

"Kantwan's brother," she responded and slipped her phone into her purse. I raised both of my eyebrows at the thought of Kill having such a nice little crib.

Finally, the door flung open, and there stood the guy that Ivy was flirting with that night at the club. His dreads were hanging loosely, and he was wearing a regular black shirt, with light blue jeans and Nike Air Max. He was real cute, tall, and had that same cocky demeanor as Kill and Kantwan; I could smell it on him.

He stared straight at Ivy even though Cheyla and I were in front of her, and when I looked back at her she was blushing. Seeing them silently flirt made me feel some type of way. What was she doing? She was supposed to be sticking by my brother.

"Welcome ladies," he said and stepped back to let us in. We walked inside, and there was a bathroom to the right, and a staircase ahead of us. "Come on, Kantwan and Kill are upstairs," he gestured up the stairs and we walked up them. "How are you, beautiful?" I heard him whisper to Ivy, who was coming up the stairs behind me.

"I'm good, you?" she responded, and I could tell she was smiling.

See hell no, she was definitely feeling this boy. I was starting to wonder if she'd been fucking with him this whole time.

We made it to the top of the stairs, and there was the living room, dining area, and then the kitchen. I saw Kantwan sitting at the piano in the living room, sipping a beer. He lit up when he saw Cheyla, and vice versa, then he stood up as she neared him. He hugged her tightly, and then kissed her temple. I thought it was so cute how they beamed upon seeing one another. Cheyla needed to quit them games before she lost out, because he was definitely a catch with his handsome ass.

"Kantwan, you know my best friend Jersey, and this is my other best friend Ivy," Cheyla pointed to us, still side hugging Kantwan.

"Nice to meet you again Jersey, and nice to meet you Ivy," Kantwan smiled.

He then took a seat at the piano again, and Cheyla sat next to him. They began to talk in low tones, while smiling giddily.

Ivy and Elijah sat next to each other on the couch, gazing into one another's eyes and pissing me off. She was obviously nervous in his presence, the same nervousness I had around Kill, so I knew she liked him. She caught me looking at her, so she cleared her throat and created space between she and Elijah.

*Where is Kill?* I wondered.

Just as the thought skated through my mind, Kill walked out of the kitchen with two bottles of Grey Goose, red cups, and a big tray of blunts.

"What's up y'all? Welcome to my crib," he smiled widely, and his teeth were so perfect and white.

He sat down next to me, and I was waiting to hear him speak again, because I'd never heard him talk until now. He was wearing a gray crew neck with a black Nike sign on it, black jeans, and socks with Nike slide ins. His beard was scruffy and sexy, just like his waves. Fuck, this nigga was bomb!

"Jersey," I stuck my hand out because I was tired of him not knowing who I was.

"Is that your real name?" he grinned.

"Yes, why do you ask?" I cocked my head.

"Never met anybody named after the state of Jersey," he licked his lips. "But I don't shake hands with beautiful women, I give hugs."

He pulled me into a hug before I could respond, and damn I never wanted to let go. His strong arms engulfed my small frame, and it felt so perfect.

Elijah got up and turned on some music, as Kantwan took the tray of blunts and started passing them out.

"You smoke, Jersey?" Kill asked me as Kantwan handed us both a perfectly rolled joint.

"Yeah, I do."

He smiled and then lit his blunt before turning to me to light mine. Was I really sitting here smoking and drinking with the nigga I'd been fantasizing about for weeks? If I woke up right now, I would be beyond pissed.

"What is this?" I quizzed after blowing out the smoke.

"Granddaddy, is it too strong?" Kill questioned.

"No, it's just some bomb ass weed. I've never had weed this good." I leaned back on the couch.

"You smoking with the wrong niggas then," he raised a brow and poured himself some Grey Goose.

I lifted my cup to him, and he poured me some as well. I took another pull on the blunt, and then gulped some Grey Goose too.

"Slow down ma, I don't want you to get too faded," Kill said.

"What? You don't wanna take advantage of me?" I flirted. *Did I really just say that?*

"That's not my style. But I think you want me to take advantage of that pussy don't you?"

Cheyla's words immediately invaded my mind, as my pussy began to drip due to his choice of words.

"No. I'm not that type of girl." I cleared my throat and tried to bob my head to the semi loud music playing.

"Not what type of girl? You don't like getting your pussy ate? You don't like getting stroked hard from the back while getting your neck slowly sucked on?"

Fuck, he needed to stop.

"Nope!"

"Yeah right, ma, you're lying like a muthafucka right now. You ain't gotta lie to kick it."

"So what if I do like all those things? Then what? You gonna eat my pussy?" I was high and a teensy bit tipsy already, so I felt comfortable.

"Yeah, I'm gonna eat your pussy, come on."

He stood up, and I just looked up at him with my mouth open. He burst into laughter, and then sat back down. I just rolled my eyes and half smiled at his stupid ass.

The six of us continued to get high and sip a little vodka here and there. I was feeling relaxed but still very cognizant. Everyone was talking in their own little world, and I was too chill to interfere with the flirting that Elijah and Ivy were doing. Cheyla and Kantwan were cute though.

"So Jersey, tell me something about yourself," Kill stared into my eyes.

He was so fucking bomb and it made no damn sense. My girl-hood was definitely noticing him too. I hadn't had any dick in years, and he was looking like a good way to end the drought; especially with the way he was just coming at me.

I couldn't though, because one I didn't know him, and two I had Tommy… sort of. I really liked Tommy, and I didn't wanna do him dirty by fucking with his homie, or whatever he and Kill were.

"What you wanna know?"

"I wanna know what you do besides show your sexy ass body to niggas that don't deserve to see it," he said.

"They're paying so they deserve to see it," I chuckled and then it slowly faded as I thought about why I'd started stripping.

"Nah, they don't. But I know you got a plan, so what is it?"

"I'm studying to become a corporate art buyer. I just strip to pay for school, rent, and other shit."

"How old are you?"

"I'm nineteen."

"Oh, and you already paying rent? Damn, you sound like me at that age."

"How old are you?" I inquired.

"I'm twenty-two right now, but I been paying my way since I was nineteen."

"Oh dang, why? We're your parents not stable?" I asked.

"Well my mom passed, and my dad has been pretty ill for a while. He had to go to a home when I was nineteen, and for a while I was able to use what money he'd left for us, but that soon ran out. Why are you on your own?"

"Because my dad is having a midlife crisis, and my mother can't afford me," I scoffed and stared at the empty wall.

"What does a midlife crisis have to do with anything?"

"He left my mother and his kids for a twenty-one-year-old girl, and we've all been struggling ever since. Now my brother is in jail, and my mom cries her eyes out every night," I said without looking at him.

"Damn, that's super fucked up, Jersey."

"Yeah, but whatever, I do okay," I half smiled and shrugged like it was nothing, even though it bothered me like crazy. I could barely sleep some nights as I thought about how my father did us.

"You look like you're doing okay, too. That's kind of dope that you got some hustle in you."

"I can't even concentrate in here," I laughed and pointed to Cheyla who was dancing on Kantwan, as Ivy and Elijah cheered them on. I *could* concentrate, but I was nervous because of his flirting.

Kill shook his head, and then grabbed my hand to lead me into the bedroom. He closed the door, and I immediately fell backwards on his big ass bed. It was huge and so soft. He just laughed at me and cut on his lava lamps, after cutting off the big light. He then joined me on his bed.

"What do you do, Kill? You're so mysterious." I turned onto my stomach, and held my head up with my hand.

"Well, I sell drugs. I usually make drops for my boss, and sometimes I collect money from trap houses."

"You're a drug dealer?"

"Yeah, I am," he nodded and snickered. "Why, is that a problem?"

"No, it's not. I just didn't expect that from you. Then again, you do have that rugged thug look." I was now on my back, staring up at the dark ceiling.

"Is that sexy or what?" he asked, and we both burst into laughter. I could tell we were both high as kites right now.

"Yeah, it's super sexy. When I first saw you in Starzz, I was so intrigued by you. You're so attractive, and you have this quiet power," I spoke honestly. I had a little liquid courage.

"I been on you since first sight, too. And the way you dance on stage, man, sometimes I felt like you were dancing just for me," he flirted back. I chuckled to myself as I remembered the night where I *did* dance on stage just for him.

"Maybe I *was* dancing for you, since you never ask for a dance."

"I don't know; I guess I enjoyed watching you from afar. I didn't like you dancing for other guys though," he admitted.

"Gotta pay them bills."

"I know, but a nigga was still low-key jealous."

"So you were claiming me without having talked to me?"

"In a way. I've been dying to fuck you and never share." He licked his full lips as he eyed my body with his low eyes.

"That's romantic. You're not supposed to tell me you wanna fuck."

"Why not? I'm an honest person. I wanna fuck you."

"Stop saying that!" I giggled.

"I wanna fuck you." He crawled over and got on top of me, lying in between my legs. "You're so bad, how can I not wanna fuck you?"

He slipped his strong hands down the back of my shorts and squeezed my ass. My panties were drenched. My breathing became heavy, and my words were caught in my throat as he kissed on my neck, whispering about how bad he wanted me. Although both dressed, I could feel his hard dick begging to be released. I spread my legs wider, because I wanted to feel it some more.

"I wanna eat your pussy. I wanna beat it up with your legs on my shoulders, while I'm licking your nipples. I wanna hit it hard from the back, while playing with your clit, and gripping your neck to suck your lips," he said in a low tone while sucking on my ear, and letting his big hands roam my small frame.

My chest rose and fell as if I was struggling to breathe. The shit he was saying sounded like a bomb ass poem right about now. It was a waterpark down there at this moment.

Rolling off of me, he laid back down next to me and squeezed my exposed thigh. He suddenly sat up and removed his crew neck and shoes. I took my shoes off as well, and then walked around the bed to his side.

I could hear "Choices" by E-40 playing in the living room, so I walked between his legs and swayed my body a little. He pulled a blunt from behind his ear, and fired it up as I danced while facing him. After he took a pull, I grabbed it from him and inhaled the smoke, as I wound my body slowly to the beat. His eyes were glazed over as they roamed all over my petite frame in the super dark room. The lava lamps gave just enough light for the current mood.

I blew the smoke out, and then passed it back to his beautiful ass. I then turned around and began grinding my ass in his lap, something I'd been wanting to do for a while now. He placed his big hand on my waist, and because I wore a crop top, we had skin-to-skin contact again. I gripped his kneecaps and kept working my body to the beat of E-40's song. I then reached and pulled my crop top over my head. I wore no bra because my titties were small enough to go without. I felt his hands rub up the front of my body and then back down as I flung my hair to the other side. I stood up to face him, and while admiring my breasts, he started to unbutton my jean shorts for me.

"Don't make no damn sense how sexy you are," he whispered as he took a pull and blew out smoke with his free hand. *Likewise*, I thought.

I just smiled and continued swaying as he pushed my shorts down to expose my blue thong. It was lace in the front, and very narrow so you had to be waxed or shaved to wear it. Thank God my occupation called for me to stay clean down there.

Leaning forward, he bit the side of my panties with his teeth, and then gently sucked and licked my pelvis. It made me shiver a little, and he smiled. I was still dancing though.

I turned around to show him it was a G-string, and he kissed all over my lower back, making me moan very subtly. He squeezed my ass, and then gripped my waist before rubbing my flat stomach. I slipped my thumbs into the thin sides of my panties, and then slid them down my golden legs. He threw me back onto the bed, and then stood over me as he removed his shirt to expose his perfectly chiseled chest. He had tattoos everywhere on his beautiful chocolate skin, all the way down to his wrists.

He dropped down on his knees, and spread my legs open. I felt my pussy dripping with anticipation, literally. He began to feast on my center, flicking his tongue over my clit. Was this really happening right now? He pushed my legs back, and went to town like he'd been starving all this time.

"Oooh shit, shit," I whimpered.

I hadn't had any attention down there in years, and he was doing the damn thing. He was licking and sucking my pussy like a muthafucka. He meant business when he said he wanted to eat me.

"Oh my goossshhhh!" I screamed damn near, and pulled on his little bit of hair. I didn't care what Ivy and Cheyla thought, because I was about to cum so hard. "Uggghh," I grunted softly as I came hard as fuck.

My body jerked, and to my surprise, he yanked me back closer to him, pushing my pussy into his mouth. He went right back to attacking my center like a wild animal, and I could feel an orgasm rising already. His mouth and my clit were one right now.

"Oh fuck babe," I called out.

I didn't even know this nigga, but right now I loved him. He spread my legs wider, and sucked my clit hard until I came again, balling the sheets in my fists.

He pecked my lower lips, and then stood up to undress himself. Once he was naked, it was the most alluring sight ever. The room was dark, but the lava lamps lit him up perfectly. My eyes darted to his dick, and it was a nice nine inches. He stroked it slowly as he stared down at my body, and I licked my lips at his beautiful pole. I got up and crawled to him, before slowly licking the tip. I'd only sucked dick once and that was when I was sixteen, around the same time I'd lost my virginity.

I started to suck on the tip like it was the best tasting lollipop in the world.

"Mmmm," he threw his head back as I started to move my mouth up and down his length.

I could tell he was a clean ass nigga, and that made me go harder. I didn't know what it was about him, because I was not the type of girl to fuck a nigga I barely knew. Funny enough, this didn't feel wrong. He cupped the back of my head, and began pumping my face. I took every stroke like a professional, until I felt his dick harden. He pushed me off and chuckled.

"Damn Jersey," he smirked.

He then rushed me, pressing his full lips against mine. We were kissing like maniacs until he was on top of me and between my legs. He gripped my hair and tilted my head back as our tongues danced, and I was feeling how rough he was. This nigga was the shit just like I knew he would be.

While we were kissing, I felt him reach in his nightstand, I guess getting a condom. *He ain't a nasty nigga*, I thought happily. Too many niggas out here didn't believe in condoms.

He pulled away from my lips, and then stood on his knees to roll the condom down.

He lowered himself on me and asked, "You sure you wanna do this?"

"It's a little too late to ask that, but yes, I want to."

He rubbed my hair back while looking into my eyes, and then slipped his strong arms under my knees. My heart started to beat fast at the thought of him entering me, since I hadn't had sex in almost four years. My legs were over his arms, with my calves dangling next to his shoulders. He kissed me hard as fuck, and then I felt his head at my opening. I inhaled sharply against his lips, and he began to suck mine. He pushed his tip into me, making me move up a little.

"Damn, it's been awhile, huh?" he whispered and kissed me again. He bit down on his lip, and then pushed the rest of his dick into me.

"Aaahh, aahh," I cried out as he filled me up.

"Shit," he said as he started to hump me slowly.

Every time he pumped me, pain shot through my pussy.

"Uuuuhh, uuuh, uuuh," I caressed his biceps as he kissed me roughly. I loved this rough ass passionate kissing.

"Fuck," he grunted as he started to speed up very little.

"Oooh, uuuh, aaah," I scrunched my face up as I felt myself cum.

He pinned my hands above my head, and then bit my bottom lip as he started to beat it up. He dipped his head down, and sucked my nipples while not losing his pace.

"Open your legs some more," he demanded in a low tone, between sucking my nipples. I spread them wider and he started going ham, making me cum immediately. "Turn over."

The way he ordered me around turned me on like a mutha-fucka. This nigga had some stamina on his ass too.

I put the side of my face into the pillow, and tooted my ass up. I felt the pressure of his dick at my opening, and then soon after, he was barging inside me again.

"Aahh, aaahh, aaahh!" I cried out as he went ham from the back, while toying with my clit.

As soon as I felt my peak near, he pressed his abs against my back, and bit down on my shoulder, making me explode. He switched back and forth between biting and sucking the area where my neck met my shoulder, while still tearing it up, and it was driving me insane.

We both screamed, and then he finally released. He flipped me over, and then wrapped his arms around my body while kissing me. His dick lied in my wetness as we kissed like two lovers who missed one another. I caressed the back of his head as our chests heaved against one another. I could feel his heartbeat as I kissed him with my eyes closed.

After kissing for about three minutes straight, he got off of me and then went into the bathroom within his room. I heard him pee and then wash his hands.

He brought out a warm towel and said, "You should go pee first."

"Okay," I replied and got up. "We used a condom though," I laughed at him trying to make me pee.

"I'm not telling you to pee because I don't want you to get pregnant, I'm telling you because it's for health reasons."

"Oh."

I peed and then he handed me the towel to wipe myself. I then washed my hands, before he scooped me up bridal style and carried me to the room. We laid down in his bed on our sides, and then resumed kissing immediately.

He trailed his lips from my mouth, to my neck, to my shoulder, and down my arm until he decided to take my nipple into his mouth. Suddenly he stopped, and then ran his finger over the tattoo of words down my ribcage that read, *Go confidently in the direction of your dreams. Live the life you have imagined.*

"Who said this?" he asked before kissing my ribcage with his soft lips.

"Henry David Thoreau."

"The poet," he stated instead of asking. I was surprised to hear he was familiar with him.

"Yes."

He then touched the one on my collarbone that read *Bonheur*, before pressing his lips there as well. The way he touched me was making me crazy. I didn't know what it was about him.

"What does it mean?"

"Happiness in French," I smiled at his inquisitive behavior.

"And this one?" he touched the one going vertically down my hip that read, *Belle vie*.

"Beautiful life in French."

I wanted to ask about his, but they were pretty self-explanatory, and he had way too many. His eyes wandered all over my naked body, and then he pushed me on my back before kissing me. "Waves" by Miguel played outside in the living room, as he slipped his fingers into me while sucking my lips. I was officially hooked. I threw my head back in ecstasy, with his teeth gently tugging my bottom lip, and his fingers thrusting into me at the perfect pace.

*woke up the next morning, and was confused about where I was until I felt the soreness between my legs. I looked back to see Kill still knocked out and looking good as hell. I smiled until Tommy crossed my mind.

*Did I really just fuck his homeboy?* I thought to myself and shook my head. *I'm such a hoe,* I thought. But it was so good, so worth it in a way. I just wished I had never talked to Tommy, because now they were gonna see me as a tossup, despite me never having slept with Tommy.

I gathered my clothes and got dressed quickly and quietly. The whole area between my legs felt like Floyd Mayweather had trained on it, and it took everything inside of me not to whimper as I got dressed.

I walked out and saw Cheyla and Kantwan cuddled on the couch asleep. Ivy was on the other end, and Elijah was nowhere to be found.

"Get up, let's go," I whispered while shaking Cheyla. Her eyes opened, and she looked around before stopping on me.

"Now? It's only 7," she whispered after checking her phone for the time.

"Yes now, I have stuff to do," I lied.

She smacked her lips and then moved Kantwan's arm off of her torso. As I shook Ivy, Kill opened his bedroom door.

"Oh umm, good morning," I chuckled.

"Where you going?" he squinted his eyes suspiciously.

"Oh I gotta go, I'm sorry."

"Without saying nothing?"

I looked back at Cheyla who was slipping into her shoes, and then walked into Kill's room. He closed the door behind me and towered over me.

"Look Kill, I enjoyed last night a lot, maybe too much. But I'm dating Tommy, well probably not anymore since I fucked his friend. Anyway, I can't do this with you."

"Tommy ain't my friend, and what can't you do? It's not like I'm asking to be your man just yet."

"I can't be friends with you nor Tommy. It's just gonna be weird now. I have to go."

"So you're this upset about not being able to talk to Tommy? You didn't mention him once last night. Especially not when I was deep inside you."

The mention of him being deep inside of me brought back so many good flashbacks of last night. My body had never felt so good, not even when I got massages.

"I know and that's why I feel so bad. If I hadn't talked to Tommy first, then I would be all for keeping tight with you, but I can't. It's wrong."

"Fine, go, I hope y'all make it as a couple," he scoffed.

"I'm sure we won't because I fucked you. Goodbye," I said before yanking his door open and entering the living room.

I wanted to rewind time and not give Tommy the time of the fucking day. I wished I wasn't so principled at times, because I would damn sure love to run back in there, lock the door, and fuck Kill until the moon showed its face again. Not only did he have good dick, but also he wasn't boring and had great conversation. I didn't even have his damn number! Ugh! *You don't need his number Jersey.*

I heard Cheyla and Ivy talking at the bottom of the stairs, so I descended them before the three of us walked out of the door.

As soon as we got into the car, I laid my head against the headrest, and adjusted myself because I couldn't sit down regularly. That nigga fucked the shit out of me, and I wasn't even sure if I could work tonight. I would be popping my ass like an old lady, and dropping it like it's lukewarm if I still felt like this later on.

"So how was it?" Ivy asked.

"How was what?" I frowned.

"Oh I don't know, the dick you got last night," Ivy responded.

"It was bomb as fuck and so passionate. But he's Tommy's homeboy, and I still sort of like Tommy," I shook my head.

"Didn't Kantwan say Kill and Tommy hated each other?" Ivy asked Cheyla, and she nodded while looking at me.

"That's even worse then." I let out a huge sigh, and sat on my hip because my pussy was crying right now. Maybe they called him Kill for this reason alone, because my shit was dead.

"So who are you gonna pick?" Cheyla quizzed.

"Neither. I was doing just fine alone."

"Kantwan said his brother has had his eyes on you for the longest, and it's obvious you like him more than old boy, so fuck Tommy!" Cheyla turned her lip up and cranked the car.

I grinned on the inside knowing Kill had been interested probably just as long as I'd been interested in him. But still, I couldn't bring Tommy anymore harm. It was bad enough that he'd really been trying with me, but I instead gave it up to charming ass Kill. I never made horrible decisions like this before. This nigga Kill had me all fucked up.

## EIGHTEEN

## Kilexis

———————

### Back Inside the Condo...

As soon as Jersey left, I walked to my window to watch she and her friends leave my street. I had no intentions on sleeping with her, despite what I'd said to Tommy to upset him. The shit just happened naturally. The way she was dancing for me just brought back all the lustful thoughts I'd had of her when seeing her dance back at Starzz. Strangely enough, I didn't even feel like dealing with any chicks last night, because I'd already had my fair share of them earlier that day.

My ex-girlfriend Margo had been blowing me up all fucking day yesterday, to the point where I had to power my shit off. I didn't know what the hell was wrong with her, but I was getting tired of the fucking games and bullshit. No woman that I wasn't claiming should feel the need to call me thirty damn times. And it's not like it was an emergency, I knew she was just doing that in case I was with a female.

I met Margo three years ago when I was nineteen, and we immediately hit it off. I thought I'd for real found the girl of my dreams. During that time, I was really going through shit, because my mom had died some years prior, and my dad was sick as fuck and being put into a home.

I was stressing, trying to figure out a way to get food for my brother and I, since my oldest brother Ka'Shea got locked up some months prior. Margo was there for me and shit, and made a nigga fall in love. You know what they say, show a nigga something he ain't never seen, or give him something he ain't never had and he'll fall in love. That shit was true, and that's exactly how Margo maneuvered her way into my heart.

Six months into our relationship, I found out she was fucking with some older cat that got her pregnant. She tried to pin the baby on me, but I knew it wasn't mine because I raw dogged no bitch. I didn't want nobody carrying my child that wasn't my wife, I don't care how much in love with you I am. Not only that, I didn't have the funds to take care of her, a child, and my little brother.

Anyway, after that shit happened, I pretty much found out she was a hoe, so I quickly cut her ass off. So now, I don't do the relationship shit at all. I just wanna get my bread and fuck a couple bitches here and there. I swore that I would never let a bitch do me dirty like that, because I would never give a woman the chance to. I just wished Margo would understand that and move the fuck on.

She and I have been broken up for a little over three years, and she still hasn't stopped trying to get back with me. And even though I wasn't looking for a girlfriend, something about Jersey had me interested. She was sexy, laid back, funny, and had that bomb between her legs. I loved how confident she was in her body, even though she didn't have the biggest ass or tits. She owned what she was working with, and that shit was such a turn on. I even liked that small bull piercing she had in her nose, and I hated bitches with shit on or in their face. But whatever, I wasn't gonna pursue her. She wanted whack ass Tommy.

*KNOCK! KNOCK!*

"Come in," I said and stood up to get some shit ready for a shower. Elijah and my brother walked in cheesing like a muthafucka. "Fuck wrong wit y'all niggas?" I frowned and continued grabbing the shit I needed.

"Yo, you fucked Jersey?" Elijah questioned with a grin.

"Nah," I lied nonchalantly.

"Bro, you lying like fuck. Baby girl was walking funny," Kantwan laughed along with Elijah.

"I mean, if that's what you believe," I shrugged.

I wasn't the type of nigga to be putting women on blast. If she wanted to tell people I fucked, then by all means, but I damn sure wasn't about to be bragging around town about who gave me the pussy. I didn't even hang around niggas who did that, because it was fucked up. Why shame her when you were probably begging her to let you fuck? That's some shit Tommy would do. See, Jersey had me hating on a nigga that was beneath me, and I ain't like that shit at all.

"It is what I believe because it happened. Now how was it?" Kantwan asked me.

I just shook my head and went into the bathroom to clean myself up. I didn't feel like talking about the shit, especially because I may never feel her in that way again. Just the thought of never being able to feel her soft thighs wrapped around my waist again had me frowning.

After a long ass hot shower, I brushed my teeth and then sprayed my favorite Gucci cologne on myself. I slipped into some light blue jeans, a gray polo with a black crew neck on top, and then some Jordan Retro 3's.

My closet was full of all the same shit because that's all I liked to wear. I had about fifty polo's and crew necks in various colors. I had more jeans than I needed, and every pair of Retro Jordan's released; some in multiple colors.

My haircut wasn't too fresh, so I pulled a snap back down on my head, and then grabbed my watch to put on. I spotted my iPhone, and powered it on to see what fuckery was popping off. I had some messages and missed calls from people who wanted to buy from me, and then some bitches including Margo and Sophie. *Damn, I don't even have Jersey's number*, I thought. I shook my head and locked my phone.

"Aight y'all!" I put up the peace sign to Elijah and Kantwan.

"That nigga got that new pussy glow!" Kantwan joked as he ate a bowl of cereal. I couldn't help but to chuckle lightly.

"Just make sure y'all lock my shit up when you leave."

I jogged to my 2012 Yukon Denali, and as soon as I got in, Margo was calling me again. I was so tired of this shit, and I really didn't understand why she couldn't get over it.

"What the fuck you want?" I questioned calmly as I reached for my seatbelt.

"Where you at?" she countered.

"Margo, what the fuck do you want? If I have to ask again, I'm gonna hang up in your fucking face."

"You had some bitches in your condo last night, Kill?"

"If that's what you calling me for right now, then I'm about to hang the fuck up."

"Well, I was calling you yesterday because I heard you fucked Amelia's home girl! What are you doing Kill? You telling me you don't want anything with me, and won't even let me see the damn dick, yet you giving it to random bitches? What kind of shit is that?"

"Bye Margo."

I hadn't fucked Margo since I found out she was pregnant by another nigga. No I hadn't slipped up and let her suck me off either; she and I were a wrap in every way, shape, or form. She hadn't felt my dick in almost three years, but still begged for it every damn time she got a chance.

"Wait, Gregory needs some diapers. I ran out this morning, and also he doesn't have any more snacks," she complained.

Yeah, the older nigga she had the baby with wanted nothing to do with her ass. He had a girlfriend and kids, who he told Margo he would leave for her. Why would a twenty-eight-year-old man leave his family, for a then nineteen-year-old girl? I shook my head at the thought. She was dumb as hell. I wonder if she would still be chasing me had he done what he promised.

"Aight, I'll stop by Target," I replied.

I felt bad for the little nigga, because it wasn't his fault that his mama was a hoe and his daddy wasn't shit. I hated deadbeat niggas, because for one it was fucked up to the woman you got pregnant. Secondly, how can you sleep at night knowing your own child may be hungry or cold? That shit was beyond me, but I was thankful that my father was who he was.

"Okay, and could you get him some outfits too, I didn't get a chance to wash," she said.

I hung up on her ass instead of replying, and then sped to the Target on Brandywine Parkway, since it was only fifteen minutes away from my crib. After buying diapers, wipes, baby snacks, and some outfits for Gregory, I headed to Margo's apartment on Fourth and Monroe. She stayed in those Inner City Living spots. Because it was fairly early in the day, there were plenty parks for me to slide into on the street.

I went into the McDonald's right across the street, and bought her son a happy meal since he loved chicken nuggets. After getting the food, I stopped by my car for the Target bags, and then headed up to her place. She saw me after looking down out of her window, and before I got to her door, she was already standing outside smiling. She had on some little ass shorts and a bikini top, with her curly hair in a ponytail.

"Hey baby," she grinned up at me with her arms folded.

"Can you let me by?" I raised a brow. She smacked her lips and moved back so that I could come in. Her house was pretty clean which it usually never was, so I wondered what the occasion was. "I got him some food too," I said after sitting everything on her bar counter.

"Oh cool, so I was thinking we could hang out today."

"No."

"Why, Kill? That shit happened three years ago, and you're never gonna forgive me?"

"I have forgiven you, that's why I buy the shit you need for a baby you had while we were together. But just because I forgive you doesn't mean I wanna be with you, because I really don't."

"So you never think about me?" Her eyes started to glaze over.

"Not in the way you want me to. I just really don't want to be with you like that, and there is nothing you can do to change it. It ain't meant, Margo," I shrugged and watched her son play with his toys, while only wearing a diaper.

"That's so fucked up, Kill," she sniffled.

"So are a lot of things." I still kept my eyes on her son. "Did you bathe him and shit yet? That's what you need to be worried about doing, not hanging out with me," I said before standing up.

She looked up at me, and then dropped her face in her hands to sob. I just shook my head and went into the kitchen to grab a plate to put her son's food on, since clearly he wasn't at the top of her priority list. I emptied the nuggets and shit onto the plate, and then set it on the table.

"Aye man, are you hungry?" I called out to Gregory as his mother continued to sob.

"Eat, eat!" he shouted and jogged to me.

I chuckled at him and then put him in the chair in front of the plate. Margo finally stood up and walked into the kitchen, looking like a sad ass puppy. She took his drink and poured it into a sippie cup, then sat down at the table with us.

"So you don't even wanna go to the movies or anything?" she asked, and touched my hand with hers.

"I have something to do today Margo, but if you wanna take him I can leave some cash."

"If you're gonna leave cash, you can leave some for my nails and shit too."

"I'm not paying for none of that shit and you know that. Stop blowing all your money on babysitters and bottles at the club. Stay yo' ass at home sometimes so you can save enough for your nails and shit."

"Whatever Kill," she waved me off.

"See you later man, and give him a fucking bath," I frowned before leaving the kitchen area.

"Say bye daddy—"

"I told you stop telling him to say that shit, Margo!" I barked, making her jump a little.

She was always doing that shit, and telling people that he was my kid like niggas in the hood didn't know what went down between us. Even if I wanted to go out like a sucker ass nigga and pretend he was mine, I couldn't because niggas from here to Pennsylvania had been peeped game long ago.

Gregory looked up at me with his mouth wide open. I just closed my eyes and exhaled before leaving.

I couldn't keep helping her, because it was only natural that he would start to think I was his father. And how would I look telling him not to call me daddy when I was acting like one? However, I refused to let Margo pin her baby on me, and I would try my hardest to make sure he understood I was *not* his father and just his mother's friend. But in order to do that, I needed to feed them both with a long handled spoon.

I made it to my truck, and then decided to pick Kantwan and Elijah up so we could go visit my father. I knew he may refuse our visits like he always did, but I still liked to try and see him every couple of months. You could never say a nigga didn't try.

# NINETEEN

# Tommy

---

A Few Days Later...

*J*ersey hadn't said shit to me for the past few days, and I was wondering what the fuck was going on. At first I was just interested in fucking, which I had yet to do, but now I wanted her as my girl. I didn't know what I was gonna do about Sasha, but I would figure something out. Shit I would just have to keep Jersey on the side until I got on my feet, because losing Sasha would mean losing my crib and car since she footed the bill for it all.

But lately Sasha hadn't been a priority at all. Maybe after I get the pussy from Jersey, I wouldn't be so interested anymore. We shall see. Even then though, I couldn't see Sasha becoming an important factor in my life again. I really didn't give a fuck about her no matter how much I tried. And the more I craved Jersey, the less I cared. And the longer Jersey held out, the more disrespectful I became to Sasha.

As soon as I heard the shower come on, I quickly got up and grabbed my keys to leave. Tonight I was gonna go see what the fuck was up with Jersey, and I didn't feel like being questioned by Sasha. She hated when I left while she was occupied, but that was the point. I'd probably book a hotel tonight since I had her credit card, just so I wouldn't have to go home to her ass.

I hopped into my Lexus, and then sped to Starzz. It was Friday night so the shit was popping like crazy. I hoped that they didn't try and charge extra tonight, because they'd done so in the past when it was live as fuck.

I found me a park, and then swaggered to the front, stunting on all the broke niggas hanging around in the parking lot. They always stood out here in the lot, because they didn't have the bread to get in, but hoped to still bag a stripper on her way out. These strippers may have been hoes, but they weren't giving any broke niggas the time of day.

After paying the regular fee, thank God, I made my way in looking for Jersey. She was walking off stage, and I was happy that I came just in time it seemed. I wished that I was able to see her dance, but I had more important things to get to. We needed to have a serious talk about why she wasn't answering any of my attempts to contact her. She was not getting away from me that easily without giving me some.

I found myself a table in the corner, and waited for her to change and come out to do lap dances. I bobbed my head to the music, and watched this thick chick with no breasts at all shake her ass on stage. I feel like her medical insurance should pay for her to get some breast implants, because to be that flat has to be a medical condition. I mean Jersey had small ass tits too, but at least you could still grab hers.

"Can I get you a drink?" The waitress walked by and I shook my head no. These assholes only took cash, and all I had right now was five dollars and Sasha's credit card.

Finally, after thirty plus minutes, Jersey emerged from the back in some little ass shit that only covered her nipples and pussy. I needed to fuck, and ASAP.

I stood up to walk over to her, until I saw that bitch nigga Kill pull her to the side. I rushed over and slipped behind the blue curtain so that I could listen in on what the fuck he wanted to talk to her about. I knew he wanted to hit, and I'll be damned if I let him get there before me.

"You look and smell good as usual," Jersey said, making my neck jerk back. *As usual?*

"Thank you. Seeing you up there brought back memories," he chuckled.

"I bet," she sighed. What the fuck kind of memories did he have of Jersey?

"You doing okay?" he asked, and when I peeked through the curtain, I saw he'd lifted her chin.

"Yes, I'm fine, just making sure I finish the semester strong."

As she talked, he wrapped his arms around her small waist, and kissed on her neck repeatedly. She just caressed the back of his head, welcoming this bullshit.

"I will let you get back to work. Text me later though." He pulled away from her.

"Kill, I told you I couldn't be cool with you."

I smiled when she said that. *Yeah, brush this nigga off.*

He pulled her close, cupped her face, and then pecked her a couple times. She rested her hands on his forearms, and I almost threw up when I saw their tongues come in contact.

"Suit yourself," he said and then walked off.

I was infuriated that this nigga had kissed on her, and from the sound of it she let him fuck. How dare she have me taking her out to expensive restaurants and shit, and not give me the pussy, but possibly let this nigga fuck. My heart rate increased as I thought about Kill having touched her before me. I was tired of this shit!

I watched her walk by, and then I walked out as well. Before she could get to another guy, I pulled her arm. She snatched it from me, and turned to me with a scowl, before realizing who I was.

"Oh shit, I thought you were one of these aggressive ass niggas," she exhaled.

"Where you been Jersey? You haven't answered any of my calls and shit."

She pulled me to the side, away from earshot.

"Tommy, it's just best if we stop while we're ahead. I'm not looking for anything, I just want to finish school and get my life together. It's complicated enough without a man in my life," she explained and pushed her hair behind her ears. It was straight instead of her usual curly style.

"Why?"

"I just have a lot going on. But you're a great guy, and if I wasn't dealing with a lot right now, I would definitely be interested."

I just nodded and then stormed past her. I was furious, and no words could express that. Kill had left, so I was gonna try and catch his ass in the parking lot. When I got out there, I saw he and Elijah standing by his truck, so I ran over to them.

"Can I help you?" Kill asked once he saw me.

"Yeah, you fucked my girl?" I seethed.

"Who is your girl?"

"Jersey nigga, I saw you kissing her on the lips and shit!" I hollered loudly as fuck.

"Well if she's your girl, why don't you ask her if I fucked?"

"Because I'm asking you," I got into his face.

"Aye nigga, you better back down before I knock your ass out," he clenched his jaw and flared his nostrils.

"Man, fuck you!"

I pushed him back and he charged me with a left hook. Blood flew from my mouth, and then we began to tussle. I was tired of this nigga sonning me, and now he'd done it in the worst way. He knew I was trying to fuck Jersey, and he ran his bitch ass out and got it first. That was a straight bullet to my fucking ego!

We were swinging fists and fighting like wild animals in the parking lot, until police sirens started to blare from afar. It caught me off guard, and Kill punched me dead in the face for the third time. Blood filled my mouth since my lip was busted, and I stumbled back because my head was throbbing. The fact that he fucked Jersey and whooped my ass *twice* had me upset, but I wasn't in a condition to keep going.

"You had enough you little bitch?" Kill gritted as I dropped to the ground with my eyes shut tightly. "Make this the last time you disrespect me, you pussy ass nigga. Out here screaming and crying over a girl that was never yours and will never be yours. I'll tell you this though, if I did fuck, you really have no chance. Her pussy would have expensive taste now, and you don't fit the criteria."

I just looked up at him with one eye open and grimaced.

"Let's go, five-o is on the way!" Elijah shouted to Kill before they both hopped into his truck.

I quickly climbed to my feet although in pain, and rushed to my car. I had blood dripping from my lip onto my shirt, and my head was pounding. I got in, and then sped out of the parking lot, almost hitting the nosey ass niggas who watched the fucking fight. Yeah, I may have gotten my ass whooped again, but Kill had it coming, and it was gonna be sooner than fucking later.

# Cheyla

***

It was so fucking dead in here that it was ridiculous. It was raining outside too, so no one wanted to come out tonight. I knew I should've stayed home, but my ass was being greedy.

I sighed as I walked to the locker room to go ahead and go home. I changed into my regular clothes, and then grabbed my big jacket to keep me dry in the rain. As I was walking through the parking lot, my foot went deep into a fucking puddle.

"Fuck!" I hollered as I stared down at my drenched shoe and pants leg. *Ain't this some shit*, I thought.

I continued to walk to the car, and slowly got in so that I wouldn't wet up my seat with my soaking pants leg. After getting myself situated, I cranked my car up but it immediately shut off.

"No, not right now," I said and tried to turn the ignition again. I just got this shit!

It wouldn't come on, so I banged on the steering wheel. Jersey was at school in the library studying, and Ivy told me she was gonna be busy tonight. I pulled my phone out, and was gonna dial AAA until I remembered they canceled my shit for not paying. I rubbed my eyes and watched the heavy rain beat against my windshield until I decided to call Kantwan.

"Hello?" he answered in his sexy deep voice.

"Hey, it's Cheyla," I said.

"I kind of guessed that ma, what's up?"

"I need you to come pick me up, my car will not start."

"Where are you? Work?"

"Yes."

"Damn, and leaving at 8pm? Alright," he said before disconnecting.

After about twenty minutes of waiting, I saw his all black Mustang pull into the parking lot. He drove next to me, and I quickly got out so I could get into his car.

"You're gonna leave the car?" he frowned as I slid into his passenger seat.

"Yes, just for now."

"You ain't scared that someone is gonna steal your shit?"

"I've done this plenty of times," I chuckled at him. I wished I could get my money back for that bucket.

"Aight, what you gonna do for the rest of the night?"

"Umm, just chill at home I guess."

"Then you can chill with me since we're both off," he told me instead of asking me, then made a quick ass U-turn towards his home.

Once we got there, he pulled his umbrella from the backseat, and then jogged around to my side to open the door for me. I smiled at how much of a gentleman he was, but then it quickly faded once I came to the realization that he was too good for me. He deserved someone that had goals and was worth something, not a pill popping stripper who had no idea what she wanted in life. I just wished I hadn't grown to like him so much, because if I saw him with another girl I might have a damn heart attack.

"Maybe we should go back to my house," I suggested with a half-smile.

My feelings for him were way stronger than I ever intended them to become. I wanted to rewind time so badly, but that wasn't an option. This was the first time in a long time that I wanted a man exclusively. Staying with him tonight would only intensify things.

"I said you're chilling with me," he responded and slammed the passenger door.

He took my hand into his, and then we walked up the porch steps into the house. He went and cut the heat on, before taking his windbreaker style jacket off. I took mine off as well, and then frowned down at my pants leg. I'd temporarily forgotten about the mishap outside the club.

"You wanna change?" he asked me.

"Yes, do you have something for me to wear though?"

He nodded, went to his room, and then came out with a t-shirt and some of his boxer shorts. I took them out of his hand, and then he went to the kitchen.

I went into his bedroom and began to undress, making sure not to let my jeans hit his carpet. I looked towards the door, and Kantwan suddenly appeared. We didn't say anything to one another; we just stared. He came all the way into the room, pulled me closer, and we began kissing hungrily. I dropped my jeans that I was still holding, and we kissed until we made it to the bed.

He immediately began pecking my stomach, while pulling my thong down my legs. Once they were off, he kissed on my thighs, and the feeling in combination with the central heating was every-thing. I threw my head back as he made his way up to my pussy. He kissed my lower lips, and then flicked his tongue over my clit.

"Mm," I moaned softly as he ate my pussy like a champion. He bent my legs back, and spread them wider as I massaged his scalp. "Shit," I whispered.

You would've thought this nigga was a gynecologist by the way he was eating my pussy. He knew just what to do and when to do it, making me cum two times back to back. Every itch I had, he imme-diately scratched without me having to utter a word.

"Damn, you got some good shit," he said in between licks and sucks.

My body quivered as he stood to his feet. He undressed, exposing his perfectly chiseled caramel body, and I got up and made him sit down. I dropped to my knees and took his nine inches into my mouth. I bobbed my head up and down, making sure to fully coat his dick as I did it.

"Fuck," he moaned letting me know I was doing it well. "Fuck girl," he groaned again as he reached down to unhook my bra. I reached up to massage and play with his balls, as I started to suck faster and sloppier. "Aaah fuck!" he hollered and then exploded into my mouth.

For the first time in my life, I swallowed. I then stood to my feet, as he crawled backwards on the bed, before getting a condom to roll down. I climbed onto the bed and then mounted his dick, which was sticking straight up. *Damn, he must be horny as fuck*, I thought.

I moved slowly down on his thick long pole, and bit my lip hard as fuck until I made it to the base. The pain hurt so good. He smacked and squeezed my ass, as I began to move back and forth, and up and down. I hadn't had sex in years, and damn was it long overdue. I threw my head back as he reached up to squeeze by perky C cups.

"Uuuh, uuuh," I screeched as I felt myself about to cum already.

I loved the way his big hands felt, wandering all over my body. It made me go harder on his dick, especially with him cheering me on.

"You about to make me nut, fuck," he panted as he watched me move.

He gripped my ribcage, and then brought one hand to the front to play with my clit. I released again, and then he spread my legs wider. I started riding him faster, and soon enough we both screamed out, exploding.

I fell down onto him, and we kissed hard as fuck. He rubbed up and down my back, and I cupped his face as we let our tongues dance. *Don't fall in love. You are not in love Cheyla*, I chanted in my mind.

"You know I want you to be my girl right?" he said.

I knew he would want this, and I knew I would want it too. That's why I should've left him alone. I needed him so much, but he deserved better than me.

I just ignored his question, and covered his mouth with mine.

# TWENTY-ONE

## Ivy

_______

The night of the little kickback Cheyla, Jersey, and I went to, I'd given Elijah my number. I felt bad as hell doing so, but for some reason that didn't stop me. For the past few days, we'd been texting here and there. At first it was nothing too much, just the little 'how was your day' and 'good morning' texts, but now we didn't go a day without speaking. And every night after I put Donovan to bed, he and I chatted on the phone until the wee hours of the morning. I really liked talking to him, and it was now at a point where I looked forward to his texts and calls.

One day he woke up late, and I was mad the whole morning thinking he was out doing shit with some bitch. I had to give myself a talk, because I should not have been tripping off one man while mine was in jail.

Tonight I was over his house, well condo, chilling with him. He lived on the same street as Kill. The night of the kickback when he went home, he asked me to come, but I was already feeling low for giving him my number so I declined. But tonight, I was anxious to see him... alone.

"Would you like something to drink?" He offered and started towards his kitchen.

I told Cheyla and Jersey that I was busy tonight and nothing else, because I didn't want them to know about Elijah's and my friendship. They'd both low-key witnessed our flirting on separate occasions, so I didn't want to put it in their face any further.

Don't get me wrong, I love Portland more than anything, but I get lonely and there is nothing wrong with having friends. I know I shouldn't be making friends with guys I'm attracted to, but I have no plans to be anything more than homies with Elijah.

Sometimes I wondered what it would be like to date someone like Elijah, and it always made me smile. He was so masculine, and you could tell he knew how to treat a woman. The things he said to me always made me grin so hard it was a shame. If we texted too late into the night, he would even start being sexual and I never stopped him. I liked hearing the things he wanted to do to me, because not only did it make me feel good about myself, but I'd been wanting to know about his sex game. Since I couldn't physically sit on it, mentally was the next best thing.

"Yes. What do you have?" I finally answered him.

"Pretty much everything. Do you like clear or dark?"

"Um, clear is best I believe."

"Not really, but it's just not good to mix them." He walked off and then returned with some Grey Goose and apple juice. "Hope you like apple because it's all a nigga got," he laughed. His smile was everything, and my nipples always got hard when I saw it or heard his laugh.

"It's fine."

He made our drinks after filling the glasses with crushed ice, and then we cut on Netflix.

"You like scary shit?" He raised a brow as he stopped on this movie titled *Dead Silence*.

"Umm yeah, I guess we can watch it," I grinned.

"Why you say it like that?" He stared at me, and he was just so fucking gorgeous.

His dreads were pulled back into a low ponytail, and he wore a white t-shirt, gray sweats, and socks. His manhood was definitely very prevalent in the sweats, and I had to clear my throat to calm myself. Portland had been in jail for a long ass time.

"Because I ain't trying to be up all night thinking about the shit," I laughed.

"Oh, just hit me up if you need me then."

He then reached for the remote and turned the movie on. He said it so seriously, and I'm pretty sure he was serious. Halfway through the movie, I started hearing shit, so he turned on *Family Guy* to relax me, while laughing hard as fuck at me.

"That is not funny! I heard something in your bedroom, you better go check it!" I pointed to his door.

"There is nothing in my bedroom," he replied still chuckling. I just rolled my eyes at him and sipped some more of my drink.

"So Mr. Camren, tell me something interesting."

"Something interesting, I'm not that interesting of a guy. I'm sure you're way more interesting than me."

"Let's see then. My name is Ivy Horne, I strip for a living, and I have a son named Donovan by my boyfriend *Portland*," I said.

"Don't bring him up."

"Why not? He's my man, you knew that."

"Where is he again?" This nigga knew exactly where Portland was, because I'd told him a while ago.

"He went to jail almost two years ago. He'll be out soon," I sipped my drink again.

"Right. So when he gets out and start acting up, are you gonna come home to me?"

"What?" I chuckled. "No, he's gonna have his act together. If he messes around on me again I'm gone."

He scooted closer to me and asked, "You promise?" I just nodded nervously. "I think you want him to fuck up, because you know as soon as he does, I'm gonna have you in that room blowing your back out, and he's never gonna see you again."

"No, no, that's not true," I said unconvincingly.

He touched my thigh with his strong hand, and then rubbed it up my skirt. The room was dark, but the TV shone on us, flickering every now and then.

"Eli," I whispered as he rubbed the crotch part of my panties.

"What's up?" he asked as if he wasn't touching between my legs.

Moving my panties to the side, he swiped his middle finger slowly between my slit. He pulled his hand up and tasted me. A moan burst through my lips just from watching him. I was paralyzed as he put his hand back down between my legs, and then moved my panties to the side again. He kissed my jawline, and then sucked it with his sexy lips. I looked down, and the sight of his tatted ass arm and hand between my legs had me on one.

As he moved his mouth to my neck, he slipped one finger inside me. My clit tingled as he moved it in and out of me slowly, while licking and sucking my neck.

"Eli, you can't," I spoke in a breathy tone.

"I already am. Relax your body," he whispered in between licking my neck.

He added another finger, and began going a little faster. He moaned in my ear as he plunged his fingers in and out of me perfectly.

"Aaaah, uuuh, uuuh, Eli," I whimpered.

"Shit, you are wet as hell," he said in a low tone as he kissed down my collarbone. "Now every time you close your eyes, you're gonna think about me."

I reached down and tried to push his wrist away as he finger fucked me like crazy. I'd cum once already, and he hadn't let up. He was too strong though, and I wasn't able to push his hand away.

"Just let me make you cum one more time," he whispered into my ear.

I just said fuck it, and lifted one of my legs up so my foot was flat on the couch. He smiled when I did that, and then kept thrusting in and out of me until my body jerked so hard I thought my neck would snap. He slowly removed his fingers, and then pulled me close to tongue me down. After a few moments of kissing, he pulled away.

"I'm gonna go clean myself up," I said and rushed to his bathroom.

As I was walking back into the living room, he said, "Damn you came all on my couch pillow."

"Are you upset?" I quizzed. I was so fucking embarrassed right now.

"Nah you good, it's kind of sexy. Plus, that means I did a good job." *You did more than a good job.* "Do you mind if I keep you company while he's away?"

"No, I don't mind." I shook my head and he nodded.

"Cool."

He got up to wash his hands, and then returned.

"Now your turn, you don't have any babies, or baby mama's, or crazy exes?" I giggled. I really wanted to forget what he'd just done to me on the couch.

"Nah, I definitely don't. I don't play that crazy ex shit. Any woman I've dated knows not to play them games with me," he responded seriously. His authoritative demeanor was sexy as hell.

"Well that's good. So what do you do for money?"

"I'm a server," he chuckled to himself.

"Like at a restaurant?" I frowned.

"Nah, like I serve drugs to people."

"Oh okay."

"What, you don't like niggas who do illegal shit?"

"I mean that's how my boyfriend ended up in jail. But he didn't sell too much drugs, he robbed people, stores, and all kinds of shit."

"Yeah, that's not my thing, but I guess neither one is better than the other when you look at it from a legal standpoint, right?"

"Right."

I didn't like the fact that he sold drugs at all, because like he said, it was illegal. But it's not like I had plans to fuck with him, so it didn't matter I guess.

We talked for a little longer, until I realized it was 9pm.

"I have to go, Elijah," I set my glass on his coffee table.

"So early?"

"Yes, I have to get my baby from his grandmother, but this was fun."

"I like how you care for your son like that." He stared into my eyes.

"Yeah, well see you later." I stood up and slipped my feet into my sandals.

He stood up with me, and when I tried to walk off, he pulled me into a hug. He smelled so good, and I could feel his hard abs against my breastplate with his tall ass. I picked my head up, and he leaned it back while looking into my eyes. He pressed his soft lips against my forehead, and then I pulled away.

"Aye, stop it," he demanded, and yanked me back.

I opened my mouth to speak, but his tongue was already down my throat. We kissed as if a pastor had just told us we were married. This kiss was so good. It was the best kiss that I'd ever had.

"As soon as you don't wanna be there with him anymore, you better leave," he said. I nodded my head, and then he pecked me once more.

Maybe being his friend was too much as well. But I didn't wanna cut him off just yet... for some reason.

# TWENTY-TWO

## Jersey

———

Tonight I was at the grocery store picking up some things that I could snack on or warm up in the microwave. All we had right now were things you had to bake or fry, and lately with me being in a rush, I didn't have the time for that.

So far I'd grabbed chips, yogurt, frozen breakfast bowls, juice, water bottles, and some other little on the go shit. After getting everything I felt I needed, I headed towards the front of the store.

As I approached the line, I saw a familiar person in the self-checkout area. His back was facing me, but I knew his style already. He wore a red crew neck, with his white polo collar sticking out at the top, and the bottom of it hanging out as well. He had on blue jeans that weren't too baggy but weren't too tight, and some white Adidas. His hat was currently turned to the back, and slightly lifted off of his head. He looked so good as he always did, and I missed him already.

I was gonna choose to ignore Kill, because I'd sworn off both he and Tommy, but I couldn't help myself. I walked behind him, and lightly bumped him with my basket. He turned around and I was smiling widely. He smiled back and then bit his full bottom lip before stroking his beard.

"What you bumping me for?" he grinned.

"Sorry, I didn't know it was you."

"Sure," he replied and we both chuckled.

I didn't know what else to say, especially since I'd made it clear that I didn't want him. But damn did I want him.

We stared for a moment, and then someone walked away from the self-checkout area so he could use it.

"Well, it was nice seeing you," I said as I turned my basket towards the regular checkout stands.

"Likewise," he responded dryly as he fed his twenty-dollar bill into the machine. I let out a deep sigh, and then went to check out myself.

"Do you need any help?" the bagger asked me after the cashier handed me my receipt.

"No, I think I will be good," I said.

I rushed outside so that I could put my things up in a hurry. It was 11 o'clock at night, and I was not trying to get robbed or some shit. I wanted to get home, make myself a little snack, and then knock the fuck out.

As soon as I got to my Nissan Maxima, I spotted Kill leaning up against it, holding his bag of things he'd just purchased.

"Hey," I said shyly as I hit the button to open my trunk.

He said nothing, and began taking bags from my basket to put into my car. I saw him eyeing my body since I had on some cut off shorts, and a spandex white t-shirt with no bra. I liked that he still found my body alluring, even though he'd seen it plenty of times at the club.

After all of my bags were in the car, he closed the trunk for me and walked off without saying a word. I just shrugged, got in my car, and then headed home. When I parked, I saw he was parking too, and I just shook my head with a smile. If this was anyone else I would've been feeling weird, but since I kind of liked him ... a whole fucking lot, I found whatever he was doing flattering.

Climbing out of the vehicle, I saw him do the same and then jog over to me. I popped the trunk, and we both began to grab bags, with him taking most of them.

"Thanks," I chuckled.

"No problem."

He trailed me up the porch steps of the apartment, and then I put my key into the knob to let us in. We took the bags to the kitchen, and he helped me unload them fairly quickly, although the house was dark and dim right now.

"Well thank you for helping me, Kill." I looked up into his sexy face, and then went to wash my hands at the sink. He did the same.

"You know I'm still checking for you," he towered over me as we dried our hands.

"I'm still checking for you too," I whispered.

"Now, I wanna help myself to you." He began pulling my shirt up.

I didn't stop him because I didn't want to. He picked me up, and I wrapped my legs around his waist as he carried me to the back. With one arm around his neck, I pointed to my bedroom using the other, so he'd know not to go into Cheyla's.

Upon entering, he kicked the door closed behind us, and then laid me on the bed faced down. He removed my shoes, and then pulled my shorts down to expose my thong.

I heard him undressing, and was about to get up but he said, "Stay right there."

I lied back down on my stomach, and waited for him to get completely naked. He climbed onto the bed, and kissed from the back of my thighs, all the way up to my neck. His lips felt so good against my skin. Once he got to my face, he craned his neck around to tongue me down while pulling off my thong.

"Put your ass in the air," he told me and then got off of me.

I did as he asked, and then I felt his lips against my lower ones.

"Mm," I pursed my lips and closed my eyes at the feeling. He ran his tongue from my clit, all the way to my hole before sticking it in. He then placed his hands on my ass cheeks, and held them apart as he feasted on my center. "Oh, oh, uuuuh," I scrunched my face up as he sucked on my clit so gently. "Kiiiill," I whimpered. Why the fuck was he so good at this?

"Mm," he moaned while eating me like a champ.

"I'm gonna uuuh, aaaaah," I couldn't even finish.

I grabbed the pillow and squeezed it tightly into my fists as I exploded. He began kissing my lower lips slowly and softly, sticking his tongue in between them every now and then. He gradually began eating me out again, making me call out to the high heavens.

"Uggghhh!" I squealed as I released again.

He finally stopped, and then I suddenly felt the head of his dick at my opening. He plunged into me, and gripped my hips tightly.

"Shit," he mumbled as he humped in a circular motion.

He felt so fucking good; too good. He sped up and began going ham inside me, making me cum so hard I felt it dripping down my inner thighs.

"Fuck," he grunted and continued to pound me as I wept damn near.

"Aahh, aahh, uuuh," I cried out until we both exploded.

We panted for a few moments to catch our breaths, and then I turned on my back. He got in between my legs, and then slipped his tongue back into my mouth as I caressed his smooth mocha skin.

"Let me take you out," he whispered in between kisses.

"Okay," I half smiled before accepting his tongue again.

"Let me make you mine."

"Okay. Wait Kill, what is your real name?"

We both burst into laughter, and then he said, "Kilexis Camren."

"I like that." I ran my pointing finger down his lips.

"And yours is Jersey what?"

"Lamyia Warren. You didn't tell me your middle name," I frowned playfully.

"Carson."

"What's your favorite food, drink, and color?"

"Steak, Jack Daniel's Whiskey, nonalcoholic is Strawberry Lemonade, and red. Your turn."

"Okay umm, lobster, Malibu rum, nonalcoholic is grape juice, and pastel pink."

He wrapped his strong arms around my torso, and pressed our

bodies together, while still staring into my eyes. Although on top of me, he made sure not to put all of his weight on me somehow.

"What happened with your latest boyfriend?" he asked while rubbing my hair back.

"It was when I was sixteen. He dated me, and then after he took my virginity he broke up with me."

I still remembered that stupid ass nigga Rory. I didn't hate him anymore though, because I was completely over the situation. I learned from it though, or so I thought.

"You haven't been with anybody else since?" Kill inquired.

"No, not in any way until you. I mean I know you're not my man but I meant—"

"Nah, you can call me that if you want to."

"Good, because I want to. What about your ex?"

"Last one was when I was nineteen, and she got pregnant by an older guy six months into the relationship. I broke up with her and I haven't looked back."

"Does she still bother you?" I questioned. I wanted to know if he had any stupid bitches on his bumper, and if he did I hoped he wouldn't lie about it.

"I mean yeah. It's been three years but she won't let go. She's harmless though." *An honest nigga... about time.*

"Oh okay. Well if she is, she better be prepared to fight, because I'm not letting you go that easy," I giggled and so did he.

"You're too pretty for that. And I wouldn't have you in a situation where you would feel the need to fight and shit."

"I know. I'm just saying," I grinned and he laughed.

"Feisty ass, I like that though," he said as he began kissing down my body. He then placed my thighs on his shoulders to please me.

I didn't wanna deny that I liked him anymore, and I definitely wanted to see where this would go. I liked Tommy too, but not as half as much... obviously. Maybe down the line he and I could be cordial still.

# TWENTY-THREE

# Kantwan

———

Two Weeks Later...

*C*heyla was on that bullshit again, so I was gonna go check her. I was getting tired of her ass always switching back and forth about what she wanted. One minute she's in my bed, and the next she's telling me that we should only be friends and nothing more. Usually I wouldn't give a fuck, but her little cute ass had my fucking feelings invested. She either needed to have a good ass explanation for her flip flopping ass behavior, or she and I were done with. I'm a grown ass man and I don't have time for little cat and mouse games.

Once I got to her apartment building, I parked across the street then jogged over. I beat on her door, and then waited for her to answer. I knew she was here because I saw both she and Jersey's cars parked outside.

"Who is it?" Cheyla yelled from behind the door.

"Kantwan," I responded somewhat angrily. I needed to calm my ass down ASAP.

"What's up?" she questioned like I was really about to hold a conversation with her from outside.

"Let me in Cheyla, I'm not about to do this with you."

A few moments of silence passed, then I heard the locks being twisted to open the door. I rushed into her apartment, and then waited for her to close the door behind me. Once she did, she just stood there with her pretty annoying ass. She wore a t-shirt dress and fuzzy socks, with her hair hanging down sweeping her shoulders. I didn't say anything; I just paced the apartment in order to calm my ass down.

"So what's up with you, huh?" I asked.

"Nothing is up with me, I just think we should be cool and that's it. We were getting too close," she shrugged.

"Are you sure that's what you want?"

"Yeah I'm sure, we should just—"

"Then don't hit me up no more. Even when you change your stupid ass mind again, don't think of hitting my fucking line. We not friends and we not cool, just act like you don't know me," I explained and her mouth stayed open as she looked up at me. "Aight?" I raised a brow.

"Kantwan, I'm just—"

"I don't care what you are. You said we were getting too close, so now we won't be. Good luck with whatever nigga you decide to get some act right for," I said before walking towards the door. She grabbed my arm but I snatched it.

"Kantwan, you don't understand! You need to be with somebody better, you're too good for me," she started to cry.

"You know what? I am. Because you're too fucking immature for me. So in a sense I guess I should be thanking your ass."

"Kant!"

Before she could say anything else, I just left her place.

She was so fucking confused, and I was not about to coddle her ass. She needed to grow the fuck up, and stop acting like some little ass baby. She needs to fuck with a little ass boy who would maybe find that shit intriguing, because I damn sure didn't. It wasn't sexy and it didn't make me like her more, so I hoped that wasn't what she thought it was doing.

Crying and shit like she's just so upset and hurt, fuck out of here. She needs to be for real and up front with me, and not do all this back and forth shit. I scoffed at my thoughts.

I went down to my car, cranked it, and then dialed my cousin Elijah.

"What's up man?" he asked.

"Aye, what you doing? I wanna smoke," I told him.

"I'm chilling right now; you can come through."

I disconnected the call and the sped off of Cheyla's street.

I was dead serious about her not hitting me up anymore, and if she did she was not getting a response. I was done with her ass. All these fucking hoops she wanted a nigga to jump through were just not fucking worth it. I didn't mind putting in the work for a woman I liked, but she was on some other shit. She needed therapy or something.

I got to my cousin's condo in about fifteen minutes, and headed inside so I could smoke my problems away for the evening. I was already stressed about work, and Cheyla just added to that shit.

"What's up with you?" Elijah dapped me up after letting me in.

"Man, stressed than a muthafucka," I sighed.

"Why, what's up?"

"Just this whole Costco shit, and you know the girl I was fucking with?" I asked and he nodded. "She's tripping hard. One minute she's all in my grill, and the next she's acting like we shouldn't talk as much. She said we're getting too close."

"What? I ain't never heard a woman complain about that," he laughed.

"Exactly," I shook my head as he handed me the blunt.

"Well her friend, Ivy, I've been spending a whole lot of time with her."

"Didn't she say her nigga was in jail? Jersey's brother?"

"Yeah, but she's not happy with that nigga. He's damaged the relationship to a point of no return. The only reason she's even sticking around is because she wants to be a family," he explained.

"Nigga, how you know she just don't love him?"

"Because I can tell. If she loved him she wouldn't be spending the night at my damn house three and four times a week."

"With the baby too?" I bucked my eyes.

"Yes with the baby. We be like a little ass family up in my crib," he grinned.

"You fucked too?"

"Nah, she won't let me. She's scared he would be able to tell. That shit had me hot when she said that."

"Well he is her nigga, fuck you expect her to say?"

"I don't know man, but I swear she better leave him as soon as he does anything, or I'm gon' be pissed."

"And what if she doesn't? These women these days don't ever leave. The nigga ends up leaving them."

"If she doesn't then I'm gon' bust off in they shit, pack her stuff up, and drag her ass up outta there," he replied and we laughed in unison.

"Man, you wild. But I don't know about this group of girls, they all on some other shit it seems."

"I know."

"Maybe we should warn Kill and tell him to stop fucking with that Jersey chick, since it seems like all the girls in that group are suspect as fuck," I said.

"You can try, but he ain't letting Jersey go," he shrugged and fired up his blunt.

## Three Days Later...

Today Kill, Elijah, and I were gonna go visit my brother in jail. He was locked up in Delaware County Prison, located in Pennsylvania. It was about a half an hour from Wilmington, so not too bad. I've heard of people traveling for six plus hours to visit a damn family member so thirty minutes was nothing.

Delaware County Prison was known for having corrupt ass guards. Half of them were on payroll for kingpins and mobsters. They'd allow anything to go on if ordered by their street boss. Luckily, my brother Ka'Shea was protected because Axel looked out for him. Axel was the guy Kill and Elijah worked for now, and he ran shit. He had everybody working for him and was untouchable. For the life of me, I couldn't understand why he couldn't get my brother out quicker, but whatever. He only had a year left.

We piled into Kill's Denali, and then took off on the road. We stopped at McDonald's for some breakfast first, and then headed to the prison. I bobbed my head to J. Cole as Kill entered the freeway.

After about five minutes, I turned the music down some and asked, "So what's up with you and old girl Kill?"

"Who, Jersey? We're bonding," he smirked.

"Bonding in the bedroom?" Elijah inquired and chuckled.

"We bonding, and that's all I'm gon' say. Think what you will," he smiled.

"Well her friend be on that bullshit so be careful," I shook my head as I thought about Cheyla. Her ass had the nerve to text me, but I deleted it without responding.

"Her friend's actions have nothing to do with Jersey. We're good, and we're working on something. You need to be hollering at this nigga, he over here tryna steal nigga's girlfriends while they're in jail," he pointed to Elijah in the backseat.

I laughed and said, "I already tried. That nigga is adamant that she's gonna leave her man for him."

"She is, watch. When y'all see my name in her Instagram bio, I don't wanna hear shit!" Elijah responded and we cackled loudly.

"Nigga, how would you feel if someone tried to steal your woman while you were locked up with a bunch of musty, sweaty niggas?" I quizzed.

"That shit wouldn't happen to me because I know how to treat a woman. If Ivy was honestly happy and wanted to be with her baby daddy, I wouldn't even press her. But after all the cheating and shit he's done, she's over it."

"So what he cheated, plenty of niggas have and their bitch still wants them," Kill frowned.

"True, but this nigga has cheated about seven times. He missed the birth of their son because he was in another state with another bitch. She got jumped by one his side bitches and her sister one week after having his kid, and the nigga didn't even come home to check on her. I know niggas who cheat, but they take care of home first and would never allow any of that shit to go down. He's a bitch. I know that's your baby's brother Kill, but that nigga is foul," Elijah said.

"Damn, he's doing her like that? Then yeah, by all means, go after her. No woman should have to deal with that shit, not even Margo," Kill replied and we chuckled.

"Yeah, I ain't know all that. He's fucked up," I nodded as I processed what Elijah had just told us.

"That side chick and her sister would've been in the ground had I been him," Elijah scoffed.

"Man, on sight too," Kill agreed.

I never understood how niggas could treat the woman they claimed to love like shit. It was one thing to dog out a chick you weren't into like that, but to claim you love her? Nah. And even if this nigga didn't love her, the fact that she got his baby should hold some weight.

We arrived at the jail in no time it seemed, since we were making conversation with one another the whole way. We parked and then went to the visitor center, and after showing them our appointment badge and identification cards, we were seated to wait for Ka'Shea.

A few minutes went by, and he finally emerged looking the same way he did when he came in, just with more facial hair. His long curly hair was in two braids, and I wondered how he was able to do that.

"Y'all niggas ain't gon' greet a nigga?" he grinned and we stood to our feet to hug and dap him up.

"Who did your hair Shea?" I frowned as we sat down.

"This little guard bitch I been fucking named Terri."

Ka'Shea slowly cocked his head, and we discreetly looked in the corner of the room to see some guard staring over at us. She looked like a young Lela Rochon, the chick that played the girl with the fucked up feet in *Boomerang*. Anyway, old girl was sexy.

"Damn nigga, that's you?" Elijah nodded approvingly.

"Nigga, for now. Soon as I get up out of here, I got a little something waiting for me," he bit his lip.

"On the outside?" Kill quizzed.

"Yes on the outside, where the fuck else nigga?" Ka'Shea laughed.

"How the hell you meet her?" I asked.

Ka'Shea could always find a way to get some pussy no matter where he was. I wasn't even that surprised about him and that sexy ass guard.

"I met her through that little pen pal shit they offer you. I wasn't with that dumb shit at first, but I decided to try it out," he replied.

"You better hope it ain't no man, nigga," Elijah said and the four of us laughed.

"She don' sent me pictures and shit so I doubt it. But ain't like we've done anything, so if it is a nigga I'll be chucking the deuces immediately," he said.

"Okay, and what about Mercedes?" I asked.

Mercedes was Ka'Shea's girl for a cool minute, all the way up until he got arrested. She claimed she was holding him down, but who knows. I ain't seen hide nor hair of her a while now.

"I know that bitch been flipping, and I'm ready for something more serious when I get out. A nigga will be twenty-five then," he grinned.

We kept talking and catching up, making the time fly by way too fucking fast. I missed my brother and I couldn't wait until his ass got free.

"Okay Shea, time is up," the sexy guard walked over, licking her lips at my brother.

"Already?" he frowned.

"Yeah, I need you to fix something." She raised both brows, letting him know she wanted some dick.

"Alright y'all, now remember, stay out of fucking trouble and don't end up in here," Ka'Shea patted the table and stood to his feet.

The three of us got up to hug him, and then he was led away by the guard. One more year and he would be out. I just hoped he stayed out.

# TWENTY-FOUR

# Kilexis

---

Two Days Later...

This was my last pick up of the day, and damn was I tired. When I wasn't pushing, my boss had me collecting money from the trap houses and solving any discrepancies. I prayed that everybody had their shit straight, because contrary to popular belief, ya boy did not feel like killing a nigga today. No one liked to kill, it's just sometimes you had to do.

It was already 7:30pm, and after I got the bag from this last house, I could go home and get ready to take Jersey out. I hadn't planned on making anything happen between us, but the attraction was too strong for me to deny. We both, I think, wanted to downplay our feelings, but I can't say that I'm not a little happy that we didn't.

I was willing to see about a relationship with Jersey's pretty ass. I think it was because I could tell that she wasn't a scheming ass little bitch like Margo. I hated to call her a bitch but she was. In hindsight, there were so many signs letting me know that she wasn't about shit, but I was young and thought I knew best. Now, I could smell a rat like Margo miles away.

I wanted to at least take Jersey out on a date, because I've fucked four times already on two separate occasions, and that shit was backwards as hell. In addition, I hadn't actually liked a girl since Margo, so it felt good to be interested in someone. Ever since she and I broke up, I've just been busting a nut and keeping it pushing. And because my relationship with Margo was so trash, I never wanted to be in another one again, however Jersey was definitely making me rethink all of that.

I don't know, I ain't wanna put too much on it, but she seemed super cool, and the pussy was Grade A for sure. I didn't like that she stripped, but for some reason it was sexy to me. Any other girl that shook their ass for money turned me off, but with Jersey it just made my dick hard. Seeing her up there stripping all her clothes off, always made me feel warm all over. That's probably why when she danced for me, only a few moments passed before I was eating her pussy. I licked my lips as I remembered how she tasted.

*BZZZZ!*

**Jersey:** *Can't wait for tonight babe.*

**Me:** *Me either baby.*

I pulled up in front of the last house of the night on Broom. I was knee deep in the hood, but this is where the money was. It was sad that we fed an already dying area drugs, but this was where you could sell the most. Everyone over here was either on hardcore drugs, or smoked so much weed they could levitate. I always wondered why Axel never tried pushing his product in the white areas, because they got high too, especially the rich ones. If I were him, my shit would be everywhere.

I threw the car in park, and then placed my gun into my waist. I got out the car and then walked onto the sidewalk of the house.

"Sup Kill," one of the workers named Robert dapped me up once I got inside the trap.

"Sup with you man, where is the bag because I have to go?" I said and looked around.

"Clay went to get it," he pointed to the back.

I sat down, and then grabbed the money counter. Robert sat down on the couch across from me, and stared at me with a nervous expression, blinking a lot. They knew if this shit wasn't right, Axel gave me full authority to kill some niggas. And if I was late to my date with Jersey because of these muthafuckas, this killing would be on some Mortal Kombat shit.

Clay brought the duffle bag out, and I quickly unzipped it before starting to count. After about an hour, I was done counting, and everything added up perfectly.

"Aight, good looking," I said as I put it back up.

I heard them both let out a sigh of relief, and after filling the bag back up, I zipped it and then dipped.

As I was driving to Axel's warehouse to deliver the money, my mind began to wander. I needed to find a way to get out of this shit. Yes, it was good money but damn, I hated having to always be on edge and shit. I wanted to get my bread the legit way, and be able to relax when I saw a police vehicle.

Speaking of police, I saw their lights in my rearview mirror and sucked my teeth. *Fuck, I hope they don't try and search shit,* I thought. I had all this fucking money on me, right when they wanna pull me over. I have never been pulled over by the police, nor have I ever gotten a ticket. I was doing too much wrong to be caught doing anything, and so far I'd been successful.

I pulled over to the side, and waited for this muthafucka to come and approach me. He finally made it to my window, and he wore a smug expression.

"Is there a problem, officer?" I questioned after rolling the window down.

He was tall as hell, pale as fuck, and his belly had to be carrying quadruplets. His thick brown mustache covered his whole top lip, and his eyes were small and beady like a rat.

"Get out the car," he responded and then placed his hands on his hips.

"Why? What did I—"

"Get out the fucking car!" another officer hollered at me with his gun out. He was shorter, but his belly seemed to be just as big.

I took a deep breath, and then I remembered my gun was still in my waist. The initial officer, Officer Oakie as his nametag read, was watching me closely as fuck, so I couldn't hide the gun. As soon as I reached in my waist, they would light my ass up. *Why the fuck was this shit happening right now?*

I climbed out of the vehicle slowly, and Officer Oakie slammed me into the car and began patting me down. I just dropped my head, waiting for him to find the heat I had on me.

"What were you planning to do with this boy?" he asked as he removed my gun from my waist. I declined to respond, and just licked my lips before blowing out hot air. *Please let this be a damn nightmare right now*, I silently pleaded. "Open the trunk Dorsey," he said to his partner.

I just dropped my head, because they were about to confiscate all the duffle bags that I'd collected tonight.

"Whoa, rob a bank?" the other officer who I assumed had the last name Dorsey said, before whistling.

I suddenly felt cuffs being placed on my wrists, and I just shook my head, still staying calm. I had nothing to say. What could I possibly say?

"Going to jail for a long time uh—" he patted my pants until he found my wallet. "Mister, let's see here. Mr. Kilexis Carson Camren, bit of a tongue twister," he joked as he pushed me towards his police vehicle. He tossed my wallet to Officer Dorsey en route to the car.

"Oh, and only twenty-two years old," Dorsey added before chortling like he was Santa Claus or something.

Officer Oakie shoved me into the backseat, and then slammed the door. I just stared out the window, wondering how in the hell this happened. They found a gun, and about $100,000 in cash in the trunk, so they knew I was into some illegal shit. I just shook my head at myself, knowing everybody who loved me would be so disappointed. Shit I was disappointed.

I saw the Dorsey guy shine the flashlight into my car, and then reach for my phone. Thank God I didn't talk business on it. He tried to unlock it, but when he couldn't he just threw it to the floor, making it shatter into pieces. Seeing him do that made me think of Jersey. I knew she was gonna think I flaked, and even though I was in the midst of such fuckery right now, her thinking that had me feeling low.

During this entire downhill slope, I hadn't said one word, because like I said, there wasn't shit for me to say.

"Fairly quiet, aren't you?" Oakie said once he got into the driver seat of the police car. I still said nothing. "Don't you hear me!" he screamed.

I just acted as if I didn't hear him. My mind was consumed with thoughts about how my life was possible over at only twenty-two years old. And what did I have to show for this shit? Nothing.

I heard him get out the car, and then he came around and snatched the backseat door open.

"You don't hear me fucking talking to you!" he shouted in my face. No response.

*WHAM!*

He went across my face with his baton, and blood spilled from my lip. I just nodded my head very subtly and repeatedly, as if he didn't just hit me. I was filled with rage, but that would do me no good in this state. I prayed that I would get a chance to fuck him up in another time though.

"Answer me!" he hollered and whacked me again, this time causing damage to my ear.

My hearing diminished slightly, as blood poured down my jaw and fell onto my crew neck. A tear slid down my face, because I was angry as fuck and couldn't do anything about it. I wanted to choke this nigga with my bare hands but I couldn't. The anger in me was coming out in tears.

"You crying? You want your mammy?" he taunted.

The mention of my mother infuriated me further, and I kicked the shit out of him causing him to stumble backward. He and the other officer snatched me out of the car, and beat me until everything faded to black. I just hoped Jersey knew I would never do her dirty.

# TWENTY-FIVE

# Jersey

---

One Hour Later...

It was now 9:30pm, and I'd gotten no call or text from Kill. I called him and text him a couple times but got nothing. The last thing he said to me was that he couldn't wait to see me either, so I was wondering what the hell was going on.

He was supposed to be by to pick me up at 8:30pm, and I have no idea what the hell is taking him so long. I was tired of waiting though, and pissed that I'd gotten all dressed up for nothing. I couldn't believe he would fucking stand me up like this. It's not like I begged him to take me out, he fucking offered!

I threw my phone onto the bed, and then got up to go wash my makeup off of my face. I'd spent forever picking out the right outfit and look for tonight, just for it to be wasted. I really liked him and I didn't understand why he would do this. After sitting up with me and letting me tell him all kinds of shit about my life, he just disses me like it's nothing. This is exactly why I hadn't been involved for over three years.

"What are you doing?" Cheyla asked as she stood in the doorway of the bathroom with her arms folded.

"I'm getting ready for bed," I sighed.

"I thought you were going out with Kill though."

"Well me too, but clearly he had other plans." I shook my head as I threw the makeup wipe into the trash. I turned the water knobs on, and waited for the temperature to become bearable, before wetting my face.

"He didn't text or anything?" she frowned as I pumped the face soap into my hand.

"Nope, and I don't care anymore." I began washing my face.

"I wish I was still talking to Kantwan, because I would ask him what the fuck was wrong with his brother."

"No need, I'm not that damn desperate."

"You really liked him though, Jersey. I've never heard you talk about a guy that much."

"So what Cheyla, I'm fine, okay?" I looked her in the eyes, trying to hold back my tears. I was so tired of getting played to the left, but I couldn't let anyone see me hurting.

"Sorry Jersey, them niggas weren't about shit anyway."

She was still upset that Kill's brother Kantwan quit her and hadn't looked back. She'd tried texting him but she said he never said anything back.

"I see someone is still upset about Kant," I chuckled to myself, trying to ease my soul.

"Don't nobody give a fuck about that nigga," she scoffed and adjusted her stance.

"Right."

After putting on my facial moisturizer, I changed into my night-gown that I'd just bought from target, and then put my hair up into a loose bun. My press was old as fuck, so it was no point in wrapping it. All I did in the morning was run my little flat iron over it, and put some edge control on my baby hairs. Maybe tomorrow I would be able to get it done after my nails. We'd have to see, because I'd spent enough money on my look for tonight already.

Sitting in the living room, I watched a couple episodes of this show titled Reign. I couldn't even pay attention to it because I was really bummed about Kill. I kept watching anyway, until I dozed off right on the couch.

———

*I* woke up around 9am, and I checked my phone hoping Kill had text me with some excuse as to why he stood me up. When my screen lit up, there was nothing of the sort, and I just rolled my eyes. *Did he go back to his ex? What the fuck happened?* I asked myself.

Surprisingly there was a text from Tommy though. He'd been off me since I told him I wasn't gonna talk to him anymore that night at the strip club, so this was unexpected.

**T:** *Hey sexy.*

**Me:** *Hey.*

I felt bad that I told him I wouldn't be talking to neither him nor Kill, yet I was fucking Kill on the low. I just couldn't bring myself to date Tommy after fucking his homie, even though Kill swore that Tommy was no friend of his, and that they'd even got into a couple fights.

I hopped up and made myself some oatmeal, because I wanted to get out, go see how my mother was doing, and talk to my sister.

I prayed every night for my mom, because it seemed she would never get over what my dad had done to her. Sometimes I wanted her to shake it off, but I knew that it wasn't that easy. Especially if what she felt was anything like what I was feeling right now.

I ate my breakfast while scrolling on Instagram, and I low-key checked Kill's page to see if he'd incriminated himself by posting last night. There was consolation in knowing that he hadn't, but I was still upset.

I put my bowl into the sink, and then headed off to shower and get ready.

I got to my mother's condo in my same neighborhood of Browntown, and just shook my head. She'd gone from living in a one-million-dollar Colonial style home in New Castle County, to a condo in Browntown. It was an abrupt change for all of us, but I'm sure it was much harder on her.

I unplugged my phone from the radio, and then slipped it into my purse before getting out. I made it to her door, then knocked four times in the same sequence I always did. My sister Raleigh opened the door and then hugged me tightly.

"About time you visited," she smacked her lips and then walked away from the door.

"I know, I've just been busy," I said as I locked the door. "Where is ma?" I quizzed.

"She's in the shower right now."

"Does she still cry every night?"

"Not every night, but she'll be really glum some days for no reason at all."

"Have you spoken to daddy?" I asked.

"He called me a day after my birthday, and we talked for like two damn minutes. He mailed me a birthday card with $100 in it."

"That's good I guess," I exhaled.

"So how are you doing over there, Jersey? Is school paid up and stuff?" Raleigh asked me.

My sister made $13.50 at a call center, and she worked twelve-hour shifts some days, just so she'd be able to help my mom. Still, she would always offer me money and try to make sure I was taken care of.

"I'm good Raleigh, but thank you," I said.

"Ain't nobody offering you money," she giggled.

"I knew you were about to so I thought I'd stop you beforehand."

"Whatever. Ma and I are gonna go to the mall and then lunch, you should come."

"I might as well since I don't have anything to do today."

"Oh that's how you feel?" She raised a brow.

"Nah, I'm kidding," I chuckled.

My mom came out of the shower, and when she saw me her face lit up. No matter how sad she was, she would always throw on her happy face upon seeing me.

"Sweetie, you should come with—"

"I already asked her and she's gonna come," Raleigh interjected.

"Okay good," my mother walked over and kissed me. "I'm gonna get dressed and then we can go." She walked to the back and began dressing.

Once my mom was ready, we got into her car and headed to Independence Mall. We looked around the whole damn mall it felt like, before we decided to leave and get some food. We settled on IHOP since it was cheap and right down the road.

"So how are things Jersey?" my mother questioned once we were seated.

"They're pretty good. My classes this semester are paid off, so any money I make now can be saved up," I replied.

"What about this boy you told me about, how is he?" she just had to ask.

"Yeah, how is he?" Raleigh leaned in with a mischievous smile, making me chuckle.

"We umm, we aren't talking anymore."

"Why Jersey? I thought you really liked him?" my mom frowned.

"I did but I decided to break it off because I need to focus. It was too much of a distraction, and plus I think he had a girlfriend," I lied.

"Dudes these days, always trying to play some damn body," Raleigh scoffed.

The thought of Kill made me lose my appetite. I was feeling okay until my mother mentioned him. Now I was sad again and feeling like shit.

*BZZZ!*

**T:** *Hey you free this week?*

I got excited thinking it was Kill who had text me, but it was just Tommy's ass. I knew it was fucked up to feel so letdown, but I was.

"Raleigh you still single?" I asked.

"She is but she's been acting weird," my mom raised a brow at her.

"I have not been acting weird," she giggled. I knew right then that she had someone she was interested in. "I've just been writing someone."

"And talking on the phone. Do you know she almost knocked me down trying to rush to the mailbox the other day?" my mom raised her brow.

"Writing someone? Are they incarcerated?" I questioned.

"No, they live in another country. Phone calls are too expensive."

"Raleigh, you're probably getting catfished," I laughed and so did my mother.

"What is catfished?" my mother quizzed with a smile. It felt good to see her beautiful face light up. She put you in the mind of actress Sanaa Lathan, just a little older.

"It's when someone pretends to be one person, when they're really someone else. So Raleigh could be talking to some fat woman from France," I replied and my mother and I cackled. Raleigh just rolled her eyes.

"I've heard his voice before, and he is all man, okay?"

"Yeah, whatever," I waved her off.

I wanted to know who it was, because Raleigh had always been picky over the years. Every time one of us wanted to hook her up, she would always decline. So whoever had her giggling like this, must've been something special.

"Well, whomever you guys choose to date, I want you to remember that you are your own person. No matter how much you love him, make sure you don't lose who you are separately from him. You know we as women feel obligated to fulfill every need and want of our men, and you should, but to an extent. Don't ever change yourself, unless for the better, just to accommodate a man. No matter how much he promises to love you forever, have your own. Don't be a shadow, okay?" she looked at us and then dabbed her eyes before the tears fell.

"Okay," both Raleigh and I answered in unison.

"I love you, mom," I added and half smiled.

"I love you too, baby."

# TWENTY-SIX

# Tommy

A Couple Days Later...

You got damn muthafuckin' right I dropped the dime on that bitch ass nigga Kill. I'd been following him all day that day, just to make sure I knew what he'd be doing. As soon as I saw him stop at the first trap, I called the police and gave them his license plate and what'd he be doing. I let them know the money would be in the trunk, and I let them know he'd probably have a gun on him. I was jumping for joy when I found out that nigga got arrested, especially because he was supposed to be taking my bitch on a date.

I'd followed Jersey a couple days prior, and when she was at the mall, she told Cheyla that Kill was supposed to take her on a date Wednesday night. I made sure to kick my plan in motion that exact day, because he had me fucked up tryna make her his bitch and shit. Jersey wasn't doing anything until she let me fuck. After that, he could take her ass on as many dates as he wanted.

I understood that Kill and I weren't the best of friends, but he knew I wanted to fuck Jersey; therefore, she was off limits. This nigga and I have clubbed together plenty of times, because my best friend was his brother, but he got the nerve to act like he had no loyalty to me. If we've hung out or rode in the car together before, you need to show some respect by not going after a girl that I clearly stated I was working on.

It's cool though, because from what I heard he may get five years behind bars at the fucking minimum! I laughed to myself as I thought about it.

I didn't care how long he got, as long as it was more than a month or two. That was all I needed in order to get my dick wet a couple times with Jersey. He could have that hoe after that. I didn't want a bitch that shook her ass for cash on my arm. But for some reason, the more I thought about the fact that he smashed, the angrier I got. Why was I so angry if I didn't even want her seriously? Honestly, I would be much more okay with him smashing Sasha. I wouldn't have even cared, as long as it didn't mess up her providing for me.

I just hated that Jersey had me working for her hoe ass, but busted it open for Kill in a matter of fucking days, if that. She met that nigga after me, so it was obvious it didn't take long. If it was any other hoe, I may have given up, but the fact that Kill got the pussy, shattered my fucking ego, especially because lately we'd taken our rivalry to new heights by throwing hands. This nigga beat my ass and fucked my bitch; I couldn't let that ride.

Sexing Jersey had taken over my got damn life. All I did was think of ways to get her to let me fuck, and when I wasn't thinking about how to fuck her, I was thinking about actually fucking her. Like right now I was in the bed with some Spanish hoe named Lizette, and thinking about how much closer I was to getting Jersey's pussy.

Lizette rolled over and caressed my chest, irritating me for some reason. I'd been fucking her for a cool little minute now. I met her a little bit after meeting Jersey, and had been fucking her just until I got Jersey. Our rendezvous had gone on way too long, but it was better than smashing Sasha's ass.

"Good morning, babe," she kissed my jaw line and I nudged her back. I was mad because I didn't plan to spend the night, and because I knew Sasha was about to be on my muthafuckin head about being out all fucking night. "What the hell is wrong with you?" She frowned and looked up at me.

"Nothing, chill damn!" I hopped up and then started slipping my jeans up my legs.

I snatched my phone and saw Jersey had responded to my text, making a smile form on my lips even though days later.

***Jersey****: I don't know.*

***Me:*** *Well can I see you today?*

***Jersey****: I'm pretty busy today. But why? What's up?*

***Me:*** *I just missed you and wanted to hang out.*

While waiting for her to reply, I finished getting dressed.

"Damn, so you gon' leave right away?" Lizette questioned.

"Yeah, I got some shit to handle," was all I said before slipping into my shoes, and snatching my phone and keys.

I quickly left Lizette's crib and sped home. When I got there I was relieved to see that Sasha was gone. I wanted to quickly get in there to shower so I could get out. She had a habit of coming home for lunch sometimes, and I didn't want to run into her. I knew if we got into it I might knock her ass out.

After showering, brushing my teeth, and changing, I checked my phone and saw Jersey still hadn't given me a response. I smacked my lips and slipped my phone into my jean pocket. I brushed my waves down, and then scooped my keys to go see Kantwan.

He and I hadn't spoken to each other since Kill and I almost came to blows the first time, but I wanted to see if I could get some details on what was up with Kill so far. I was gon' take one shot tonight for every year that he was possibly gonna be locked up.

I pulled up to Kantwan's house, but I didn't see his car there so I dialed him.

"Sup," he answered.

"Aye man, where you at? I'm at your crib."

"What you at my crib for?"

"I wanted to talk to you my nigga, that's all," I replied and shook my head at him.

"I'm at the store, I will be home in like five."

"Cool."

I hung up the phone and then checked my texts to see if I missed the reply from Jersey. Nope, my 'I miss you' text was still sitting there unanswered. She was really working my nerves at this point.

I fired up a half smoked blunt that was resting in my ashtray, and finished it off while waiting. As soon as I dropped the roach back into my ashtray, I saw Kantwan pulling into his driveway. I got out around the same time that he exited his vehicle, and he nodded to say what's up. We walked up the steps, and took a seat on his porch.

"What brings you over?" He raised a brow as he twisted the top off of the Jack Daniel's bottle.

"I know I was acting stupid, but I realized I didn't wanna lose a homie over some bullshit."

"Oh alright," he replied dryly, and almost like he didn't believe me. I could tell his brother's arrest was on his mind.

"So what's been up with you my nigga? You looking like your dog died," I chuckled.

"Man, some shit don' popped off that got me hot as fuck."

"Damn, like what?" I asked even though I already knew.

"My brother got arrested, and it's looking like he's gonna get ten years in the pen," he sighed and it took every muscle in my body to contain my smile.

"Damn, ten years? That's crazy. Why the fuck they arrest him?"

"Man, stop acting like you care. You and Kilexis have never liked each other. Plus, I ain't wanna talk about this shit," he low-key snapped on me.

"Alright damn, my bad."

We sat there in silence while he took swig after swig from his bottle. I could tell he wasn't in the mood to talk, and I had already gotten the information I needed, so I was gonna bounce.

"Well, I'll holla at you tomorrow or something son," I stood up and put my fist out to dap him up.

"Yep," he said and kept staring out into the street, ignoring my hand. He was starting to act just like Kill's ass, and I ain't have the patience for it.

## Later That Evening...

It was now around 7 o'clock at night, so I wanted to go and see Jersey. When I got to her crib, I decided to call her because I wasn't sure if she was home yet. Sometimes you didn't have the luxury of being able to park right in front of your crib, so I wanted to see if she had parked further down, or if she just wasn't here.

Just as I put the phone to my ear, I saw her Nissan pulling into an empty park, a little further up towards Columbia Street. I got out and waited by my car, until she hopped out of hers and hit the alarm.

"Jersey!" I boomed, making her look in my direction.

"Tommy, you scared the shit out of me."

She walked closer to me, and her sweet perfume hit me like a ton of bricks. My dick started to get hard just from looking at her in the skirt and top she had on. Even her small breast made my mouth water, which never happened. It was go big or go home for me in that department, but Jersey still had me lusting.

"So what's up?" She threw her hands out and let them fall back against her legs.

"Look Jersey, I know you fucked with Kill, but I'm telling you I don't care about that. All I'm asking is that you give me a chance baby girl," I pleaded.

"Who told you a-about Kill and me?"

"I just know aight, but that don't matter. Just give me a chance, unless you'd rather be with him," I raised a brow.

"I don't wanna be with anybody," she said somberly.

I knew she was kind of mad about that nigga not taking her out, and this was perfect because I could play on that. I was about to be captain save a hoe in this bitch. And fucking her would be all the more better now that I knew Kill had some genuine feelings for her. He never tried to take a bitch out, so he had to be into her.

"Come on, I've taken you out, given you space, what else can I do to make you see that I'm really interested in you. Plus, I came at you before him," I smiled and so did she.

"So you don't think I'm a hoe?"

"Nah, I don't think that," I lied.

I hella lied, because she was a for sure hoe. Any bitch that talked to two niggas that ran in the same circle was a hoe. And any bitch that took her clothes off for money was a hoe too.

I had to fuck though… I had to. I was tired of dreaming about what the pussy felt like. If it had this nigga Kill about to spend bread on a date, I knew it had to be good. Bump that, the shit had to be phenomenal.

"I guess I will think about it," she sighed.

"You should, especially since Kill is back with his baby mother."

"Baby mother? What? What are you talking about?"

It irritated me to see how hurt she was when asking that. Why did she like him so much? That nigga really wasn't shit!

"Margo, you don't know his baby mother?" I frowned in confusion and she shook her head no, slowly. "Yeah, he has a three-year-old son with Margo. I saw them together a couple days ago."

"No, he told me about her. She sounds like his ex." *Fuck*, I thought. *Think Tommy*.

"I'm sure he said that to get in your panties, no offense. They break up all the time, and then get right back together. Plus, they have a kid together so they will always love each other. You know how that goes."

"No—"

"Jersey, I grew up with the nigga. Margo is his girl, now you can ignore this information if you want to. But you probably aren't gonna be able to talk to or get ahold to him now, because he's with her. He always has little flings when they break up."

"He sure wasn't acting like I was a fling. But whatever, fuck him. I gotta go Tommy." She turned around to leave.

"That means you will start replying to my texts and answering my calls?" I called after her.

"You haven't hit me up in forever until recently!"

"I know but I'm just making sure that when I do, my efforts won't go unnoticed."

"They won't," she blushed, but I could still the sadness in her face.

I pulled her sexy ass into a hug, and squeezed tightly. I pulled away just a little and tried to peck her lips but she turned away. *Oh, but you let that whack ass nigga kiss you.* She let me kiss her the night I took her out, but now that Kill had gotten to her, she was acting like she didn't remember that shit. Bitch. *Her pussy would have expensive tastes now.* Kill's word replayed in my head.

"Talk to you later Tommy," Jersey patted my chest and moved from my embrace.

I watched her run into her condo, and smirked because I knew I'd be smacking out soon. I walked to my car with a little more pep in my step too.

I'd been out all damn day just bullshitting and robbing a couple grannies by the mall, so I was tired. I'd come up on $600 from this one old bitch. She was easy because she needed a damn cane to walk, so all I had to do was snatch her fucking purse. I didn't even have to draw my heat out on her.

I thought about buying something to eat, but decided to see if Sasha had cooked. I sped home listening to Kevin Gates, and when I got home I saw Sasha's Jeep. *Yes, food,* I said to myself as I shut the engine off.

I made it up to the door, and when I walked in I smelled no food. My expression immediately turned to a scowl, as I rushed to the back in search of Sasha's trifling ass. I checked the bedroom and she wasn't there, and then I realized I heard the shower running. I went to the living room, and sat down to wait and bark her ass into the kitchen when she got out.

Ten minutes later she emerged, wrapped in a towel and looking sad yet mad as hell. We made eye contact, and she was angry as fuck. Storming to the back, she began to rustle through some shit in the bedroom, before coming back out and marching towards me.

"Really nigga?" she threw a paper into my lap.

"Fuck is this?" I frowned as I read the paper. I knew what it said, but I was gonna play dumb.

"Not one STD, but two? How the fuck did you give me chlamydia *and* genital herpes?"

"Man, I ain't give you shit! I don't how the fuck you got that shit! Probably one of them niggas you been out here fucking!"

I honestly had no idea who I could have gotten that shit from. I was fucking so many bitches, and I never strapped up so who knows. Maybe I didn't have it though, because I was feeling fine down there.

"You's a muthafuckin' lie Tommy!" she hollered through tears.

"Ain't nobody lying! I ain't got shit! My dick is feeling fine."

"What bitch is it?"

"I ain't fucking nobody but you, so I really don't know what the hell you're talking about, ma. You better talk to your other nigga!"

"I can't do this shit with you," she plopped down on the other end of the couch, and cried hysterically with her face in her hands.

"Well who the fuck else you gon' do it with? Ain't nobody gon' want you now," I laughed lightly.

She didn't say anything, she just got up and walked to the room, slamming the bedroom door. I shook my head and then pulled my phone out.

**Me:** *Wyd? Can I come through? I need some food and head.*

**Lizette:** *Okay, but what am I gonna get? lol*

**Me:** *This dick, on my way.*

**Me:** *Goodnight beautiful.*

**Jersey:** *Night.*

She was still acting cold, but I wasn't tripping because I knew I would have her soon. And shit, if Kill found out she had something, maybe he wouldn't want her anymore. Shit, because I would definitely be hitting her skins raw!

# TWENTY-SEVEN

# Cheyla

---

*When I think about you, I think hoe. When I dream about you I think hoe. It only took me some hours to hit, I think hoe.*

The lyrics to "Hoe" by Kirko Bangz blared over the club, as this one chick named Miami worked her body to the beat. I chuckled because she was a big time hoe, and the song fit well. She was one of those strippers that you could throw a little extra cash at to get some pussy. Niggas would come just for her, because they knew they could fuck her in the private dance room. She was balling because of it too.

When I first started I used to think she was the shit because she had a nice car, nice clothes, nice shoes, and everything else that cost major money. When both Jersey and I asked her for advice on how to squeeze more bread out of this stripping thing, she told us we needed to start fucking. From that day on, I never looked at her the same. I actually felt bad for her man sometimes; yes, she had a man. I was surprised that word hadn't gotten back to him about what his girlfriend was doing in the club. But I heard she was the breadwinner, so maybe he approved.

I moved lazily in some man's lap who was old enough to be my daddy, and it disgusted me. You had to do what you had to do though, because believe it or not it was hard to get niggas to cough up the cash for a dance. They only threw small bills at you while on stage, and then would only want to pay more if you would fuck them. I may be a wild, but selling pussy was just not how I got down.

Once the song ended and switched to "Down in the DM" by Yo Gotti, I got out of grandpa's lap and he pressed thirty dollars into my palm. He kept his grip on my hand, and yanked me closer to him so he could whisper into my ear.

"I got way more where that came from at my house in Alapocas," he whispered into my ear. Alapocas was a rich neighborhood just north of Wilmington.

"Oh, I'm okay, but thanks for the invite."

"I'll be here late in case you change your mind," he smirked as I stepped back from him. I just chuckled because there was no changing my mind.

As I was walking, I spotted my favorite customer Monty waving me over. I loved him because he always spent big money on me, and only on me. After I gave him his dance, he usually left, and if he did stay, he didn't entertain any other strippers.

I strutted over to him, dancing to Yo Gotti, and a cute shy smile appeared on his face. "Hey boo," I kissed his forehead.

He grabbed onto my waist, and rubbed up and down my back. I usually didn't let him touch, but because he'd been dropping top dollars on me, I felt obligated to.

"You know I want a private dance," he said.

"I got you."

I grabbed his hand and led him to the private dance area behind the red curtain. He hiked his pants up and sat down, as "She Goin Up" by Chris Brown started to play. I was happy the song was fast, since I despised giving lap dances to slow shit because it was too intimate.

As I swayed in Monty's lap, my mind drifted to Kantwan. I'd been missing him but I hated to admit it, even to myself. I had a problem with being with people as boyfriend and girlfriend, which is why I'd never had a man. As soon as guy showed me that he liked me and wanted to be closer than fuck buddies, I ended that shit.

Every person that I've loved has abandoned me, from Sonny to my own mother. The only person that has been by my side for forever was Jersey. To add insult to injury, seeing her mother so damn miserable just further proved why I didn't wanna fall in love.

Kantwan had gotten farther than most niggas though, because he actually fucked. Usually I cut it off before we even got to the bed, but Kantwan was determined and he got the panties. And along with my panties, he might've taken my heart too.

I had no idea why I couldn't stop thinking about him. What was so special about him? I think it was the fact that he was a thug, but the classy kind. He didn't go around shooting bullets in the air or sticking his chest out every chance he got. However, I knew he would knock a nigga out at any given moment if he needed to. I saw it with my own eyes when he saved me from getting raped and choked out by the guy who sold me pills.

Kantwan was the perfect balance that all women looked for. He was rugged, sexy, smart, and thugged out, but he wasn't some rude asshole who mistreated you. I really fucked up by bullshitting with him, and the thought alone would keep me from sleeping at night. This was so new, because in all of my nineteen years, I'd never felt this way about anyone. No man had ever caused me to lose sleep other than my brother Sonny.

"Damn, I hope this ain't extra," Monty said, snapping me back to reality. "Switch Lanes" by Tyga was now playing, and I was still dancing for him.

"Oh sorry, I guess I just like dancing for you," I chuckled and got up.

"You good."

He reached into his pocket and handed me $50. This was on top of what he'd already paid Joey for the private dance.

"Thank you boo," I smiled at him and tucked the fifty in my little bag. He just nodded and stood up.

I walked out of the dance room, and it was nothing out there but broke niggas watching the home girl Bunny up there dancing.

She got that name because she had a huge ass bunny tatted on her ass cheek. Anyway, they weren't even throwing any money, and I knew it was time to fucking go, because Bunny could work the pole well.

After changing, I checked my phone to see if I could think of anyone else who had some pills for me. I lost that last plug after Kantwan beat his ass, for obvious reasons, but I found this one chick named Candy, so I text her. She'd sold to a couple other strippers at Starzz, so her resume looked pretty stellar to me.

After hitting her up, I grabbed my shit up and headed outside to my car since it was fixed now. My phone buzzed when I got outside, and I saw it was Candy.

**Candy:** *Yeah I got something. I'm right outside of the Almanzar grocery store on Maryland and Stroud.*

**Me:** *On my way.*

She was right around the corner from my house, so it all worked out.

I clutched my phone tightly, and as I ran by this one car, someone grabbed my arm and yanked me back. It was that old nigga from Alapocas.

"What the fuck!" I yelled and snatched my arm back.

"Come with me."

"I already told you I'm good, now let my arm go," I shouted and tried to remove myself from his grasp.

I kicked him in the shin, which made him slap the shit out of me. I felt blood drip from my nose as he dragged me into the backseat of his car.

*WHAM!*

He smacked me again, and then climbed inside his car with me. He pinned my hands down using only one of his big hands, and then reached under my dress to yank my thin underwear off with the other. *Not again, no!* I screamed in my head.

"Please no! I'll go with you!" I hollered and cried.

"Too late bitch!" he growled and finished ripping my panties. He spread my legs open as I squirmed, screamed, and cried, and then began to unbuckle himself with one hand. "That looks like some good pussy," his old ass smiled down at me.

Suddenly, the door opened behind him, and he was yanked out of the car. I quickly sat up, leaving my torn panties to dangle around the top of my thigh. I climbed out and saw he and Monty going at each other. Monty was getting the best of him even though he was a skinny guy.

"Go Caramel!" he shouted for me to run off.

I did as he told me to, and booked it to my car.

"Please crank up," I said as I twisted the key, and thank God it did.

I sped out of the parking lot and went straight to where Candy said she was. I really needed the pills now, to calm me down. I didn't even care that my nose was all bloody. Thank God for Monty.

# TWENTY-EIGHT

# Ivy

I woke up to the sound of my phone ringing, and hit around the bed looking for it. Once I realized I wasn't going to be able to blindly locate it, I picked my head up from the pillow. I found it right next to me, jammed into my rib cage and I rolled my eyes. I turned it over and quickly answered when I saw who it was.

"Yes I accept the charges!" I hollered into the phone damn near, and then jumped out of the bed to rush to Donovan's room. He was still asleep on his little fat belly, and I just rubbed his back.

"Hey baby girl," Portland spoke into the phone. My body became warm all over at the sound of his voice.

"Hi baby, I missed you," I said as I walked out of the room.

"Same, but all we got are a couple more months and I will be home to you."

"I know and I'm just smiling thinking about it already."

I was happy as hell that he was coming home, and even happier that his sister Raleigh had gotten me an interview to work at the call center she worked for. If I got the job, I would be working there by the time Portland came home. I would be making considerably less, but with Portland home, he would be contributing to the household more than now. So it would all work and balance out.

"So how is everything?" he questioned.

"It's going okay. You know I may be getting a job working with Raleigh."

"Oh yeah? That's good babe, you're not fucking with the clothing store no more?"

"No, I'm tired of standing on my feet for hours at a time. It's time for me to get a sit down job."

"I feel you baby," he laughed and it made me smile.

I missed hearing that laugh so much. I missed hearing another laugh too, but I had to give that up as of late.

"So what do you have planned for when you come home?" I quizzed.

"What do you mean?"

"Like as far as work and stuff like that. Is anything set up?"

"Nah, ain't nothing really set up right now, but that's not something I need you worrying about. You just make sure my son is good and that's it. Let me do me, and everything will be straight."

"Oh alright, well I love you," I said trying to lighten the mood.

Portland hated for me to question him about work. Ever since he got locked up for that robbery shit, he never wanted to talk about the ways he got his money. In a way I felt like I deserved to know, because his arrest came as such a fucking surprise to me. I knew he was out doing illegal shit, but he always made it seem like he had that shit under control, when obviously his ass didn't.

"I love you too, baby girl. But I have to go, and I should be calling you around the same time tomorrow."

"Alright, I will be waiting."

"Wait, where is Donovan?"

"He's still asleep right now. I would wake him, but I wanna take a shower and stuff first, because you know he takes up all my time," I giggled.

"Yeah he sounds just like me, he loves him some Ivy."

I blushed upon hearing him speak so sweetly about me.

"Awwww babe, stop, because you're making me sad that you're not here."

"Don't be sad Ivy, I'm coming home sooner than later, and we probably need to start looking at some rings," he said catching me off guard.

"Like engagement rings?" I removed my legs from being in the Indian style position, and sat at the edge of the couch.

Strangely, the first thing that came to mind upon him mentioning getting engaged was Elijah.

"That's exactly the kind of rings I'm talking about. But aye ma, I love you and I miss you and all that other shit," he laughed in his raspy voice that always made my pussy wet.

"Love you too daddy, bye."

After hanging up, I let out a deep sigh because I missed him so much. My little vibrator thing had been putting in major work lately, so it was time for the real thing. I just recently had to put it to use, because beforehand Elijah was satisfying my needs. I would be spending the night with him multiple times a week, and he was always finger fucking me or eating my pussy. Damn I missed it.

At the thought of my toy, I hopped up and rushed to my dresser drawer to retrieve it. I then grabbed my shower caddy and baby monitor, before rushing to the bathroom to clean myself.

I let the hot water run over my body, and then powered my toy on. It was very small, about the size of my thumb, which I loved. I placed it against my clit, and then threw my head back in ecstasy. I began to reminisce about all the times Portland had dicked me down and how bomb it was. Behind my eyelids, I envisioned him flicking his thick tongue over my clit, and sucking the life out of my pussy. Once he made me cum that way, he always kissed up my body, and then positioned his dick at my opening. I bit down on my lip as I continued to use the toy on my button.

"Mm, shit," I moaned softly as I felt myself about to cum.

I imagined Portland thrusting in and out of me, with my legs on his shoulders. That was my favorite position and he knew that. My breathing became heavy as this little toy flew me to new heights.

This was about to be the best orgasm that this little thing that ever delivered to me.

"Oh, oh, fuck!" I whimpered as I sped up, eyes still closed.

Suddenly, in my mind Portland changed into Elijah and I came hard and long before I could erase him. My eyes flew open, and my chest rose and fell quickly while I stared at the drain.

"What the fuck?" I asked myself aloud. I had never fantasized about Elijah, especially not while I was masturbating. "Get it together Ivy," I said as I began to lather my loofah. I think because I'd been ignoring Elijah, my mind was missing him.

After my shower, I brushed my teeth, and then submerged my toy in scalding hot water to clean it. I then cooked some breakfast, and just when I finished, my baby boy had woken up crying. I walked into his room, and just like always, his full baby lips were trembling.

"Aww, look at you," I chuckled and scooped his chunky butt into my arms.

I took him to his high chair, and we shared my plate of pancakes, eggs, and sausage. I then took him to the bathroom for a nice warm bath, and while I was washing him my phone chimed. I placed my hand on Donovan's shoulder to hold him in place, and when I looked at the screen I saw it was Elijah. Seeing his name reminded me of my shower. I slid open my phone to read it.

**Elijah:** *Long time no talk. I miss tasting you.*

I quickly changed his name to Erica, and then ignored the text. The longer we went without talking, the easier it would be to hold out for Portland. I'd already let Elijah do more than I should have.

# TWENTY-NINE

## Jersey

___

### A Week and a Half Later...

Tonight I agreed to chill with Tommy. I think it was because I felt bad for him, but of course I wouldn't tell him that. It was the fact that I had dissed him for Kill, when clearly I shouldn't have. Kill had stood me up for his baby mama, whom he tried to pretend was his ex-girlfriend. I didn't even know the nigga had a child!

They must've been having a funky good time together too, because that nigga hadn't posted shit on Instagram. He wasn't a super poster, but he would give a little something every now and then. I know because I looked forward to his posts. They were always subtly sexy. I would always look at the picture, and then scroll through the thirsty comments that females left while rolling my eyes.

A part of me didn't believe this whole baby mama story, because Kill didn't seem like the type of guy to lie about shit. Nor did he seem like the type to disown his baby just for sex. He seemed like a very blunt and honest person, and I just can't see him fibbing so that I would let him fuck, especially since he'd already smashed prior to telling me that. Then again, maybe I was just trying to make up excuses for him because I still really liked him despite him disappearing on me. And because Cheyla no longer talked to Kantwan, I had no one on the inside to tell me anything, other than Tommy. Tommy knew Kill better and longer than me, so I'm sure he was just as good a source as Kantwan.

I put on some jeans, and then a simple heather gray t-shirt. I grabbed my slide-ins from Victoria's Secret Pink, my phone, and then my purse before heading to the door.

"Where are you going?" Cheyla asked as Ivy sat on the couch.

"Chill with Tommy," I sighed.

"Why? Didn't you fuck Kill?" Ivy frowned.

"Yes I did, and I have no plans to fuck Tommy, I'm just being nice. I mean he did get at me first. It's kind of fucked up that I overlooked him for dog ass Kill."

"Yeah, that bitch ass nigga stood her up," Cheyla rolled her eyes and plopped down next to Ivy.

"Right, and I haven't heard from him since," I added.

"And the nigga has a fucking baby and baby mama that he can't leave alone!" Cheyla shouted and sucked her teeth.

"Damn, for real? How do you know?" Ivy stared up at me.

"I mean Tommy told me, but he could be lying to make himself look better. Remember he hates Kill."

"Or maybe you just want him to be lying so you can still lust after Kill," Cheyla smirked.

"Or maybe you should worry about how you can get Kantwan to let you suck his dick again," I raised a brow, and there was silence before the three of us all burst into laughter.

"Damn, it looks like none of us are talking to that crew," Ivy shook her head, making Cheyla and I cock ours.

"Us? You were talking to Elijah?" Cheyla bucked her eyes.

"No, no, I don't mean talking like y'all were to Kill and Kantwan. I meant like he was the homie."

"Then what happened? Why y'all not homies no more?" I quizzed suspiciously.

"Oh, because I didn't feel right being cool with him while my man is away," she responded. Cheyla and I made eye contact, diverted our attention back to her, and then nodded.

I'd been skeptical of Ivy's relationship with Kill's cousin since the day I saw her in his lap back at Starzz. She seemed way too flirty, but if she said it was nothing then it was nothing. Since I met Ivy she'd been all about my brother, so I had no reason not to trust her now.

Truth be told, after all the shit my brother put her through, if she was talking to Elijah in that way, I couldn't even be too mad. Most women in her place, including me, would have long ago given Portland his walking papers. He took advantage of Ivy because she loved him, and it made me physically sick sometimes. My mother, Raleigh, Cheyla, and I had all tried to convince her to leave him before, but she never wanted to. I know that's my brother, but he was a German Shepard for real.

"Alright y'all, well I will be back," I said.

I stopped before opening the door, and jogged to the fridge for some water. Lately I'd been feeling parched a lot, and my stomach had been hurting. I think I consumed some bad seafood, and it was starting to take effect. This would be the second time that I got sick from seafood, and that was so nasty to me. I turned my lip up as I pulled on the door handle.

I grabbed a bottle of Arrowhead from the fridge, and then rushed out. I got to Tommy's in no time, since he lived in Browntown as well. It was a nice little place, and not something I expected him to have on his own. I think it was because I had no idea how he got money. I heard he was a stick up kid, but you didn't get a Lexus, condo, and nice clothes from purse snatching.

**Me:** *Here.*

**T:** *Here I come.*

After a few moments, he appeared in the doorway, so I got out of the car to meet him. As soon as I neared him he pulled me into a hug. He looked and smelled good, so I didn't mind.

"Happy to have finally gotten your ass over here, beautiful," he grinned. His beautiful hazel eyes lit up as he smiled, and it was super cute.

"Oh really?" I raised my brow.

"Yep."

We walked into his home, and for some reason it had the touch of a woman. Something in my gut told me he didn't live here alone. Maybe I was just paranoid since Kill had possibly pulled the wool over my eyes with Margo.

I looked at the coffee table, and it was adorned with two champagne glasses, and a big cheese and fruit plate that they sold at the grocery store. I was starved so I booked it to the couch.

"Can I?" I pointed to the tray.

"I bought it for tonight so help yourself."

He didn't have to tell me twice. I immediately began piling cheese onto a cracker, and then threw it into my mouth. He chuckled at me, and then walked around to cut some music on. August Alsina came through, and I could feel Tommy staring a hole through me as I attacked the platter. I just kept my eyes on the snacks, because that was a priority right now.

"Hungry?" he quizzed.

"Yeah, I haven't eaten much today, only lunch and that was at school," I responded.

"Oh alright. Well keep going, I need to get my money's worth."

After having enough, I sat back and took a huge sip of my water. That little platter hit the spot. My phone began buzzing, and it was the same *Unknown* flashing across. I didn't answer unknown calls, so they needed to just give up, or find a different line to call me from.

Suddenly the lights cut off, and I snapped my neck to look over at Tommy. He had the biggest grin on his face, and he was so adorable. He reminded me of a taller, lighter version of Bow Wow.

"What are you smiling for?" I questioned, smiling myself.

"I just think you're so damn pretty."

"Thank you. I guess you're cute too."

"About time you give me a compliment back."

I was about to speak, but my phone started to ring again.

"What the fuck!" I said and turned my lip up.

"Who is that?" Tommy furrowed his brows.

"I don't know, but they call me every night around this time, and always twice. I don't answer unknown numbers, but they clearly won't take a fucking hint."

"I got you."

He reached over and took my phone from me. He set it on the table next to him, and then scooted closer to me. I leaned back a little since I had no room to actually scoot back. He began kissing on my neck, and rubbing my back slowly.

"Tommy," I said in a low tone. I was trying to push him, but he was determined, making himself really resilient. He didn't say anything as he began to lick on me and grope my legs. "Tommy I —" I couldn't finish my sentence because I began puking all over him, the couch, carpet, and my jeans. "Ah!" I stared down at my ruined pants in disbelief. I was embarrassed, floored, and disgusted.

"What the fuck! Are you sick?" he asked me as he looked over his sweater. It was a nice sweater that was now drenched in my vomit.

"I'm sorry Tommy. I-I don't know; I think I have food poisoning."

I wiped my mouth and then stood up. Throw up dripped onto the floor, making Tommy hop up off the couch and run to the back. He re-entered the living room with a towel and some carpet spray.

"I'm gonna go, but can I use the restroom?" I asked, but he didn't respond as he cleaned the floor with his eyes wide as saucers.

I rushed to his bathroom, and then rinsed my mouth out. I grabbed a whole bunch of paper towels, and began wiping my pants off. I spotted some Bath and Body Works hand soap, confirming that this was the home of a woman. It wasn't his mother, because he'd already revealed to me that they weren't on speaking terms after she sold his stuff for drugs. I didn't care though; I clearly had bigger problems.

I hadn't realized how sick I was until just now. After rinsing my mouth again, I left out of the bathroom and grabbed my purse and phone.

"Tommy, I'm gonna leave."

"Nah, don't leave, it's cool. It's cool baby."

"No I need to shower and brush my teeth. I need some Pepto Bismol as well."

"I got a shower here for you. And I can go get you some medicine baby," he neared me with a smirk.

He began kissing on my cheeks and I nudged him off. Was he seriously trying to kiss and shit after I just vomited everywhere?

"No Tommy, we can chill another time," I said before leaving out of the house.

"Jersey! Jersey!" he hollered after me, but I just got into my car. Damn nigga, what the fuck?

I sped home, and when I got there I didn't bother speaking to Ivy and Cheyla. I just went to the bathroom, stripped down, and hopped into the shower. I have never been so embarrassed in my life! I knew one thing for certain, I was never going back to that Red Lobster in Talleyville again! Nor was I going back to Tommy and his girlfriend's house!

THIRTY

## Cheyla

Two Weeks Later...

Today was gonna be the greatest day ever! I would finally have some family home with me, that wasn't Jersey's family. My brother was bringing his ass home from the pen, and I could not fucking wait. I missed him like crazy, and I was so ready to chill with him like the old days.

It was 9:30am currently, and I was getting up to shower. He was to be released and ready to be picked up around 12pm, but I couldn't sleep because of all the damn excitement inside of me.

Once I was done cleaning myself, I went into Jersey's room so that she could wake up.

"Rise and shine boo, it's time to go get my brother!" I shouted over her.

"What the fuck Cheyla, you don't have to yell!" she shouted back. After inhaling and exhaling sharply, she finally sat up. "What time is it?"

"You look pale, Jersey, are you okay?" I frowned.

Her usual caramel complexion looked flushed out and she was sweating, even though the house was really cool.

"Yes I'm fine, I just need some soup and shit," she waved me off.

"You've been sick for weeks Jersey, you should go to the doctor."

"I will."

I was starting to worry about her, because she'd been sweating, looking pale, and throwing up every now and then. I hated to ask her this but I had to.

"Did you take a pregnancy test?" I quizzed.

"For your information, I took one three days ago and it was negative."

"Oh okay, well I wonder what it could be then." I twisted my lips up as I pondered over her symptoms.

"I don't know, but let me go to the shower, because you know I can take a while."

I nodded and she stood up to gather her things. Jersey showered while I whipped up a small breakfast for us. I made waffles, grits, and eggs. Jersey and I loved waffles, so I knew she'd be happy to see that I'd made some.

"Mmmm, it smells good," she smiled as she entered the kitchen. She wore shorts, a crop top, and some black and white Adidas.

"It's waffles," I smiled and set the plate down in front of the chair she was pulling out.

We ate, talked, and reminisced on the good times we had with Sonny and Portland. We cleaned our plates, and then got in my car to head down to the jailhouse.

We got there around 11:45am on the dot, and then waited impatiently.

"I cannot wait to wrap my arms around his neck," I cheesed.

"I know. I miss Sonny too. I can't wait until both he and Portland are home though, because that will be paradise."

Finally, around 12:05pm, he emerged causing Jersey and I to hop out of the car and wave our arms wildly to flag him down. Once he spotted us, he jogged over and scooped me up.

"Oh my gosh!" I squealed as I squeezed his neck. I kissed his cheek repeatedly, making him laugh. I missed his laugh.

"Damn sis," he chuckled and set me down. He turned his attention towards Jersey, and they embraced for a few moments.

"We have so much to talk about Sonny, umm, are you hungry?" I asked once we all got back into the car.

"Yeah, I could use some pizza from Gino's," he responded.

We peeled out, and finally made it back into our area after an hour or so. We pulled into the shopping center parking lot on Lancaster where Gino's was, and parked. The three of us walked in, and Jersey and I sat down at a table as Sonny ordered his favorite slices. The lady gave him his ticket, and then he sat down with us.

"I can't believe I'm looking at you!" I grinned.

"Man, likewise. How are you though, Cheyla? Is mom still on that bullshit?" he inquired.

The last time I talked to my mother was a year ago. Him asking me that just made me realize how long he'd really been gone.

"Yes, she's been on that same bullshit since the last time I talked to you."

"Damn, so how are you getting money and shit? You still working with Ivy at the clothing store?"

I swallowed the lump in my throat, because I didn't know if I wanted to tell him about my work as a stripper. I knew he would get upset, but I had no plans of quitting, so I might as well come clean now.

"No Sonny..." I started, and Jersey stared into my eyes with a worried expression. "I've been working at Starzz," I finished.

"Starzz?" he frowned. He stared at me for a couple moments, and then his facial expression changed, letting me know he finally realized what I was saying. "Tell me you're a waitress or bartender," he grimaced.

"I'm too young to bartend, and I'm not a waitress."

"Cheyla, you gon' quit that shit right now!"

"No Sonny, I'm not! It pays my bills and I'm gonna do it until I find something else that does!"

"I can't have all these niggas watching you take your clothes off! Don't tell me you do this shit too Jersey?" He diverted his attention towards her.

She opened her mouth to speak but "Number 55!" cut her off, causing Sonny to get up and go get his food.

"I can't believe you told him," Jersey said.

"I had to, I mean I don't plan on quitting anytime soon, do you?"

"No, so I guess as soon as Portland comes home I have to tell him."

"You do," I nodded.

Sonny returned with his food, and he didn't say a word more as he scarfed it down. Once he was done, the three of us got up to leave.

"Do you wanna stay with us?" I smiled at him as he stared out the backseat window of my car.

"Nah, take me to Marley's crib. That's the place that's approved by my P.O."

Marley was Sonny's baby mother, who claimed she was gonna make sure to stay in contact with me so I could see my niece. She lied because the bitch moved and didn't even tell me where. I've hated her ass since the first time I met her, so I wasn't too surprised about what she'd done.

"Where does she stay Sonny? She moved on me."

"She stays off of Read and Harrison, I'll direct you," he stated dryly.

Right down the muthafuckin' street from me. I'm surprised I haven't seen her hoe ass out.

I blew out hot air and cranked my car up so that I could drop him off.

After dropping my brother off to Marley, Jersey and I headed home because we were tired as fuck. We were both off tonight, and a nap sounded heavenly right now.

I was a little bummed at my brother's reaction, but I'm sure he'd get over it in a little. I'll be damned if I'm out here alone with no blood family because he wants to act stupid. I was looking forward to him being there for me, so I didn't want something so small to come between us.

"You okay?" Jersey asked me as she walked towards her room.

"Yeah, his ass will get over that shit, shoot, he better," I replied and we both chuckled.

"Alright, well when I wake up we should invite Ivy over for a movie night."

"Sounds like a plan."

We both retired to our rooms, and I immediately lied down after placing my phone and purse on my nightstand. I swear my body was jumping for joy right now at the feeling of rest.

Before I closed my eyes, I picked my phone up, and went into my text messages to read Kantwan's and my old conversations. I chuckled at some of the funny things he'd said, and got warm all over at the sweet things. I licked my lips upon reading all of the freaky shit he'd said, and then gave a warm smile when I came across the comforting words he'd typed when I was missing my brother. I missed him so much, and now he hated me. I would never forget him. My stomach felt queasy at the thought of being out somewhere and seeing another girl enjoy the benefits of being with someone like Kantwan.

I locked my phone, set it on the dresser, closed my eyes, and then clasped my hands together before saying, "God, please let Kantwan forgive me. I miss him, and I promise if he forgives me, I won't act stupid. Please, I think I love him, and right about now love would do me some good."

# THIRTY-ONE

# Sondre "Sonny" Austin

*I* watched Cheyla drive off, and then I walked up Marley's three little steps. I knocked a few times, and then I heard someone behind the door, toying with the locks. Slipping my hands down into my pockets, I was overcome with anxiety, worried about what was to come of Marley and me.

The door opened, and Marley was standing there with a blank expression. She wasn't happy, sad, angry, or anything from the looks of it.

"What's up ma?" I grinned.

"Sonny, you- what is today?"

"My release date, I shouldn't have to remind you. Good thing I had Cheyla pick me up, you would've forgotten me," I joked.

She didn't say anything in response, and just closed the door behind me. I looked around and she'd been doing pretty well as far as the inside. This was still the hood, but she did a damn good job on the interior; too good.

"When did you get all this nice furniture?" I asked as I ran my finger across her nice coffee table. I sat down and waited for her response.

"I bought it a little after I moved in here." She sat down. "Sonny, I'm happy to see you baby."

"Why didn't you write me? Or answer any of my letters and shit?"

I met Marley when I was about sixteen years old, and she was fourteen. She was beautiful as hell with long brown hair, smooth dark skin, and a body sent from heaven.

We'd been together since we met, and of course we had our share of problems because we were young and I was dumb, but we made it this far. I was still doing a little bit of dirt here and there before I got locked up, but Marley never knew about it. In fact, she's never known me to cheat on her. The only arguments we had were about me doing illegal shit, which she didn't like.

Right before I went to jail, she told me she was pregnant, and that we were having a daughter. It broke me up that I couldn't be there for the birth, and that I couldn't see my child for two years.

At first Marley and I corresponded heavily, especially while she was pregnant, but after she sent me the newborn pictures, everything seemed to slow down. I thought it was because she had a new baby and couldn't tend to me as much, but here we are two years later and she was still up with that bullshit.

"I was busy Sonny, I didn't have as much time," she explained.

"You didn't have as much time," I repeated. "So I mean where do we stand? Because I haven't spoken or heard from you in over a year."

"Well—"

"And where is Sonaya," I frowned looking around for my daughter.

"She's—"

The sound of jingling keys in the door interrupted her. We both looked towards the door, and in walked some nigga holding a baby that looked just like Cheyla. I knew she was mine right then.

"Hey, Sonny?" the guy pointed to me.

"Yeah that's me, who you?"

The guy just looked at Marley, as Sonaya stared at me,

wondering who I was. It hurt me to see that she didn't know me, but it was no one's fault but mine.

"Sonny, this is Wyatt," Marley gave a shy smile.

"Who is he Marley?"

I was starting to get angry because it was obvious who the hell he was. I can't believe she would do me like this, and while a nigga was locked up? I tell you these bitches ain't worth shit! And they wonder why we fuck them over! I no longer felt bad about the shit I was doing to her on the low.

This homecoming so far was proving to be some bullshit for real. First Cheyla and Jersey telling me that they strip, and now I find out my girl been fucking some other nigga and playing house.

"M-my boyfriend Sonny, but it ju—"

"Nah, fuck that!" I barked and snatched my daughter from this nigga. Sonaya burst into tears, and began reaching for him. That shit almost made a nigga burst into tears too. How dare she have this nigga playing daddy to my kid?

"Give her here Sonny, she doesn't know you!" Marley shouted.

"Nah, fuck that! She gon' get to know me! And how dare you have this nigga playing daddy to my fucking kid!"

"Let's lower our voices now, you're scaring her," Wyatt said.

"Nigga, don't tell me what the fuck to do!"

"Marley, I'm gonna give you guys a chance to talk, but let me know if you need me and I will be right here," Wyatt told Marley, but was staring right into my eyes.

"Man, get yo' ass on!" I hollered before he turned around and left.

Sonaya was still crying, so I just kissed her cheek softly and hugged her. She began sniffling, and then finally the crying stopped. I pulled her away from me, and then smiled as I looked into her cute little face. Upon seeing me smile, she began to smile and giggle as well.

"This is your daddy Ny-Ny," Marley rubbed her back.

I moved Sonaya from her touch, and then walked to the couch to sit down. Marley followed me, and then sat down next to me. No words were spoken as I stared at my beautiful daughter, while Marley stared into the side of my face.

"Sonny, I'm sorry. I had every intention on waiting for you to get out. It's just that after I had the baby I was struggling to make ends meet. The money you sent wasn't doing anything, and eventually I got evicted from our place. I met Wyatt because my co-worker introduced us, and he was just trying to help me. He got me into this place, bought my furniture, and he was really good with Sonaya. Over time feelings developed, and we became a couple." I should've known something was up, because her last letter to me over a year ago was from a different address than the one I'd left her at.

"Whatever Marley, I don't even give a fuck," I scoffed and shrugged as I bounced my daughter in my lap. I tickled her making her laugh, and Marley joined her.

"Sonny, I know you're upset but I want you to forgive me. I still love you."

"You still love me," I repeated and chuckled. Was this bitch really still trying to be together? Nah, she couldn't be.

"Yes I do. Wyatt was just a placeholder if you will. I wanna be a family though, for Sonaya and because I love you."

"I don't know, Marley, I need some time." I handed Sonaya back to her, and she took her while staring at me.

"You don't know? Sonny, I—"

"Just give me some time."

"Where are you going? You just got here, you need to spend time with us," she said once she saw me walking to the door.

"I'll be back in a couple of hours, I need some air Marley."

Before she could say anything, I left her crib. I spotted one of my old homies named E-Way, and threw my hands out to say what's up.

"Sonny? Nigga when you get out?" he shouted, looked both ways, and then jogged across the street.

"Nigga today, and it feels good as hell."

"Nigga your girl been entertaining."

"I already know, but thanks for looking out for me. Aye, but can you give me a ride to Chestnut and Van Buren?"

"I got you."

We walked back across the street, and then got into his car. He drove me to my requested destination, and pulled over to put on his hazards.

"Thanks son."

"You need me to wait?" he asked.

"Nah, I'm sure I can get a ride."

"Aight, hit me if you change your mind. It's a little party popping tonight too, ya know. Some bad thick jawns gon' be up in that thang."

"Oh word? Shit, I may try and see what's up with that then."

"Fasho, see you later pimpin'."

I dapped him up, and then got out. I ran onto the sidewalk, and once I reached the front door I was looking for, I knocked.

"Baby!" Raleigh squealed and jumped into my arms. She wrapped her legs around my waist after I lifted her.

"I missed you, ma," I said as I kissed on her neck. "Ya mama home?"

"No, she's at work. I took today off just for you."

"You love me?" I questioned as I kicked the door closed with my foot.

"You know I love you, I just wish you loved me the same, Sonny."

I met Raleigh when I was sixteen, after I became friends with her older brother Portland. Marley was already my girl, but Raleigh was not something a nigga could pass up. I didn't love one more than the other, it's just that Portland would be furious if he found out I was smashing his little sister. That's the only reason Raleigh was a secret, well not the only, but the main reason.

She'd kept up with the letters, and always answered my calls, so she had one up on Marley before I even found out about Wyatt. The fact that Marley was out here busting it open for another nigga just made my decision easier. I knew Raleigh would be happy to know that it was about to be just her and I from now. Fuck Marley's hoe ass.

"I'm done with her, baby," I smiled as I neared her bedroom.

"For real?"

Raleigh was so fucking beautiful. She had smooth caramel skin, a nice slim thick body, short curly hair, and the sexiest fucking lips a nigga had ever seen. I loved this girl.

"Yes for real."

We made it to her bedroom, and I let her down so she could get undressed. I watched closely as she got naked, and damn did I miss her body. Even though it'd been years since I touched her, I remembered every damn crevice.

"I love you, baby," I said before towering over her, and slipping my tongue into her mouth.

# THIRTY-TWO

# Elijah Camren

---

Three Days Later...

*I* was going to see my cousin today and I couldn't wait. His ass had been locked up for a little over thirty days now, and I had some good news for his ass. I couldn't wait to see his face when I told him, because when *I* found out I was beaming like a light pole.

Initially, he'd been sentenced to seven years in prison, but now he would be coming home much sooner, thanks to his fucking boss. I was happy that this nigga came through for Kill, because he hadn't done that shit for Ka'Shea. I wasn't sure why either. Especially because he lost way more bread behind Kill than he did with Ka'Shea.

I sat in the waiting area until the inmates began coming out and sitting with their people. Kill came out, and he appeared to be mad as hell. He looked the same, except he had something tan in his ear. I guess that was because the policemen had hit him in it with their baton, so he lost some hearing according to Kantwan.

"What's up?" I smiled as he sat down across from me.

"What's up man, how are you?" he asked me.

"Nah, how are you? You're the one behind bars and shit."

"I'm straight, I guess. I can't believe a nigga gon' be in here for seven fucking years." He pursed his lips and shook his head.

"That's what I came to talk to you about."

"What you mean?"

"Axel is getting you out in two fucking months, son. He tried to sooner, but that's the earliest his people could get you out of here," I explained.

"Wait, why?" he frowned.

"He wouldn't tell us, he just said it was important that he get you out. But you know Axel loves you like a son."

"I guess I shouldn't care about the reason. It's good to hear, but I won't believe it until I see it," he sighed and ran his hands over his face.

"I said the same thing. But stay positive, Kill. What's going on with your ear man?"

"Fucking officer clocked me, and the little jail doctor said I had some hearing loss."

"Is it major loss? Like, can you not hear shit or what?"

I swear these policemen got away with fucking murder, literally. There was nothing they couldn't do. I just hoped Kill was able to get back at their asses. I was all for helping out too. Shit if the law wasn't gonna take care of them, then we would have to.

"I can hear really well if you're in front of me, or sitting on the side with the good ear. If you're by the damaged one, it's really low and almost inaudible. I'll live though."

"I know you will. I'm just pissed about the shit happening in the first fucking place," I scoffed.

"Me too. But have you spoken to umm—"

"Margo?"

"Nigga, hell no. I don't give a fuck about that girl. I was gonna ask about Jersey," he furrowed his brows at the mention of Margo. Kill couldn't stand Margo, but he helped her with her son occasionally, so she couldn't complain too much.

"Oh, nah man. We don't fuck with them girls anymore. I think she and Tommy are a thing now though. That's what I heard."

I was still a little salty that Ivy had stopped talking to me before her nigga even got here. I knew it was because she felt we were about to cross the line, but so what! That nigga didn't deserve her at all, if even half of the shit she told me he'd done was true. I could only do so much though, so I wasn't gonna go completely out of my way to pull her from something that she wasn't ready to leave yet.

"Damn, for real?" He chuckled angrily and shook his head. Kill was really into Jersey. Shit, the three of us were into all of them complicated ass girls.

"I mean I don't know how true it is, but that's what people have been saying," I nodded.

"Tommy though? Damn. Anybody else would've been better."

"I agree, because that nigga is a bitch. Plus, I heard he gave his girl herpes," I clenched my teeth and Kill's jaw dropped.

"I ain't even that surprised. That nigga will stick his dick in a meat grinder if it had a pair of thick thighs around it," he laughed and so did I.

"Damn shame."

"I hope Jersey knows that before she let that nigga hit," he smacked his lips. "Fuck, I hope she don't let him hit."

"You ain't tried calling her?"

"Yeah man, every fucking time I got the chance I called, and even twice a night. She would never answer, so after two weeks of trying I gave up."

"Nigga, pull out that pen and paper."

"Fuck that, that's doing too much."

"Suit yourself my nigga, but you sound like you got it bad for her. If it were me, I wouldn't give up until I exhausted all options."

"I don't chase nobody."

"Sometimes the woman may be worth you changing things up my nigga."

"Well I ain't even know her that long, and she was trying to push up on both Tommy and I anyway."

"You ain't got to throw on the nonchalant act for me Kill, I know you. I can see all in your face that you buggin' just thinking about her being with Tommy," I chuckled.

He dropped his head, and then ran his hands over his unkempt fade. He blew out hot air, and then picked his face up. His eyes were closed, as he shook his head.

"Nah, I'm good. I'm good. She ain't even came looking for me."

"Looking for you? Nigga, how? None of us talk to them, so it's not like she would find out."

"I know she don' heard it in the fucking streets."

"Okay, and what if when she heard it, you had stopped calling by then, huh?"

"You think you know every fucking thing, don't you?" he grinned.

"You right about that," I chuckled.

We chopped it up for a bit more, and then it was time for him to go back. His whole mood changed at the mention of Jersey fucking with Tommy, and initially I didn't know why. I mean I knew they'd fucked around a couple times, but clearly it was deeper than I thought. This nigga was in love, which was shocking. Kill didn't fall for women easily; shit, he never did. So the fact that he only spent a night or two with her, and now had it this bad, was mind blowing to say the least. Either she put some voodoo on this nigga, or her pussy was that damn good. Maybe she put them stripper moves on his ass. I laughed at the thought.

Kill would keep it pushing though, because he was never the type to chase a bitch or dwell on a situation too long. If she in fact was with Tommy, he'd be upset at first, but he would overcome it. Kill wasn't a soapbox type of nigga. I swear he was the creator of the saying, 'don't cry over spilled milk'. He hated to sit and complain about something that was already done, because of the simple fact that it happened and there was no way you could change it. It made sense, but it was hard to do for me.

After I left from visiting Kill, I decided to just go home and chill. A lot of shit was on my mind and I didn't feel like being out. I was always the type of nigga to need solitude every now and then. I couldn't be around anyone twenty-four fucking seven. I'd been that way since I was a kid, and my uncle Clarence would always say, 'Boy how are you gonna have a wife?'

I didn't have any parents really, because my mom died during childbirth, and my dad committed suicide when I was six months old. My uncle Clarence, Kill's, Ka'Shea's, and Kantwan's father, said that's just how attached my father and mother were. They'd been together their whole life damn near, and my dad just couldn't take the fact that she was gone.

After my mother passed, my dad was so depressed that he had to be committed twice, just for the hospital to let him go and say he was fine. The last time they let him go, he went straight home and hung himself in the bedroom. Uncle Clarence found his brother, and he said it was the most horrifying thing in the world.

It was sad to think about, even though I had no idea who my parents were. There were pictures of them all around my uncle's home, but unfortunately it was the first time a picture didn't say a thousand words.

I was raised with Kill, Kantwan, and their oldest brother Ka'shea as if they were my brothers. Their mother and father were basically my mother and father. When their mom Laurie died, I was paranoid that my uncle would react the same way as his brother, but thank God he didn't. He did however injure himself at work, and he hasn't been able to provide since. He doesn't like for us to visit him in the home he's in, just because I think he is embarrassed, but we try to see him at least twice a month. He was a great father to my cousins, and an even greater father figure to me, so he had no reason to be ashamed.

After uncle Clarence injured himself and quit working, it was like a downward spiral, because Ka'shea started pushing weight, which soon landed him in jail. The three of us had been fending for ourselves ever since, and by the grace of God we had a pretty nice income at this point. Neither of us were rich, but we didn't go hungry, we had somewhere to lay our heads, cars, and pretty nice clothes. I was doing just fine, and because of what I came from, I would never complain.

I arrived at my complex, and quickly rushed upstairs to my

condo. I sat down on the couch, and then picked up my phone. I was frustrated that Ivy had stopped returning my texts, even though a nigga wasn't even trying to care. I guess Kill wasn't the only one intrigued off minimal impressions. Ivy could continue to kick rocks though, because I was not about to continue to try and be there for her, when she clearly didn't want me too. When she realizes that any nigga that would treat her the way her baby daddy does couldn't possibly love her, she would come to me. I just hoped she wasn't too late.

# THIRTY-THREE

# Jersey

_______________

*I*t was early May, and my last class of the semester was at 8am this morning. All we had to do was take a test and then we could leave. I loved days like that, because it made it easier to go to class, knowing you wouldn't be there the usual length of time.

I had a doctor's appointment later today, because I was still feeling sick. I'd lied to Cheyla and told her I'd made one a while ago just to ease her mind, but shit now I was worried. I'd never had a sickness last this long. It had come and gone a few times, but recently it'd been sticking around like glue. And every damn pregnancy test I took came back negative, so I was dumbfounded.

I was sweating all the time, throwing up, and I even fainted in my room, breaking my wrist on the dresser. No one was home with me at the time, but luckily I woke up and was fine. The doctors that fixed my wrist up wanted to run some tests on me, but I wouldn't allow them to. I only used one doctor, and they weren't her, so it was a no go.

I heard the mailman shoving the mail through the door, so I threw the crackers I was shoving into my mouth to the side. I'd emailed my Dad for some money, and since I didn't get a response, I was hoping he mailed it. I tried dropping by, but Hannah his house-keeper said he didn't want any visitors at the time. He hadn't seen me in a while, but I guess he didn't care.

I rushed to the door, but slowed down once I started to get light headed. I picked the mail up off the floor, and sifted through it. One stuck out to me, because it had a handwritten address on it. I recognized the sender's name, but the address appeared to be from the same place Portland was, so I was confused as hell.

"Kilexis," I whispered. I can't lie, a warm sensation took over my body. Over a month later and I was still crazy about this nigga for some reason.

I dropped all of the other letters, and then rushed back to my room and sat down on the bed. I shoved a cracker into my mouth, and munched it as I opened the letter.

*Jersey,*

*I know I probably shouldn't even be writing you because I heard you're taken, but I just felt the need to. It's probably my fault as to why you went ahead and got you a man. I guess I just didn't want you to think that I stood you up for our date, although you should know in your heart that I would never do anything like that to you. I sweated you way too hard to do some fuck nigga shit like that. But anyway, I'm sure you can tell by the sender address that I'm in jail. The night I was coming to get you, I got popped for a gang of shit. I won't get too much into it for your protection. I was sentenced to seven years in jail, and that was like a stab in the chest. My cousin came to see me though, and he let me know that I'd be home sooner than that, but who knows. I was pretty much caught red handed, so I doubt it. On the bright side, I get to see my older brother Shea daily. I'm sure you don't care by now, but I just felt the need to tell you. I know we didn't know one another that long, but I find myself thinking about you and what we could've become CONSTANTLY. I liked your style beautiful, lol. Anyhow, feel free to write me back baby, if you want. It's no pressure; I just wanted to talk to you. You don't answer my calls from here, so I had to go 1800's style on your pretty ass. But if you don't respond, I just ask that you please stop fucking with a nigga like Tommy. He ain't what you think he is, and I'm not just saying that because I'm feeling you. Ain't like I can be your man from behind bars, and I damn sure don't expect you to hold me down when I ain't never even taken you out on a date. But yeah, please find somebody better baby girl, you deserve way more than that nigga could ever give you. I don't wanna throw too much salt in his game, because to be honest I was low key jealous when I found out he got you. If you ever need someone to talk to, answer my calls or write me back, I'll be here ... Obviously lol. Hope to talk to you soon.*

*Love Kill Cam...*

I smiled as I read the letter, and then let out a sigh of relief to know he hadn't stood me up. I tried to be over it, but the truth was that I was still bothered to this day. I was really into him, and to think he dissed me to go chill with his baby mama hurt my feelings.

Now I was looking at Tommy kind of sideways even more, because he told me that bullshit about seeing Kill out with his baby mama. Something in my gut wouldn't allow me to get close to him, and now I knew why. He was a fake ass nigga, and I bet he had a woman of his own. Scratch that, I *know* he has a woman of his own.

That house he had me in had too much of a woman's touch to be his own. What nigga shops for hand soap at Bath and Body Works? Shoot, you're lucky if a man even washes his hands after using the restroom; I know, I have a brother. I'm glad I threw up on his ass because he deserved that shit. I wish I could go back and throw up on his stupid ass again.

My high immediately came down once I realized Kill would be gone for seven long ass years. I really wanted to chill and feel him out some more, but I guess it wasn't meant. That didn't mean I couldn't get to know him some more while he was in jail though. And now that I was done with school, I would have all the time in the world to sit and write him. Thank God I didn't injure my writing hand.

I looked at the clock, which read 10am, and decided to write him a letter now. That way I could drop it off at the Post Office on my way to the doctor. I wanted him to get it as soon as possible, so he would know that I felt the same way he did about me.

I sat at my desk, and pulled out my pretty stationary. The paper was mint green with gold detailing, and so were the envelopes. I picked up my favorite purple pen, and began to write.

*Kilexis,*

*I'm so happy you wrote me, because I'd had the wrong impression this whole time. I definitely thought you stood me up, and I'm happy to know that you didn't. I do want to let you know that I'm NOT with Tommy, and I NEVER will be with Tommy. I would have much rather gotten to be with you, but I guess I can't, huh? Anyway, I've kind of been missing you even though we've only known each other for a little while. I still remember you pulling into the parking lot in your black Denali a couple months ago. I've been into you ever since. Every time I hear "Yeah, I Said It" by Rihanna I think of you, because that was the song that I danced to just for you that night at the club. I'm beyond bothered that you won't be home for seven years, but you have to promise to keep in contact with me. I promise I will answer all of your calls and letters, no matter what my situation is. And seven years from now I better be the first person, after your brother and cousin, that you come visit! Although I won't get to see you for a while, I'm happy that I got to spend the time I did with you, especially those nights we spent exploring one another's bodies in more ways than one. I can still feel your lips pressed against mine, even though we've only kissed on what, three occasions? You for real came through and rocked my world baby, and I want you. I want you so bad. I dream about you every time my head hits the pillow, and before you contacted me I was kicking myself for it. Now, I can't wait to go to bed tonight so I can see you in person. Anyway, as soon as you get this you better write me back! Even if we've talked over the telephone already, write me back Mr. Camren! Oh and by the way, add me to your visitors list or something, I would love to come see you if it's okay!*

*Love Jersey Lamyia Warren.*

After putting up my purple pen, I re-read the letter to make sure I'd said everything I wanted to say. I then grabbed my body butter that smelled like strawberries, and rubbed a dime-sized amount all over the page. I put some red lipstick on, and then kissed the page before folding it up. I grabbed his envelope to double check the address, making sure I was sending it to the right place, then licked the back of mine to seal it up. I grabbed my purse and phone, and then headed out to the Post Office and doctor's office with a smile on my face... for some reason.

## THIRTY-FOUR

## Ivy

———

One Month Later...

"Come on Donovan, today is the big day," I said to my son as I picked him up off of the bed.

I had him all dressed up because we were going to pick his daddy up. I was so damn happy that I couldn't stop smiling. My cheeks were starting to hurt from cheesing super widely.

"Are you excited to see daddy? Are you, huh?" I tickled his little belly as he chuckled. "Me too." I kissed his fat cheek, and then carried him to the living room where Jersey and Cheyla were waiting.

"Why do you keep checking your phone?" I questioned Jersey.

"She's waiting for Kill to call," Cheyla answered for her.

"Oh, you guys are talking again?" I cocked my head.

"Yes, he's in jail so we write and talk on the phone," she nodded.

"In jail? Wow, what the hell!"

I don't know when this shit happened, but I did notice that she was always checking her damn phone for the past month. Some nights I would try to go out with her and Cheyla, but she would be in her room, laid up talking.

I was wondering how the hell he ended up in jail, and it made me wonder how Elijah was doing. I hoped he hadn't gotten locked up too, because he and Kill often ran together. *Ivy, that's not your man,* I told myself. I should not be worrying about another nigga the same day my man was getting released. I needed to get it together.

"Yeah, and I miss him," Jersey sighed.

"How cute, but are you guys ready to go?" I asked.

They both nodded in response, so we headed out the door. Once Donovan was all buckled in his car seat with a filled sippie cup, we were good to go. I stopped at the gas station to fill up and get some snacks for the drive, so that we wouldn't have to stop midway. Even though the jail was only a thirty-minute drive, we hadn't had breakfast or anything, and we were bound to get hungry.

"Somebody is gonna have their back blown out this week!" Cheyla clapped her hands and laughed from the backseat.

"Ugh, that is so nasty!" Jersey chuckled.

"I'm not even about to get into that," I shook my head.

"And now that you quit the club, you have nothing to worry about," Jersey changed the subject thank God.

"I know," I nodded as I thought about it.

The call center hired me on the spot, and paid training was to start next week. It was like perfect timing since Portland was coming home today. Because they hire a month before training, I was scared I wouldn't have a job by the time Portland came home, but it all worked out. I didn't think I would have to tell Portland about my old job, which had me ecstatic.

I had the rest of the week off to spend with him and Donovan, and then I would start my new job next week. The rent and utilities were paid up this month, and the money Portland had gotten to me filled up the fridge. I was good and on cloud nine right now.

The only problem I had was the fact that I couldn't stop thinking about Elijah, especially at night. He was different from Portland in the sense that he cared about my thoughts and opinions on things. He never made me feel dumb like Portland did either.

Portland didn't give a fuck about my views, he just wanted to me to cook, lie on my back, and not ask any questions about his actions. Elijah was different and saw me as an equal, while still being able to take the lead as a man. I never knew that there was a balance like that until I met him. I thought a guy could only be either or. Then on top of that, his finger and head game was bananas! I could only imagine what his dick was like. Don't get me wrong, Portland could eat pussy too, but it just feels better when the person who is doing it, treats you good outside of the bedroom too.

"I can't wait to see my brother," Jersey said excitedly as she stared out the window.

I entered the freeway, and picked up my speed hoping to get there quicker. We made it to the Delaware County Prison about an hour later, and it was about forty-five minutes before Portland emerged.

He was just as fine as the day I met him, except he had more facial hair, which was sexy. He was definitely more cut up, and I didn't mind that either. He walked over to us, wearing the last outfit I'd seen him in two years ago. He had a big ass smile on his face, when he saw me take Donovan out of the car. He gave Cheyla a side hug, before Jersey jumped into his arms with so much force that he stumbled backward. He squeezed her small torso tightly, and closed his eyes before kissing her head.

Cheyla and I were silent as the two just hugged one another. He finally put her down, roughed up her curly hair, and then swaggered over to me. He took Donovan from me, who just stared at his father with his eyes bucked. He was only five months old when Portland got arrested, so he probably didn't remember him.

"Hey man," Portland smiled at our baby.

Donovan just stared with his little eyes wide, and his small lips parted. Portland kissed his cheeks, and then turned his attention toward me.

Jersey rushed over and said, "I'll take him," referring to Donovan.

After she took my son, Portland wrapped his arm around my neck, and I gripped his torso as we squeezed one another. He pulled back just a little, and pressed his lips against mine. I closed my eyes because I hadn't felt his lips in forever. I could feel his snake hardening on my leg, which caused a smile to creep across my face. He bit his lip and then kissed me again.

"I missed you," I said in a low tone.

"Can y'all save that for later?" Cheyla barked playfully, before yanking the back door open.

She got inside the car, and Jersey walked around to the other side to get in the backseat with Donovan. She buckled him in, and then Portland and I got into the front to head back home.

We went to TGI Fridays to have lunch, and then I dropped Jersey and Cheyla off at home.

"Did you wanna go see your mother and sister?" I questioned Portland as we pulled away from the curb.

"Nah, I will see her tomorrow, I have other plans right now," he squeezed my thigh. I chuckled at him and then drove to the apartment we shared.

By the time we got there, Donovan was asleep, so Portland just carried him upstairs to the door, and then took him into his room. He kissed his face, and then grabbed my hand to lead me into the bathroom.

He started removing his clothes, and if jail did anything, it did his body well. Portland was always a fit guy, but now he belonged in some type of catalog.

I licked my lips once he exposed his dick. He walked over to me and pulled my dress over my head, before unhooking my bra and pulling down my panties all in one motion it seemed.

"I need to shower, but I can't wait to slide up in that, so we gonna do both at the same time," he flashed me his beautiful smile. He turned the water on, and then got in with me following him.

We stood under the showerhead, kissing to make up for all of the months and years that we couldn't.

"I love you, Ivy," he whispered with his lips still crushed against mine.

"I love you too," I said.

He picked me up and began sucking on my neck, before sliding me down onto his long thick pole. I hadn't been penetrated with a dick in almost two years, so it was painful to say the least. Portland was very well endowed, and damn did I miss it. This was part of the reason why he had such a hold on me.

"We can go as slow as you want," he said before sucking on my jaw line.

I tightened my grip around his neck using my forearm, and locked my ankles on top of each other. He held me as if I was equal to a feather, and moved me up and down very slowly.

"Damn, you are so fucking tight. You've been holding me down in more ways than one," he said.

Elijah immediately entered my mind, but I did my best to shake him. Portland could not find out that I'd been entertaining him.

I bit down on my lip as he thrust into me with slow but powerful strokes. My legs trembled every time I hit the base of his dick.

"Shit," he grumbled.

"I'm so fucking backed up, that you may get pregnant tonight baby."

I couldn't respond because he had me paralyzed right now. He turned the water off, and while still inside me, stepped out the shower to carry me to the bedroom.

"What are you doing?" I asked even though I could barely talk.

He said nothing; he just laid me down on the bed, without removing his dick. He stood on the bed using his knees, and spread my legs as wide as they would go. Gripping my waist, he began to move in and out of me at a nice medium pace.

"Uuuh, uuuuh shit," I whimpered.

I'd been waiting for this day and it was here. My pussy salivated every time he slammed into me, causing me to make the ugliest faces ever. As soon as I came, he stared down into my eyes and began beating it up. The pleasure had taken over the pain by now, and he was hitting every spot that had been neglected while he was away. My little vibrator could not even begin to compare itself to Portland's dick game. Elijah's fingers were a close second though. *Stop Ivy*.

I was dripping to the point where the area under me was

drenched. He slipped in and out of me quickly, until we both grunted from exploding.

"That's over a year of back up," he chuckled and slowly pulled out of me. "I had to get out the shower so I could fuck you how I wanted," he added.

My pussy was sore, and I was out of breath so I couldn't say anything. He scooped me up, and then carried me to the shower so we could really wash off.

Thank God it had a seat in there, because right now a bitch could not stand. It was so fucking worth it though.

Now that Portland was home, forgetting about Elijah would be a breeze, or so I hoped.

# THIRTY-FIVE

# Portland Warren

---

The Next Morning...

*I* woke up next to Ivy, and slipped my arm from under her head. She was sleeping so peacefully and I didn't want to wake her up. She'd been through it while I was locked up, and I wanted her to get all of her rest.

It was a little after 9 in the morning, and I wanted to get up and get out. I had a few people to see, namely my sister Raleigh, my mother, Sonny, and maybe my father. That nigga didn't give a fuck about me though, so that may be something I do at a later time, if at all.

I climbed out of bed, and quietly walked to the closet to choose something to wear. Not having to wear that damn jumpsuit was a luxury in itself. I chose some black jeans, and an all-black t-shirt. My black Chuck Taylors were looking at me begging to be chosen so I did. After pulling some fresh boxers from my drawer, and pulling down a belt, I headed to the shower.

Once I was clean and ready, I went to kiss Donovan goodbye, then grabbed Ivy's keys to dip out. Slipping into her car, I immediately cut the radio on and blasted the music as I pulled off the street.

"I need some fucking weed," I said to myself as I drove down Chestnut.

As I was driving I spotted the homie E-Way spitting to some chick. I knew he would be able to help me get some good shit to smoke.

"E!" I shouted out of the window. He paused and scanned the street, before stopping on me.

"Portland?" he furrowed his brows.

"Who else, bruh?" I grinned.

He put his finger up to tell the girl to hold on, and then jogged to me.

"Damn homie, I forgot you was getting out this month."

"Yeah man, and I'm happy to fucking be here too. You know somebody I can cop some smoke from?"

"Yeah son, let me get his number for you," he said before reaching into his pocket and pulling out his phone. "I know you made Ivy quit the club now that you back. Honestly, I was surprised you were even cool with her working there."

"What?" I frowned.

"Oh shit, never mind. I got the number for you right here—"

"Nigga, what the fuck are you talking about with Ivy and working at some fucking club?" I seethed.

E-Way sucked his teeth and then blew out hot air. "Man, Ivy was stripping down at Starzz."

My heart dropped into my stomach after hearing those words leave his lips. He could not be fucking serious right now. Ivy showing her body to niggas was not cool at all. This shit couldn't be true.

"What? How you know?"

"My boy Hump seen her giving a couple lap dances."

I wanted to go in there and strangle Ivy right now. She lied to me about what she was doing for money and that shit had me on one. I should've known that working for a clothing store was not paying the bills like her ass said it was.

"Why you ain't tell me, man?" I frowned.

"Nigga how? Call the damn jailhouse?"

"You right. Let me get that number though," I shook my head.

"Aight, his name is Elijah, and it's (302) 555-7784."

"Cool, thanks man."

I sped off down the street, deciding not to approach Ivy right now because I was too mad. If I went up and talked to her right this second, I may put hands on her. Right about now I was feeling like she deserved a little slapping up and down though.

After stopping at the liquor store for a few things, I headed to my mother's crib. I was wondering if they knew how Ivy was getting her money. If they did, that shit was gonna piss me the fuck off.

I found a park right in front since it was the time that people were at work, and then exited the car. I said what's up with a head nod to a few people, and then knocked on the door. I started to feel happy about seeing my mother and sister; I'd missed their asses. Although they did visit me a lot, it would feel good to hug them for more than two seconds without a guard barking for us to break apart.

"Baby!" my mother beamed and hugged me tightly as hell. I just carried her inside, and closed the door behind me.

"Portland!" Raleigh ran to me, and as soon as my mom let go, she took her place. "I know you got out yesterday, so why the hell are we just now seeing you?"

"Because I wanted to spend time with Ivy and shit. I knew y'all could wait," I smiled and sat down on the couch.

"Oh baby, I missed you so much," my mother rubbed the side of my face.

"Likewise, ma. So what's everyone been up to?"

"Same old stuff. Working hard, just for our money to be swallowed up with bills," Raleigh sighed and plopped down next to me.

"Dad still on his bull I see. I got y'all though, stuff is gonna be different now that I'm back."

"Oh yeah, how?" my mother folded her arms across her chest.

"Because I'm gon' be giving all of y'all money. You two and Jersey."

"I asked you *how* Portland?" my mother replied.

"It shouldn't even matter, just know you gon' be good, the both of y'all. We don't need dad and we're gonna continue to show him that."

"We shall see," Raleigh huffed.

"I found out that Ivy was stripping while I was locked up, and I hope neither one of you knew anything about this."

"Portland, she needed the money and the only reason we didn't tell you—"

"I don't wanna hear y'all excuses! How do y'all let something like that go on and not say nothing to me? Huh? Because you knew the shit was wrong!" I hollered.

"First of all little boy, lower your got damn voice when you're talking to me. You are not too old for me to knock the shit out of you. Secondly, like I said, she needed the money and that was the only way she saw fit to pay the rent and stuff. We didn't tell you because we didn't want you acting out in jail. Don't be mad at her Portland, she was just trying to make ends meet. She could've easily gone out and met some guy to help out," my mother got me together, but I still didn't agree.

"For real Portland, you know Ivy loves you. She would never do anything for malicious reasons; she just needed the money. Just like Jersey and Cheyla need the money," Raleigh said.

"Jersey and Cheyla? Fuck you mean? Don't tell me you letting my baby sister strip, too?" I hissed. What in the entire fuck was going on? I go away and come back to half of the women in my life being hoes?

"Letting? Jersey is an adult, we don't let her do anything. She has a lot of bills including expensive ass college, so she had to do what she had to do," Raleigh replied.

"I can't do this shit right now," I said before standing to my feet.

"You don't want to eat or anything? I can make some shrimp scampi for you, I know you love it," my mom offered.

"I'm good. I'll holla at y'all later."

I went and picked up a phone, then drove to scoop Sonny from his baby mother's house. I couldn't call or text before, because I didn't know what number he had, or if he'd even gotten a phone, but thank God he was there.

"Damn man, we finally out of that shit," Sonny grinned as we peeled down Read Street.

"For real. I feel so damn good. Well I felt good until I found out Ivy, Jersey, and Cheyla were shaking their asses down at Starzz."

"Yeah, they told me that shit the day I got out. I couldn't even talk to Cheyla for a couple days. I tried making her quit but she refused."

"Crazy, but I'm about to hit this guy up for some smoke, you down?"

"Yeah, I am. But man, what you gon' do about Ivy?" he quizzed.

"I don't fucking know. I'm gon' talk to her tonight."

I hit this guy Elijah up, and he told me to meet him on the corner of Maryland Avenue by the liquor store. I drove over there, and saw a guy that looked like it could be him so I parked.

"You gon' stay in the car?" I asked Sonny and he nodded as he texted on his phone.

I jogged around to the sidewalk, and then slowly approached the guy I assumed to be Elijah. He turned to me, and his facial expression was weird. It was like he knew something about me, and whatever that something was, he didn't like.

"Elijah?" I inquired and he nodded slowly.

"Yeah, who told you about me?"

"My boy E-Way, I wanted some smoke, what you got?"

"How much are you looking to spend?"

"Well I just got out of jail, so my money is slightly funny. But whatever you can give me is good. I found out a lot of shit today, and I just need to relax," I chuckled but he didn't crack a smile.

"Fasho," he finally said.

I didn't know what his problem was, but maybe he was just having a bad day. Shit, maybe that was how he was. I didn't give a fuck though, I just wanted the product. He could let a therapist figure all that other shit out.

"'Thanks son," I said after making the transaction. He declined to respond, but I was already jogging back to the car.

## A Few Hours Later...

I was feeling a little better, so I decided to drop Sonny back off at Marley's so I could go spit at Ivy. I wanted to ask her why she lied, and why she was *still* lying. Did she think that I was never gonna find out?

"Where have you been?" she quizzed when I walked into the house. She was holding Donovan with a slight scowl on her pretty face. Her blue eyes were glossy as fuck.

"I had shit to do."

"You didn't even ask if I had something to do Donovan. You can't just take my car out like that!"

"Aye, calm the fuck down! You forgot who runs shit up in here obviously! Ain't shit you have to do that can't wait with yo' lying ass!"

"Excuse me?"

"Yeah, the homie told me you was down there showing ya pussy for money Ivy!" I barked.

She paused for a few moments and then said, "Portland, let me explain. I—"

"I don't need your fucking explanation, Ivy. I already know you needed the money and all that other shit. I sent you money!"

"It wasn't enough, Portland. All it paid for was food and some necessities for Donovan. I still need things, my car needs things, and I need a place to stay too!"

"Watch your fucking tone, Ivy!"

She just shook her head, and then adjusted Donovan in her lap. "So now what? We're done? You don't wanna be with me no more?" she sniffled.

"You know I still wanna be with you. I love you Ivy, I just don't want you lying to me anymore. That shit is not cool. You got me out here looking like a sucker. I don't even know my girl is stripping? Come on, man."

"You're right, I should've at least told you once we got home from the jail. I'm sorry baby." She stood up and laid a sleeping Donovan on his stomach.

"You good," I smirked and then yanked her close for a kiss. I was still mad as hell, but I knew she wouldn't have done it if she didn't need to. Ivy would never fuck around on me, and I had nothing to worry about with her. "Aye, but E-Way is outside, and he's gonna take me to get a rental."

"Okay, hurry back because I'm making shrimp pasta for dinner, just for you," she cheesed.

"I can't wait." I kissed her lips, dropped her car keys into her hand, and then rushed down to get in the car with E-Way.

"Where does this chick live?" E-Way asked after I slid in.

"Lynford."

He nodded and then took me to go spend the night with my baby... well my other one. I knew Ivy would be mad that I didn't come home tonight, but she would forgive me like she always did. Plus, she lied to me, giving me room to act up.

# Cheyla

---

$\mathcal{I}$ pulled my baggie of pills from my locker, and slipped one into my mouth before washing it down with water. It was almost my turn to go on stage, and I needed something to relax me. I'd done this plenty of times, but the pills always made it easier. I even felt like they helped me dance better.

I fixed my booty shorts, and then strutted out to wait on the side of the stage. As soon as " Or Nah" by The Game started, I sauntered onto the stage. The pill was taking effect already, making a smile appear on my face.

I threw my hands up slowly, and then dipped down with my back against the pole. I then grabbed it tightly into my hand, and kicked one leg up in the air, before wrapping it around. While upside down, I spotted my favorite person- Monty.

I twirled until I hit the floor in a splits, and then popped my ass making the men hoot and holler. I got back onto my feet, and swayed side to side while pulling my bikini top to the side, exposing my nipples.

As money flowed onto the stage, I continued to work my magic until I saw the light flash, letting me know my set was over. I walked down off the stage, and then went to the back to wipe all the sweat off of me so I could go talk to Monty. I think he'd been out of town, because I hadn't seen him in a while.

Not only did I wanna dance for him to get some more bread, but I wanted to thank him for helping me that night. If it weren't for him, I would've gotten raped for sure. I was thanking God for him that night.

I walked out and saw him sitting in the same spot that he was in before. Next to his VIP, I saw Kantwan chilling and bobbing his head to the music. I'd tried texting his ass, but he really meant it when he said he was done. No matter what I said he didn't respond. I contemplated texting 'Help!' but I don't even think that would've worked. That was way too desperate also.

I thought Sonny being home would make me forget about Kantwan, but it did nothing of the sort. I still thought about him a lot, and it even seemed to intensify. I thought not talking to him would make me lose feelings over time, but it seemed to be doing the opposite. I needed to get over him fast, because I did not want to see him with another girl while I was feeling like this.

"Hey boo," I smiled at Monty as I entered his section. I felt Kantwan's eyes on me, but when I looked over he turned away. *He's looking*, I smiled on the inside.

"You know what to do." Monty waved a $100 bill in the air, and pointed to his lap with his free hand.

Some song by Dej Loaf came on, so I got into his lap and began to rotate my hips. He held onto me with one hand, and placed a soft kiss on my back. I didn't mind him touching me, because like I said, he paid well. I wasn't gonna trip over a few touches and body kisses, when he was paying $70 over for a lap dance that wasn't even private.

Every so often, I would glance over and make eye contact with Kantwan, but neither one of us said a word to each other. Once the song went off, Monty stuffed the $100 bill into my booty shorts' waistline.

"Thank you," I said before kissing his forehead. "And thank you for coming to my rescue that day Monty."

"Oh no problem, I would never let anything happen to you, ma."

"I appreciate you for that. I hope you didn't get hurt that night. I probably should've stayed to check on you, but I was too shaken up," I covered my mouth and giggled lightly at my actions.

"You're good, ma, I whooped his old ass. I don't think he will ever be back."

"I hope not, but thank you again." I turned around to leave, but he grabbed my hand into his.

When I turned to look at him he said, "Let me get your number."

"Monty, I don't think that's a good idea—"

"What, I'm not cute enough?" he grinned.

"No, it's not that, I just have feelings for someone else right now and it would be wrong for me to begin something with you. Especially when I know if the guy I'm feeling ever wanted me again, I would go back in a jiffy," I said in a low tone, not wanting Kantwan to hear me.

"I see. Well fair enough, I just thought I'd ask."

"See you later, Monty."

I walked down the steps, and slowed down when I got in front of Kantwan's section. I decided to try my luck. I don't know why I was so hell bent on making him talk to me. I usually felt relieved when the guy stopped calling, but with Kantwan I felt like I just couldn't let it go. This nigga had me begging God for him, which was something I never saw myself doing.

"Would you like a dance?" I smirked at him. He cleared his throat, stared into my eyes, and then turned his attention elsewhere. "Kantwan please," I walked up into his section.

"Fuck you want, Cheyla? I thought we both agreed that we weren't gonna be cool anymore?"

"No, you chose that, not me. I wanted to be cool but as friends," I whined.

He gave me a toothless smile, and then stood up, towering over me. He took my hand into his, and power walked towards the private dance area. He was walking so fast, that I had to lightly jog since I was shorter than him. He smashed some money into Joey's hand, and then yanked me into the room. He abruptly turned around, and pulled on the curtain to close it.

"What—"

Before I could say a word, his tongue was down my throat, and he was pulling my bandeau top down. He rushed me into the wall, yanked my bottoms down, and then crushed his lips against mine, cutting me off before I could talk again.

While he kissed me, I heard him unbuckling his pants with the quickness.

"Are you- aaaah."

Mid-sentence, he lifted me in the air and brought me down onto his long, thick dick. He had me pressed against the wall as he went ham in my center. I'd almost forgotten how good the dick was. I'm lying, I could never fucking forget. He had me clenching my thighs together just last night when I was reminiscing.

"This feel like a friend to you?" he asked me as he rammed me, making me cum immediately. He was strong, the way he held my legs open, while also holding me up in the air. "Shit," he groaned.

"Ohh, oooh, uuuuh," I tried to keep my moans in, but it was hard. He was going in on my pussy and it felt like heaven. I thought I would never feel this bomb shit again. "Oh my gooosshhhh, Kant, shit," I called out.

"Oh fuck!" he shouted as he released.

He humped me a few more times, and then slipped out of me. He let me down, and I immediately fell to the ground because my legs were no good. He stared down at me as he buckled himself back up.

"Now if you can go without that, then let me know and we can be friends," he said and then left the room.

I sat there in disbelief, all the while trying to catch my breath. Did this nigga just come through here, fuck me like that, and dip? I think I'm in love... No, I know I am.

Walking out of the private dance booth, I bumped into Miami. She was wearing a big ass smile, with her arms folded across her chest. We stared at each other for a little while, as I leaned up against the wall for support. My legs were on noodle status and shaking like I had a damn illness. You would've died laughing, watching me put my clothes back on just a minute ago.

"What?" I finally asked.

"I see you're making that extra cash now," she smirked and nodded approvingly.

"What are you talking about?"

"You just let that guy fuck for cash," she giggled. "It looked like Kill's brother Kantwan. He is fine girl. He must really like you to be paying for pussy, because he doesn't have to."

"He didn't pay me to fuck him, he paid to have alone time with me. He fucked me because he likes me."

"Right. Whatever makes you feel better about it. But do you mind sharing clients? Because had I known that he would pay for pussy, or *alone time*, I would've been pressed him. I remember a couple months back he shooed me like a fly."

"He is not a fucking client Miami, that's mine. I better not catch you sniffing behind him," I gritted. The thought of her pushing up on Kantwan had me ready to knock her ass out.

"And if I do, what the fuck are you gonna do?" she neared me.

"You don't wanna know. Plus, he would never fuck with a hoe like you. He's taken, by me."

"Don't no nigga on Kill or his brother's level want a stripper for a girlfriend, boo. You better sink your teeth into one of these sucker ass niggas if you want a man. They're too dumb to care."

"Miami, get out of my face and stay out of Kantwan's." I started to limp off because my legs were still weak and the pill was still taking effect.

"I'll think about it. He's really sexy, and I really wanna suck his dick. I know it's nice and big."

*WHAM!*

I punched her ass so hard, that the back of her head hit the piece of wall behind her. She brought her head back up, and then charged me. She grabbed two handfuls of my hair, and I began choking the shit out of her as we spun around, bumping customers and tables. She sucker punched me with the side of her fist like a dumb bitch, but it still pissed me off. I let go of her neck and began punching her in the face, to the point where she let my hair go and dropped down to grab my waist. I kept raining blows on the back of her head as we moved all around the club like wild animals.

"What the fuck!" someone yelled as we knocked their table over.

Miami and I fell to the ground, and even though she was on top of me, I was tearing her face up still. I felt her blood drip onto me but I didn't care. Suddenly, I felt a pair of hands that looked like my manager Rick's, pulling on my wrists.

"Let her go!" Rick yelled to me.

"Cheyla, let her go!" Joey hollered as he tried to pry my fingers from Miami's weave. She had stopped trying to hit me by this time, but I was too angry.

"Cheyla!" Rick screamed in my ear, with his hands still on my small wrists.

I finally let her go, and Joey scooped her up. Her face was a mess, and her weave was sticking to her face because of the blood.

"Bitch, I'm gon' beat your fucking ass! I'm gon' fuck that nigga too! Watch!" Miami shouted over the club as Joey carried her away.

Rick helped me up and then said, "Go home, Cheyla."

"A-am I fired? She provoked me Jo—"

"You're not fired, just please leave."

"I wanted to do some more—"

"Cheyla, leave before I decide to fire you."

He started to walk away, as Joey returned to help pick up some of the tables that we'd knocked down. The music was still playing, but all the customers had their eyes locked on me. I scanned the room, embarrassed, until I felt my belongings being jammed into my chest. I turned to see Parrish, the guy who helped collect the stage money.

"Here you go, Cheyla," he said. I clutched my shit tightly, and then walked towards the door. This was one hell of a night.

# THIRTY-SEVEN

# Jersey

---

$\mathcal{I}$'d just come from Scrumptious, a frozen yogurt spot, and all I wanted to do was eat it and kick back. I was done with school, and I couldn't go to work tonight. I needed the money though, so I may go this coming weekend. I felt ashamed to go at first, but I needed to get my fucking bread so oh well.

I locked my vehicle, then stepped onto the sidewalk, heading up to my door. I waved to this girl named Amelia, and then proceeded.

"Jersey!" I turned around to see Tommy jogging over to me.

"Yes?" I raised a brow.

"Lazy day," he smiled and gestured towards my big sweater that I'd bought from my school's website.

"What do you want, Tommy?"

"What's going on with you baby? I thought we were working towards something?"

"Working towards something? Uh no, I don't like liars," I shook my head.

"What did I lie about?"

"About Kill having a baby mama that you saw him hanging out with. You knew he was in jail, didn't you?"

"What? Nah, he must've gotten locked up after the fact," he shook his head repeatedly and so did I.

"And you have a bitch Tommy, why are you chasing after me?"

"I ain't got no fucking girl! What is you talking about?" he frowned at me.

"I saw the Bath and Body Works hand soap, and the bathroom had pink plush rugs nigga. Who do you think you're fooling? Does she know you're always coming 'round here trying to fuck?"

Kill had finally let me know the things that Tommy was saying about me to him, Kantwan, and Elijah. He kept trying not to throw salt on Tommy as he would say, but it was already salty as fuck. I knew Tommy saw me as some hoe that he wanted to slide up in and dip out on afterward. Little did he know, he was never close to fucking me, even before I found out he was a jealous little bitch.

He stared at me with his mouth open. He was about to speak, but he paused for a second and looked off.

"That's my sister's crib, and she—"

"Bye Tommy!" I waved him off and turned around.

He hugged me from behind, but quickly jumped back. I turned around to him, and after we made eye contact, a scowl burst through his face.

"Wow," he said and rushed off to his car.

I went inside my apartment, and was happy to see the mail on the floor behind the door. I set my frozen yogurt down, and quickly dropped to my knees to sift through the letters. I spotted a letter from Delaware County Prison, and squealed with excitement.

Over the past months, Kill and I had been writing letters and having talks on the phone nonstop. He was able to get a cell phone inside there, so he could talk to me for longer at nighttime. It was a little Motorola Razr though, so he didn't like to text on it.

Since I hadn't been going to work, I wasn't making any money obviously. I was tired of asking my dad, because he went in on my ass every damn time. Plus, I refused to be treated that way just to get some cash. On top of that, he wasn't even giving me enough to pay the bills. By saying that, Kill was paying my portion of the bills, rent, and my car note. I don't know how he was doing it from behind bars, but every other week, this guy named Edward would drop off an envelope of money to me from Kill. It was spending money in there too. I hated to have him paying my way while he was the one locked up, so that's why I wanted to start going back to work.

I stood up, and then grabbed my yogurt from the counter before heading to my bedroom. I noticed Cheyla was in her room knocked the hell out. Ever since she whooped Miami's ass back at Starzz, she'd been a homebody.

I closed my bedroom door, got comfortable on my bed, and then opened the letter.

*Baby girl,*

*You got me wondering what the hell you need to tell me. I know you wanna wait until I get out, but shit I don't know when that'll happen. Axel said in a few days, but it sure and the fuck doesn't seem like it. Anyway, can you give me a hint? I'm becoming anxious as fuck. I wanna see your face so bad and kiss every inch of your body like I used to. You got me acting like a damn fiend, especially with the shit you be writing in these letters, talking to me like you low key love a nigga and shit. Lol. Is it weird for me to say I miss you? I miss feeling your soft body under mine, and how good your pussy felt, especially the last time I was in it. I'm gonna call you tonight. Lol. I know I wrote this way before you read it, but I call you every night so it all works out. Send me a picture in the next letter, because this cell phone I got doesn't show picture messages baby, but thank you for trying the last time. Anyway, I miss you (I don't care if it's weird, it's true.) And when I come home, hopefully soon, I'm claiming you as mine. So get all the ratchet shit out your system because when I get out, you're all me.*

*Love, Kilexis Carson Camren.*

I smiled at the letter, and read it two more times. I took a picture of myself using my laptop, and then put it onto a USB. I grabbed all my things, and then headed to Target to develop it. I hoped it made it to him before he was released, but I also hoped that Axel came through with what he'd been saying this whole time.

## Later That Night...

I woke up to the sound of my phone ringing, and when I picked it up I saw it was 11pm. The caller ID showed a Philly number, and I grinned because I knew exactly who it was.

"Hello?"

"Hey baby, are you willing to talk or are you too tired?" Kilexis asked.

"No, I'm not tired. I always wanna talk to you."

I got up and left out of my room to go make myself some tea. With the extra money that Kill got me, I was able to buy a Keurig. I felt like I shouldn't have been buying things like that with the money, but he said to go ahead and that was why he'd given me extra.

"Good, how are you feeling? I know you said you've been sick."

"I'm good now. I'm not in school anymore until August, so that took some of the stress off. How are you?"

"I'm doing alright. Some days are great when I think I'm getting out soon, and other days are miserable because I feel like I'm never getting out until my seven years have been served," he sighed.

"Don't say that, you have to come home so we can hang out."

"Oh, I'm definitely trying to hang out with you. And touch you and do all kinds of shit. But you got my latest letter already?"

"Yes, I did," I chuckled. "It made me smile like always."

"So you're cool with being mine when I get out?"

"No."

"Too bad," he said and we laughed in unison.

"I'm super good with that. I just hope you don't change your mind." I grabbed my tea, and then went back into my room, closing the door behind me.

"Why would I change my mind?"

"I don't know. You know how men change once they have their freedom back."

I started to get sad as I thought about it. I've heard plenty of stories where the guy gets out and then he breaks every promise he made to the girl that was holding him down.

"Those are niggas who let their surroundings change them, and make decisions based off emotions. That's some female shit, no offense. But don't worry about me changing my mind, I'm not the indecisive type Jersey."

"Good, because I was gonna be mad."

"You miss me? Was it weird that I said I missed you even though we only spent a couple days or nights together?" he questioned.

"No, I miss you too. I think we became attached to one another really quickly."

"We definitely became attached quickly," he laughed. "I was all in that pussy."

"Not like that Kill!" I snickered at his nasty ass.

"I know what you mean. I felt like I knew you. I haven't sat and talked to a girl in a while, so the fact that I was able to talk with you let me know something was there. But I like being attached to you in the other way too," he said in a low tone. My pussy began to throb at the sound of his sexy voice talking to me in that way.

"I like being attached to you in that way too," I finally responded after a couple moments of silence.

"You sure?" he chuckled.

"Yes I'm sure, I was just thinking."

We kept talking until we both started to doze off. We didn't wanna hang up, so that it would seem as if we were in the bed together. Kill had me feeling things I'd never felt before, and I just hoped that when he got out, he'd still be interested in what we'd built so far.

# THIRTY-EIGHT

# Kilexis

_______________

*I* walked outside, and the sunlight beaming down on me made me smile. Although in a city that I had never been to before getting locked up, I was happy to be out in the streets again. I would never be caught slipping again, especially once I eliminated the snitch that got me knocked.

I spotted my brother Kantwan, and my cousin Elijah, standing by Kantwan's Mustang and shook my head.

"Why the fuck did y'all bring this little ass car to get me?" I frowned.

"Nigga, you need to be happy you getting out and stop complaining," Kantwan dapped me up.

"All of us are over six feet and we got to fold up in this shit. I'm riding shotgun," I said.

"You know, since I'm in a good ass mood I ain't gon' fight you on that shit," Elijah smiled.

"You better not. But thanks for agreeing to ride uncomfortably for half an hour," I laughed.

"I'm finna lay across this muthafucka just like this here," he responded and stretched his long ass across the backseat.

"Aye nigga, don't scuff my leather," Kantwan furrowed his

brows as he slid into the driver seat. I smiled because I missed our little banters that we always had with one another.

"Let's go get some food," Kantwan suggested.

"I guess we can eat and then hit the road," I nodded.

We stopped by an IHOP, and luckily it wasn't too packed. After getting our table, we placed our orders and resumed having conversation. I've never wanted pancakes so damn bad in my life. Jail food really made you appreciate the simple fucking things about living out in the free world.

"Man, I'm so happy right now, because I really thought you were going down for seven fucking years," my brother Kantwan shook his head.

"Nigga, me too. I don't know what Axel did, but I'm grateful," I said.

I was actually surprised that the nigga wanted to get me out, since I got all his money confiscated. Shit, maybe he got me out because he wanted to kill me himself. Whatever the case was, I wasn't gon' trip. I feared no one, and that meant no nigga would ever have me shaking in my Robin jeans, ever. I don't give a fuck how much power they had, the only person who could make me feel any type of emotion relating to fear was God himself. I just wondered why he didn't do the same for my brother.

"So Axel wants to see you tomorrow morning," Elijah let me know.

"Yeah? Did he say why?"

"Nah he didn't, he just said it was important and that's why he needed you out on the streets," Elijah said.

I scoffed at his response, because I found it low key shady that the only reason Axel got me out after only serving three damn months was because he needed me for something. Thank God he did though, because I didn't wanna stay in that muthafucka at all.

"Anybody talked to Tommy recently?" I questioned.

"He dropped by when you first got knocked, asking questions and shit like he cared," Kantwan answered me.

"Why?" Elijah squinted his eyes.

"Because that nigga set me up," I said matter-of-factly.

"What? Tommy ain't that type," Kantwan smacked his lips.

"Lil bro, I know that's your best friend but the nigga set me up."

"How can you be sure?" Elijah inquired.

"Because that nigga has been my number one hater since I met him. I ain't stupid, I know a snake when I see one, and the only reason I even let his bitch ass breathe this long was because he was your best friend," I pointed to Kantwan.

"Man, what exact reason would he have to set you up? Name one thing other than y'all always going at each other's necks," Kantwan folded his arms and raised his brow.

"Jersey," I replied.

"Jersey? Man, he just said he just wanted to fuck, so why would he be dropping dimes over her?" Kantwan turned his lip up, disgusted by my accusations.

I was disgusted too, because Tommy was really doing the most over a woman. Yeah, Jersey was everything a nigga could want, but nigga, she's not interested, let it go. You supposedly don't even like her like that so why do all this? Why seal your fate over a girl you only wanted to hit and quit?

"He sure and the fuck did run up on Kilexis in the parking lot of Starzz, hollering about him smashing Jersey first," Elijah backed me up.

"Nah, I refuse to believe that," Kantwan shook his head just as a waitress began setting our meals down in front of us.

"Kant, he told Jersey that he saw me out with Margo and her son Gregory, but made it sound like Margo was my bitch and Gregory was my kid."

"So," Kantwan shrugged. I could see in his eyes that he was starting to believe what I was saying, but he didn't want to.

"Well, whether you agree or not, I'm murking that nigga for even trying to fuck with my freedom like he did. I don't know what the fuck he thought this was, but they don't call me Kill just because it's an abbreviation of my name and you know that," I stared into my brother's eyes, and he just nodded slowly before eating a strawberry off of his pancake.

We ate our food and then got back on the road. As soon as we got back into town, I couldn't stop smiling.

"Man, hurry up and take me home, my legs is cramped!" Elijah shouted making us laugh.

"Just an hour ago you was bragging about being so comfortable," I chuckled.

"Well now I'm not," he barked and then mumbled to himself, still complaining.

"Aye, drop me off at Jersey's bro, I will find a way home," I told Kantwan since we were already on Harrison.

"Okay."

He pulled up in front of Jersey's apartment building, and when I got out I looked up and down the street to see if her Nissan Maxima was there. When I saw it I smiled.

I hopped onto the sidewalk, and then waved to my brother and cousin to let them know they could bounce. I was hoping no one yelled my name to say what's up, because I wanted surprise her.

I ran up the three little steps, and when I reached her door I knocked. I covered the peephole when I heard someone lean against it. After a few moments the door flung open, and there stood Cheyla.

"Ah—" she was about to speak but I put my finger to my lips to tell her to be quiet.

"Where is Jersey? I wanna surprise her," I whispered.

"She's in her room, but I think she is dressing."

"So, ain't nothing I haven't seen before."

I walked to her bedroom door, and slowly twisted it before pushing it open. She had her back to the door, while pulling her shirt off. It was dim in the room, but the sunlight provided enough light. I crept behind her, and wrapped my arms around her body before kissing her neck.

"Ah! You scared me!" she jumped.

I expected to feel her toned stomach, but I was met with a very little bulge. I turned her around and stared down at her naked body floored.

"How many months are you?" I quizzed.

"Three," she responded in a low tone.

"By..." I just pointed to myself and she nodded with a worried expression. I was happy this wasn't a repeat of the Margo situation. I think I would've been way more pissed though. I walked to her bed, and plopped down on it. "This was what you had to tell me," I stated versus asking.

"Yes, are you mad? I didn't know how to tell you, Kilexis. I was sick, but when I took a pregnancy test, it was negative. I took another the day of my doctor's appointment and it was negative again. When I went to the doctor, they tested me and said I was pregnant. I showed her the test and she said one line was dark, but there was a faint one which still meant positive, so I'd been reading it wrong. I'd been spotting a little, so I assumed it was my period," she explained.

"I didn't strap up the last time," I mumbled. No wonder that shit almost had a nigga's toes curling. I've never raw dogged a woman in my life, but I was just in the moment with Jersey.

I picked my head up and she was tearing up. I reached out for her hand, and pulled her over to me. Placing my hands on her small waist, I gently pressed my lips against her stomach. She caressed my hair as I kept planting kisses on it.

"Don't think I'm mad or angry about this at all Jersey, I'm just surprised. I still want you to be my girl, so don't start thinking that I'm gonna dip on you, aight?" She nodded in response. I pulled her down to the bed, and laid her down. I placed my hand on her soft face, and then kissed her lips before slipping my tongue into her mouth.

"I know everything is moving faster than either of us planned but—"

"Don't think like that, Jersey. A baby is a cause for celebration always. And you look good too," I bit my lip before kissing her again.

I got on top of her, groping her body and breasts before standing up. I stripped out of my clothes, and then climbed back onto the bed. I pulled back the comforter and sheets, and she got under them. I got under them as well, and made my way between her legs. I pushed with all my might, until my dick made it into her tight hole. She hadn't been fucked since the night I got her pregnant, I could tell.

"Mmmm," she tucked her bottom lip into her mouth as I moved in and out of her. She then scrunched her face up, obviously in a little pain.

"Should I stop?" I asked her.

"No it's not the baby, it's just been awhile," she half smiled.

She then cupped my face, and we began tonguing each other down as I plunged in and out of her. I didn't plan on having kids, shit I thought I would never have any, but I guess God had other plans for me. I'm happy it included Jersey though.

## Later That Night...

We were still in her bed, looking at the TV on mute. We'd went to get food, and then came back to eat and fuck again. I wanted to get in her once more, but I could tell she was tired.

As I looked around the room, I saw one of her stripper outfits hanging up on the outside of her closet.

"Why do you have that out?" I asked and pointed to it.

"Oh, I was gonna work this weekend," she looked over at me.

Her stomach wasn't too big to where she couldn't go to work, but she wasn't about to be giving out lap dances and shit with *my* baby in there.

"Nah, that's not a good idea."

"I know but I need the money right now and—"

"Jersey, I got you. I been having your back while I was locked up, so what makes you think I wouldn't while I'm out. I really do not feel comfortable with you dancing and shaking your ass for niggas while carrying my baby. You're not going."

"Yeah, I guess that *is* doing too much."

"Don't you wanna quit?"

"Kill, I already told you about my parents. I don't want to depend on you for everything and then end up struggling."

"Jersey, I'm not saying to quit school, I'm saying to quit dancing.

I will help you with school. I would never do you how your father did your mother, but even if by some chance I did, you would have your degree and your job. I would never ask you to quit your career. I'm asking you to leave something behind that you don't like doing anyway."

"I understand. I guess I'm just paranoid. I think I would do better in school if I didn't have to dance every night until three and four in the morning."

"Exactly, so just leave that shit in the dust."

"I thought I would never have you here with me like this again. I find myself wondering if it's a dream."

"It ain't so get used to me."

She smiled and then scooted closer to kiss my lips. She rubbed my head, and then pushed her lips into mine again. She then leaned up to kiss the ear with the diminished hearing, before going back to my lips.

"You gon' make me want another round, ma."

"No, I'm too sore and tired," she giggled.

"Then you better stop."

"Okay, one more," she said before sucking my lips. We kissed hungrily for a few more moments, and then she turned her back to me to go to sleep.


## The Next Morning...

I woke up the next morning, and realized I was still lying next to Jersey. She was sleeping on her side, looking so fucking pretty. Her curly hair was in a disheveled bun, but it didn't take away from her appearance at all. Her forearm was covering her small breasts unintentionally, and her full lips were somewhat poked out.

I pushed the covers down just a bit to expose her stomach. It wasn't big at all, but because it was so flat before, you could definitely see the difference. I leaned down to kiss her stomach, and then brought the covers up over her.

I sat up completely and stared out her window, although I couldn't see much because of the tall trees next to her building. I had a lot of shit on my mind already, and now that I had a baby on the way, shit was gonna get much more complicated.

Before, I knew I needed to find a way to lead a more stable life, but now I knew I had to actually come through. I needed to be stable for this baby that was coming shortly. I couldn't fail, I had to provide and do the right thing. I'll be damned if my child and girl are out here struggling because I can't get my shit together. I hated to admit it, but the drug game couldn't be left right now. I sighed because I had so much shit to get together, and on top of that I had to go see Axel.

I had no fucking idea what was so important, but because his money was taken while in my possession, I knew it couldn't be good. I needed to stop by my house and get my heat before I saw him, because I wasn't gonna go down without a fight. It'd be a shootout in that muthafucka before I let him light me up.

I stood up from the bed, and then started to put my clothes on. I was gonna go get Jersey some breakfast, and then see about getting my ass to my condo. Elijah let me know that Axel was paying the rent for it while I was away, which alarmed me. Why was this nigga doing all this for a muthafucka that cost him $100,000? That nigga must need a kidney or some shit. I was more than able to pay it myself, so Elijah just put the money I did send for my rent in a safe place.

I finished putting my clothes on, and then quietly left the apartment. There was a McDonald's around the corner on 3rd Street, and it would take me no time to get there even on foot.

As I was walking down the street, I saw a whole bunch of people just outside chilling. There were niggas who just sat outside on their porches, waiting for a cute bitch to walk by so they could holla. I never understood that, because no woman with any sense would respond back. Not unless she'd never seen you porch sitting before. But if you were a professional porch sitter, which Wilmington had plenty of, you weren't get any play from the women who were about something.

I finally hit the corner, so I just ran the rest of the way until I reached Mickey D's. I got some food for Jersey, Cheyla, and myself, and although a Saturday, the workers moved pretty quickly.

As I was leaving, I spotted Margo chatting with some nigga. He got really close to her, and she tilted her head back so that he could kiss her. He looked old enough to be her daddy, but he definitely wasn't.

I didn't even care, but the shit was funny how she stayed in my face about being a family, but was probably fucking someone else the whole time. I really don't know why she was so adamant about being with me, because we hadn't had any love between us for years. I didn't kiss her, say sweet things, or dick her down, so what was keeping her around? She knew I would still help her with Gregory without being together, so that couldn't have been it. I refused to believe it was because she loved me though, because if she did Gregory wouldn't be here, and I mean that in the nicest way possible. I was tired of her acting as if she would die without me though.

I was able to get past without her seeing me, and after ten minutes I made it back to Jersey's. Because my hands were full, I couldn't use her key, so I needed to be let in.

"Who is it?" I heard Cheyla answer my elbow knock.

"It's Kill," I answered.

Cheyla opened the door, and after I walked in she said, "Hey Kill, do you know what's wrong with Jersey?"

"What you mean?"

"Like, she was sick for a cool minute, and now she's a little better. She hasn't been to work in the longest, and is about to get fired. She stays in her room most of the time, unless we go out for dinner, and she never dresses in her shorts and crop tops anymore. We used to walk around naked in this house, and she hasn't done so in a while."

"Oh, you miss that?" I grinned.

"No fool," she giggled. "I'm just saying she's not acting like herself. I think you going to jail depressed her."

"Oh damn, let me talk to her," I said and handed Cheyla the bag containing the food I'd gotten for her.

"Oh shit, thanks Kill. I'm hungry as fuck," she beamed and then plopped down onto the couch.

"Welcome."

I didn't feel it was my place to tell Cheyla that Jersey was having my baby. She needed to tell her on her own, especially because after a while it wouldn't be something that she could hide. I was not about to cause any rifts in their friendship.

I went into Jersey's bedroom, and then lightly shook her so that she would wake up. She stirred a little, before finally opening her eyes. She smiled at me, and then closed them back to yawn.

"I thought you coming home was a dream until now," she said again.

"Nah, thank God it's reality, baby. But sit up so you can eat." She got up and brought the covers over her body.

"You want a t-shirt?" I asked.

"Yes please, they're in the top drawer." I stood up and walked to the dresser to get a shirt for her. After she put it on, we both began to eat.

"Jersey, when are you gonna tell Cheyla about the baby?" I quizzed.

"I guess today. I wanted to tell you before I told anyone else, so that's why I held out."

"Good, because she's getting suspicious, and I'm not the type to lie," I smiled and so did she.

"When I tell my mom and sister, will you come?" She looked into my eyes while chewing the hash brown.

"Of course."

After I ate, I used the phone to call my cousin to come get me since Kantwan was working. He picked me up and dropped me off at home so I could wash my ass and get myself together. I didn't mind showering at Jersey's, but I wanted to be in my own home.

Once I was clean and dressed in a white t-shirt, gray crew neck, light blue jeans, all white Jordan 11's, and a white snapback, I was ready to go see Axel.

"You ready?" Elijah asked me when I walked into my living room.

"Yeah," I responded as I locked my heat into my waist. "After Axel, if I make it out alive, can you take me to Hertz? I need a rental."

"I got you bruh."

Them policemen torched my Denali, and that shit hurt. I loved that whip and it was the first car that I bought and had paid off with my own money. I shook my head at the thought, as Elijah and I descended the stairs.

We got to Axel's house on Summit Lane in New Castle, and once Elijah let security know who we were, we were granted access into his gates.

"This nigga is living large," Elijah said as he found a place to park.

"Tell me about it, the drug game has been good to this nigga." I chuckled.

We exited the car, and a middle aged white woman stepped out of the front door. You could tell that in her younger years, she was definitely a looker.

"Mr. Johnson asked me to escort you in," she smiled.

She led us through the never-ending foyer, until we reached a big ass wooden door. She turned around to put her finger up, signaling to give her a moment, and then entered the office alone. Elijah and I waited until she finally returned.

"Okay, so only you, Mr. Camren. Your friend must wait," she said.

"You good?" I looked at Elijah.

"I'm straight."

"Yes, you can follow me to the kitchen area if you'd like a snack while you wait?" the pretty old lady asked.

"I'm always down for a snack," Elijah rubbed his stomach and followed her.

I chuckled at him, and then walked into the office.

"Kill, welcome home man."

Axel stood to his feet with a cigar hanging from his charcoal colored lips. He was a light skinned guy, hella light skinned actually, but his lips were another story. He told me he burned them with a crack pipe when he was in his late teens and doing hard drugs. After that he got his shit together, and now he was the biggest kingpin in Delaware.

"Thanks, I appreciate you getting me out the way you did."

"That was nothing, sit down," he waved me off. I took a seat across from him at his desk, and waited as he poured himself a glass of Hennessy.

"Would you like a glass?" he offered.

"I'm straight." I was anxious to know why the fuck I was here.

"I'm sure you're wondering what's so important that I had your charges dropped," he chuckled but I kept quiet. "I found out I have lung cancer, and its evolving pretty fast within my system."

"Damn man," I sighed. *Why are you puffing on a cigar right now then?* I wondered. He bet not be asking for a body part of mine, because it wasn't happening.

"Yeah, I know. And since I'm gonna start going under pretty intense treatment, I can't really be a kingpin anymore."

"Uh huh," I nodded.

"So I sat and thought, who could take over and make sure it runs just as smoothly as I've been able to? And you immediately came to mind, Kill. I need you to assume position."

"Wait, me? What about your sons, man, Dante and Ahmad?" I frowned. Maybe he'd forgotten he had kids.

"This shit will go down in flames if I let one of them knuckle-heads take over. And if my shit goes down, that's taking money out of everyone's pocket, including yours."

"I don't know about this man, I was thinking of going legit soon, and this shit is way left."

"Kill man, you're built for this shit and you know it. Just accept the gift that God has given you," he grinned.

"I highly doubt that God has given me the gift of being able to run a drug empire."

"Well, maybe not that specifically, but he gave you the smarts, cleverness, and most importantly heart. I need someone who wouldn't go out crying like a bitch if shit hit the fan, and that's you. I could put a chopper to your head right now and you still wouldn't let me disrespect you. That's the same type of nigga I am, and that's why I want you to take charge. You're quick-witted, and you can read people well Kill. You know a snake in the grass even when it's still just a little egg."

"How long do I have to think about it?" I quizzed.

"Ten minutes."

# THIRTY-NINE

# Tommy

---

*I* sat outside of the Independence Mall, parked right next to Jersey's car. It'd been two weeks since I touched her fucking hard ass stomach. I wanted to murder that nigga Kill for not only fucking her, but also for getting her pregnant. For some reason I was jealous as fuck!

Yeah, I only wanted to bang her, but it was a pride thing at this point. He should've never stepped on my toes and smashed her ass, and I can't even believe she let his ass. Not only that, she let him get it with no hat? That was supposed to be me.

*BZZZ!*

**Lizette:** *I'm gonna fuck you up!*

**Me:** *I'd like to see you try.*

**Lizette:** *Herpes? Really asshole?*

**Lizette:** *Where are you? I swear I'm gonna fuck you up! I'm gon' get my brothers on yo' ass!*

I was gonna reply, but Jersey walked out of the mall, and stopped at the edge of the sidewalk to let a car pass. She wasn't wearing her big sweaters anymore, she had on a tight t-shirt dress today. I guess she was proud of her stomach now. Hoes these days, man.

I'd heard that Kill was home, but I couldn't be sure. Kantwan wasn't returning my calls, and everybody else acted like they weren't too sure. I kind of knew that they were keeping a secret from me on purpose, but I hadn't seen him around.

As soon as Jersey neared her car, I slipped out of mine and rushed over to her.

"What Tommy?" She turned her lip up and sighed like I was the most annoying muthafucka in the world. *Don't hit her Tommy.*

"I see you're gonna be a mom soon," I folded my arms, frowning.

"Yeah, you figured that out a while ago. What's new?" she shrugged.

"How the fuck you gon' get pregnant by this nigga, Jersey? I thought you and I were building something. Then all of a sudden, you letting him fuck you, and raw too?"

"I didn't plan this Tommy, it just happened. I'm not gonna act like I don't have strong feelings for Kill because I do. I had sex with him because I liked him, it just felt right."

"Oh, and it didn't feel right with me? You didn't feel nothing with me even after I took your ass out and damn near begged you to come through to my crib?" I was mad as fuck right now, and had to keep my arms folded in order not to choke her ass out here in broad daylight.

"No, I mean I thought you were cool and shit but I just didn't feel as attracted to you. From the first time I saw Kill I felt something. And you have a girl, maybe you should spend more time checking for her versus me."

I just nodded and stared off to the side as I let her words sink into my mind. I hated that I couldn't get over this shit, and I also hated that I didn't know why I couldn't.

"So you gon' hold him down while he's in jail?" I raised a brow trying to figure out if he was released or not.

"That's none of your business. And why do you even care? I'm having his damn baby. There will never be anything between us because of that," she frowned.

"I am not that nigga's friend so I don't care! Stop acting like you ain't ready to give me the pussy because I know you are! If you want me to leave you alone, then you know what to do!" I hollered down into her face. A couple people looked our way, because that's how loud I was. I'd even given myself a headache.

I was pissed that she didn't confirm whether or not that nigga was out of jail, and because she wouldn't let me fuck. She was standing here like she was some saint, knowing she probably let niggas hit all the time. I knew how those stripper bitches were, so she couldn't fool me.

"If you think I'm gonna fuck you so that you can leave me alone, you have some mental problems," she waved me off. She turned her back to me to walk to her door, and I grabbed her small arm roughly. "Move Tommy," she yanked from me but wasn't strong enough to escape my grasp.

"We can do this the easy way, or the hard way Jersey, but I'm getting up in that one way or the other."

She stared up into my eyes with a look of fear, which made me smile. I kissed her soft cheek, and then let her go. I walked around her car, and then got into mine.

Speeding out of the parking lot, a smile spread across my face, because I was happy that it seemed I had finally gotten through to her ass. I would just sit and wait for the call, but after a while, I'd take the pussy if I had to. I just wish I knew for sure if Kill was home or not.

After stopping to get something to eat from KFC, I headed home since I was pretty tired. I woke up hella early because I rushed over to Jersey's house so that I could follow her wherever she went. That's how we both ended up at the mall. I thought I would see her and Kill together, but that didn't happen.

I pulled into the driveway of Sasha's and my home, but decided to eat my food in the car. I wanted peace while I ate, and I knew peace and Sasha did not go together. Especially lately, because of the STD, and the fact that I'd been damn near obsessed with Jersey for some fucking reason.

I didn't love the bitch, and I definitely didn't wanna be her man, but for some reason I couldn't get her out of my mind, nor my damn dreams. I was so tired of waking up with a hard dick from dreaming about fucking the shit out of her little ass. Even though she was pregnant, my lust for her hadn't died out. Pussy had never meant this much to me. Something was not right with me and I knew it. I could feel it.

I finished my chicken sandwich and wedges, then balled up all the trash and got out. It was around 12pm in the afternoon right now, so the sun was really doing its thing. As soon as I walked into the door, Sasha muted the TV and sat up. I let out the deepest sigh ever, and locked the screen door behind me.

"Can you sit down for a second?" she quizzed.

"I wanted to take a nap Sasha, I got shit to do today."

I was supposed to be meeting up with this little jawn I'd just met a couple days ago. I needed to snatch a few purses before I did though, and I wanted to rest before all of that.

"This won't be long."

I sucked my teeth, and then made my way over to the couch. I was still holding my trash, as well as my drink, so I sipped it.

"Speak," I said right after I gulped some of it.

"I'm just gonna come right out and say it. I'm pregnant."

"With what?" I snapped my neck to look at her with a surprised expression.

"A baby, fool! So that means you need to step up, Tommy! I'm gonna need help with the baby and more of the bills," she whined. "And you need to cut out all the fucking cheating!" she teared up.

"Man get out of here with that shit. I ain't taking care of no fucking babies right now, you need to get rid of that shit!" I spat.

"Excuse me? I'm not getting rid of anything! This is *your* baby, and *you're* gonna man up and take care of it!"

I set my drink and trash on the coffee table calmly, and then abruptly pounced on her with my hands wrapped around her skinny neck. I squeezed as tightly as I could, and watched her squirm and silently plead for me to stop.

"I'm not taking care of shit, like I just said," I gritted. "I should just get rid of the both of you right now," I smiled and squeezed tighter. "Is that what you want, huh? You wanna die?" She couldn't respond, and when I felt like she was about to slip away possibly, I let her neck go. She immediately began coughing and panting heavily, with tears coming from her eyes. I just sat back and watched her after picking my soda back up. "Get rid of it Sasha, aight? If you keep it, I'm gonna kill you both."

She just nodded, slowly rose to her feet, and then limped to the back room. Dumb bitch.

# FORTY

Ivy

———

Portland hadn't come home for the past six days, and I was angry as fuck. I'd been calling his cell phone, and he hadn't been answering as usual. I was getting so tired of this shit, especially because I knew he was out doing shit that jeopardized his freedom, or worse, cheating on me.

He'd not come home a couple times since he'd gotten released, but he'd never been gone for six damn days in a row. The first time, the night he approached me about being a stripper, I cried all night as I sat at the table with his favorite meal. He came home the next evening talking about he was hitting the pavement trying to make money. Sure, okay. This was the fifth occasion that he'd stayed away from home since he'd been released, and I was just about fed up.

It was around 2pm on Saturday, and my baby was knocked on my lap. With this new job, I had every weekend off which was a relief. I had never worked a job where my shifts and off days were set and not variable. It was so much easier for me to plan things and such. I just wish I made the same amount of money I made while stripping.

I caressed my baby's back as I stared at the TV, not even paying attention to what was showing. My phone buzzed, and I saw *Erica* flash across the screen. I rolled my eyes, but decided to answer since I was interested to know why Elijah was calling. I did miss him a lot.

"Hello?" I answered.

"Whaaat, she answered the phone?" he laughed, which in turn made me laugh.

"Yes I did, now what do you want?" I chuckled.

"I just wanted to check on you. I hadn't spoken to or seen you in a while, and I was just wondering how you were doing?"

"I'm doing good, I guess."

"Why do you guess? I noticed you don't work at Starzz anymore; you should be happy."

"Yeah, I'm happy about that, even though I miss the money."

"Damn, it must've been good to you," he snickered.

"It definitely was. But how are you?"

"I'm doing good, about to get a promotion in a way, so I'm just getting all my duckies in a row."

"A promotion? I thought you worked in the pharmacy area," I cocked my head as if he could see me.

"I do, but there are still levels to the game, baby. I'm gon' be higher up than what I was."

"Oh damn, well congratulations even though I don't agree with that type of work."

"Thank you, and I know. Sometimes neither do I, but it's all I know. I'm gonna invest my money though."

"Oh, you're not gonna have the flashy cars, clothes, and homes?" I laughed.

"Oh, I'm gonna have a little of that here and there, but I'm gonna make sure I put my money into something that will have me getting bread even when I retire."

"That makes sense. I guess you have to make the best out of certain situations."

"That's right. What you doing?" he asked.

"I'm just watching television, why?"

"I wanna get some food. I have a taste for Chelsea Tavern, but no one to go with," he replied.

"Where is Kill? I know he is out of jail."

"He's busy working right now."

"Kantwan is busy?"

"Yeah, they're together. And I wanna go with you, not them."

"Elijah, you know I have a man and I can't go." Even though I was upset with Portland, I still couldn't entertain Elijah. I wanted to though, damn.

"I'm not asking to be your man. I'm asking you to come with me and get some food. Just think of me as Jersey or Cheyla," he chuckled and so did I.

"But even if I do, my man will not see you as Jersey or Cheyla. You know he's home now."

"I really don't care if he's home Ivy, it doesn't change the fact that I'm gonna be at your house in like fifteen minutes, so be ready."

"I have Donovan here with me," I giggled like a schoolgirl.

"That's cool, I like that little nigga anyway. He's cool people," he responded and we both laughed.

"Aight, be here in fifteen or less, or I'm not going," I stated sternly.

"Walking out of the door now."

I hung up, and then gently lifted Donovan so that I could lay him next to me. I knew I shouldn't be going out with Elijah, but I was pissed at Portland. Nigga just got out of jail and had the nerve to be ripping the streets, not coming home for multiple days at a time.

When I was younger I would let that shit slide, but now he needed to shape up or get the fuck on. I was not gonna be dealing with him going in and out of jail, fucking every bitch in Delaware, and talking to me crazy, baby daddy or not. I was done with that shit, and if he was still on it then he could just let me know now.

I stood up off the couch, and went to my closet to grab some jeans. I slipped some on, and then put on a white halter-top. I opted for some white strappy sandals, and then put a white headband on my fresh press. My golden blond locks looked vibrant since getting a clear cellophane, and it looked so much better and healthier.

Just as I unplugged my phone from the charger, I saw a text from Portland. I unlocked my phone, and then went to my texts.

***Portland:*** *Who is this?*

I jerked my neck back because I was confused as fuck.

***Me:*** *What are you talking about?*

Instead of responding, he called me.

"Portland, where the fuck have you been?" I answered.

"Who are you?" a female responded, catching me off guard like a muthafucka.

"No, who are you, and what the fuck are you doing answering my man's phone!" I hollered as my heart rate sped up.

I'm sure she saw my name stored in his phone, so she must've been playing dumb. Then again, I wouldn't be surprised if Portland didn't store me in his new shit.

"Your man? Bitch, you got me fucked up! Make this the last time you contact my nigga, aight?" she spat. I just hung up in her face, and dialed back because I had to be tripping. "Are you deaf!" she screamed when she answered. Tears were streaming my face by this time. I could not believe he was doing this shit to me again. "Hello!" she hollered.

"Who are you to Portland?" I sniffled.

"I'm his woman, I just told you that. Who are you?"

"How long have you been with him?"

"Like six months, why?" Her tone was dripping with attitude but I didn't care.

"Six months? How, when he was in jail?" I cried.

"So is my brother, and I met him when visiting my bro. Now again, who are you?" she barked. *She must've been the bitch staring a hole through Donovan and me that day I visited Portland*, I said to myself. I just pulled the phone from my face and hit the end button.

I heard a knock at the door, and it startled me. I cleaned my face, and then walked to the living room.

"Who is it?"

"Elijah."

"Elijah I can't go, umm, Donovan is sick and—"

"Why the fuck are you crying?" He cut me off.

"Elijah just go, I have to take care of my son," I yelled from behind the door, still attempting to mask my broken heart.

"I'm not leaving until you tell me why you're crying."

I bit down on my lip so that I wouldn't wail loudly. I shut my eyes, and cried soundlessly while covering my mouth. After a few moments, I took a deep breath, and then answered the door.

I looked up into his sexy face, and he searched my eyes with a sympathetic expression. His dreads were hanging loosely, and he wore a quarter sleeve button up, with some jeans that were jogger material at the top, but jeans on the bottom. They were weird but looked nice on his lean yet muscular frame. His light complexion was very luminous, and his full lips made my mouth water.

He walked in and closed the door behind himself before hugging me tightly. I couldn't hold my tears in anymore, so I just started bawling.

"You good?" he asked as he caressed the back of my head. I just hugged his torso tightly. After my tears slowed down a bit, he pulled away and wiped my face. "Please tell me you're not crying because of that nigga."

"A girl answered his phone Eli, and he's been gone with her for six days!" I sobbed.

"So what's the deal now then, Ivy? Are you gonna sit here and cry over this nigga who doesn't even have the decency to make sure his bitches don't answer the phone when you call? Or are you gonna press on, and show that nigga he's not gonna treat you any kind of way."

"I know I look stupid crying, huh?"

"Not stupid at all. I understand that you love him and you care, so of course you're gonna cry."

"I don't wanna be with him anymore," I shook my head as tears ran down my face. "I can't do this. I don't want to do this." I was still hugging his torso, and he was looking down at me. "Can I have a kiss?"

"Oh now you want a kiss because this nigga is still doing dirt?" he chuckled.

"No, I've wanted a kiss from you for a while now, but I couldn't get it. I missed you, Eli. I tried to forget about you this whole time but it didn't work. I know you probably don't like me anymore by now, but can I just get a kiss. I missed kissing you."

"Only if you come spend the night with me."

"Donovan too?"

"Yes, I'd rather him stay over you," he joked and I lightly pinched his strong back. *Damn*, I bit my lip in my mind.

"Okay, I will stay. Now kiss."

I took a deep breath, inhaling his cologne on the way, and he cupped my face before pressing his lips against mine. We graduated to lip sucking, and then soon enough it was full on tongue action. I'd been needing this for a long time, and Portland's touch just wasn't doing it. I could feel the way Elijah felt about me through his kiss, making it so much better. I was so into the lip locking, that I didn't even care if Portland decided to come home at this point. Elijah's hand moved down and squeezed my ass, making me jump and giggle.

"Let's go eat. Did you wanna make an overnight bag for the two of you?" he questioned.

"Yes, and can you help me?"

He walked to the room and helped me pack enough stuff for three days. I tried to stop him but he insisted. Once we had everything, he carried it all down to his car, while I carried Donovan. After Elijah put all of our stuff in his truck, he got Donovan's car seat from my car, and I instructed him on how to put it in, before buckling Donovan in it. He was so cute even though he had no idea what he was doing.

The three of us ate dinner at Chelsea Tavern, and the whole time Donovan wanted to sit with Elijah. I kind of felt bad, because he didn't seem to have that same attachment to his own father. Donovan was a sweet baby who didn't fuss too much when people held him, so you couldn't judge by that. I could tell when my baby liked people by how he acted while with them. If he was very smiley and playful, he liked them. When he didn't know them, he just sat in their lap staring at them. When he didn't like a person, he just sat in their lap while staring at me, silently begging me to take him.

Whenever he was with Elijah, he was always giggling loudly, and talking to him non-stop in his gibberish. I liked that Elijah talked to him as if he could understand too. When Donovan was with Portland, he just sat in his dad's lap staring into my eyes hoping I took him. And if I didn't take him in time, he would begin to cry. Portland didn't talk to him though, he would kiss him sometimes, but other than that he didn't interact with our son. Maybe that's what made the difference.

"Can we get the chicken fingers for him?" I told the waitress.

"You don't want that, right man? You want a pizza, huh?" Elijah smiled at Donovan and he chuckled before speaking in baby talk to him.

"No, the chicken fingers please," I chuckled as well and shook my head.

"He said he'll get them now since you won't let him have any fun," Elijah said making everyone laugh, including the waitress.

"You guys' baby is so cute," she said.

"Oh it's—"

"Thank you," Elijah smiled up at her. She nodded to say you're welcome, and then skipped off. "She don't have to know everything woman," he smiled.

After dinner, we went back to his place, and I laid a sleeping Donovan down on this little bed thing in his room. I was slightly upset that Portland hadn't called me or text me back, but it just further proved that he and I weren't meant, and that he didn't care about me.

"I love how good you are with Donovan," I said as I sat down on Elijah's big ass bed.

"He's a good baby though. He's easy to get along with."

He smiled at me, and then removed his shirt. His body was so fucking cut up it was ridiculous. I'd seen it plenty times before when I used to spend the night over his house, but every time was like the first time.

He slipped out of his jeans, and his dick was definitely the main event at this point. Even though he had boxers, I could see it under the cloth.

"You want a t-shirt, baby?" he asked.

"No I brought something, remember?" I smiled and stood up. I grabbed my bag and then pulled my little nightgown out. I felt him watching me, and I had no plans to leave the room.

I pushed my jeans down, and then pulled my shirt over my head. Before I could get my gown on, he scooped me up and carried me to another room. He laid me down on the bed, and rushed between my legs. We kissed passionately, as I ran my hands through his dreads, and he ran his all over my body. I'd been wanting this for way too long.

He kissed on my neck, and then pulled my panties down. He then unhooked my bra, since the clasp was in the front, and immediately began flicking his tongue over my nipples.

"Mmmm," I moaned softly and threw my head back.

He stood up, and then pushed his boxers to the floor. His dick sprang up, and stared me in the face. We got into the middle of the bed after he took a condom from his drawer. He rolled it down, and then lowered himself onto me before kissing my lips.

"Once I get inside you, it's over for you and him," he whispered before starting to suck my lips again.

I draped my arms over his shoulders, and spread my legs wider to let him know I was with that. He bit his lip and then slipped his tongue into my mouth. I was so into kissing him, and the way he was touching me, that I didn't tense up when he pressed the head of his dick at my opening. He eased into me and I almost came on contact.

Thrusting into me, he pinned my hands above my head while keeping his lips against mine. He started off slow, and then once I came, he began going in. It wasn't too much though, it felt bomb as hell.

"Aaahh, uuuh, uuuh," I called out and pressed my fingers into his back.

Although he was kissing me nonstop, I could breathe fine. He wound his hips, slamming into me but pulling out slowly. He took his lips off mine, and then trailed them to my neck, shoulders, and down my arms. He took my nipple into his mouth, and sucked hungrily without slowing up his pace.

"Fuck," he finally made a sound, and then tucked his bottom lip into his mouth.

"Ugghh!" we both called out as we released.

My body trembled, and he bear hugged me before our lips met again. I'd been dreaming of this moment for a while and I was happy it'd finally come true. As bad as this may sound, I was sort of hoping Portland messed up so I could move on to better things.

# FORTY-ONE

# Kantwan

---

*I*'d just gotten home from running errands with my brother, because he had to get a new car and shit since those officers burned it down. Kill worked hard to get that Denali, so I knew he was pissed about it. Shit I was pissed for him.

He also had to go to the doctor, because he'd loss 40% of his hearing due to that officer whacking him in the ear the night of his arrest. Just thinking about that shit infuriated me. Also the fact that these niggas got away with beating him until he passed out was ridiculous. There was no need for all that, since to my knowledge he was cooperating. Officers were drunk with power out here, and they were always running around here doing whatever the fuck they wanted to people. I shook my head at my thoughts, and turned up my beer.

I heard a car pulling into my driveway, so I slowly scooted to the edge of my couch. I listened intently, and the engine shut off. It was too loud to be out on the street, so I knew they were definitely in my driveway. *Who the fuck?* I said to myself.

I stood up and walked to the door, before pushing the curtain to the side to peep out the window of it. I saw it was Cheyla, and she was walking across my grass with her sexy ass. She wore jeans that stopped in the middle of her calf, a top with no straps, and some black Nike Roshe sneakers. Her shoulder length hair was hanging down, and it was bouncing around letting me know she'd just gotten it done. I only knew because she told me whenever her hair moved and flowed it was fresh, and when it was stiff and still it was old.

As she walked up my steps, I gripped my doorknob, waiting for her to knock or ring the doorbell. She pushed her shades up, and then looked around for the doorbell. I chuckled at her ass. I let her search for a few moments, and then pulled it open surprising her.

"Fuck you want?" I asked angrily, although I was happy as fuck to see her.

We hadn't spoken since I fucked the shit out of her in the club that night. Even though she hadn't said anything to me since, I knew I had her head gone with the way I handled her ass. I knew it'd be only a matter of time before she was dragging her sexy ass back to me. And it looked like today was that day.

"I just haven't seen you in a while, and I was wondering how you were," she shrugged one shoulder.

"I'm good."

"Oh okay, good. Umm, what have you been up to?"

"Doing me."

"Oh that's always good, I guess," she chuckled but I was stone faced. "Well me, I've been okay. I've just been working a lot, and saving my money and stuff. I haven't been getting high like before. I went down to Delaware Tech and—"

"Cheyla, what the fuck do you want?" I growled.

"I just told you I'm here to see how you're doing." She was still standing on my porch, and I was in my doorway. She wasn't coming in my house with her bullshit.

"I told you I was good, and now I know you're good. You could've texted me that."

"I wanted to see your face though," she shrugged and looked down at her feet.

"For what, woman?" I shouted. "For what? You told me you just wanted to be friends, and I've told you on countless occasions that I didn't want that. There is nothing more to say. I like you and I don't want to be your friend, sorry." She moved closer to me so that we were chest to chest. "You need to be honest about you how you feel instead of trying to play this stupid ass game with me. I know you wanna be my girl, but you're too scared so you're trying to settle for being my friend. Well I'm not accepting that so if that's what you want out of me, you can just keep it pushing."

"You really want a stripper who pops pills as your girlfriend?" She asked, now tearing up.

I stared down into her pretty face, and thumbed away the tear traveling down her smooth caramel skin.

"I want Cheyla Austin to be my girlfriend. You're more than that and I need you to see that. You won't be popping pills while you're with me, and we gon' figure something out for you so you can eventually leave Starzz behind."

She grinned, showing her perfect smile, and I kissed her cheekbone.

"You wanna work with me, huh?" she chuckled.

"I don't need a ready-made girlfriend, but you're definitely gonna have to work to make yourself better along with me, aight?"

"Okay. And it's been a week since I popped a pill by the way. And like I said, I went to Delaware Tech with—" I cut her off by thrusting my lips against hers.

"We can talk about that later, we got some making up to do."

I pulled her into my house, and closed and locked the door behind her. We kissed passionately until we made it the bedroom, where I began to remove her clothes. Once I got her naked, I pushed down my basketball shorts and boxers, then pushed her onto the bed.

"There's no going back from this, Cheyla," I stared into her eyes with a serious expression.

"I know, and I don't wanna be without you anymore. I can admit it."

# FORTY-TWO

# Jersey

---

I sat in the bathtub relaxing, wondering what the hell I was gonna do for money. I couldn't strip, and the little hundred bucks my dad threw me here and there every other month, sure wasn't gonna do it. I knew Kill said not to worry, but I just couldn't stop.

I've been taking care of myself for the last three years damn near, right after my daddy left. I never wanted to go back to the days where I had to bathe in washing detergent because I had no soap, make pads out of toilet paper, or put baking soda under my armpits because I had no deodorant. Yes, it got that bad when my dad left us high and dry.

He always footed the bill for everything, and shit I didn't expect him to stop; especially while I was only sixteen years old. My mom constantly blamed herself for not making more of her life, because she couldn't provide for us the way that she wanted to. If she had finished school instead being a full time supporter of my father's dreams, she would've been able to stand on her own two feet she said.

In a way I agreed, but I didn't blame my mother at all. She

didn't make the wrong choices because she was lazy, she made them because she loved my dad. She thought she was doing the right thing by focusing all of her attention on him and what he wanted. She never thought he would wake up one day and tell her that he didn't wanna be with her anymore. To this day, my mom couldn't give a legit reason as to why he left her. She says he never told her anything other than what he'd said to us in the study that horrible day.

I tried my best not to hate my father, because for most of my nineteen years he did take care of me and love me. The fact that he didn't call me or check on me at the least, was unlike the man that raised me. He was the most caring father in the world, and did everything for us. I just wished he would tell us why he chose to leave everything behind for Trixie. And even if it was because he didn't love my mom anymore, what about my siblings and I?

We had nothing to do with their relationship. He could've divorced my mom and kept being a father to Portland, Raleigh and I, people do it all the time. I just don't get how he could be in our lives for that long, and then just not want it anymore. I used to think he would eventually realize his mistake and come back to his senses, but here we are three years later and he's only gotten worse.

I washed my body down with some Dove liquid soap, and then got out of the tub. My stomach wasn't too big at all, but it was definitely poking out. I loved my baby, but I was worried of what was to come. One thing was for sure though, I would not make the same mistake my mother did.

Kill could be the sole provider as a man should, but I was gonna make sure that if he and I decided to part, I would be able to still live comfortably. It was good to know that he supported me going to college, graduating, and getting out into the workforce. I loved that he could me a man, but still allow me to be who I was. Believe it or not that was hard to find. Most guys were either too weak to take the lead, or too masculine to let you think for yourself.

I put my towel wrap on, and buttoned it. After I brushed my teeth and rinsed, I walked to my room so I could pick something to wear for tonight. Kill was taking me to dinner, and I was excited.

We had done everything else but go on a damn date. I guess everything was gonna continue to go backwards. It's crazy how your life never goes according to your plan or timeline.

I chose a red strapless dress, and red sandal heels to go with it. After spreading lotion all over my body, I sprayed a few spritz of perfume, and put my dress on. As I was buckling my shoe around my ankle, I heard Kill knocking on the door. I quickly finished fixing my shoe, and then walked to answer it.

"Hey beautiful," he grinned down at me and then kissed me. I backed up to let him in, and then closed the door behind him. "You look sexy as hell," he said in a low tone and pulled me close to him.

He sat on the edge of the couch, and I threw my arms over his shoulders as he rubbed up and down my back. We just stared into one another's eyes, and then I pecked him again. He was way too fine for his own good, and it was kind of bittersweet for me. It was sweet because my nigga was finer than the law allowed, but it was bitter because I knew bitches salivated every time they laid eyes on him.

I admired his smooth mocha skin, facial hair, long ass eyelashes, the tattoo that read Hilltop on his neck, the small nose stud in his left nostril, and his perfect full lips. His cologne traveled up my nose with every little move he made. His dimples appeared as he flashed his perfect smile at me.

"I'm starting to get excited about the baby," he said.

"You weren't before?"

"No, I was, but now I'm anxious to see it."

"Oh, well that won't be for months so relax," I smiled.

"I'll try." He squeezed my butt when I turned around.

"Well, let me do something to my hair and then we can go," I said and he nodded.

I walked to the back, and moved my curly hair around as I stared into my closet mirror. I decided to just pull half of it up into a ponytail, and leave the rest down. I slicked down my edges, and then walked back out into the living room.

We drove to this place called Domain Hudson, a nice little

restaurant on Washington Street in downtown Wilmington. It was a very quiet place, and it made me not want to say anything.

As the hostess walked us to our seat, there were four of five tables with businessmen sitting at them, looking like they were discussing the millions in their bank accounts.

We were seated at a booth by the window, and I was happy the space between the seat and table wasn't small. I needed room even though I wasn't even big like that. I'm sure most people didn't even think I was pregnant. Or maybe that's just how I saw it.

"You feeling okay?" Kill quizzed.

"Yes, I'm good," I nodded and smiled. "How are you feeling?"

I asked since he asked, and because I'd been wondering how things were going for him. I knew he had to meet with his boss, and I was scared for him. Portland spent many a nights telling Raleigh and I how vicious kingpins were, especially over stolen money or product. I was just glad that God had answered my prayers by keeping my baby alive.

"I'm great, I'm adjusting right now. I wanted to talk to you about some things though." He stared into my eyes and waited for me to give him the green light. I was scared of what he was about to say.

"Waters?" the waitress interrupted.

"Yes, please, and do you have flavored lemonades?" I inquired.

"Yes, we have raspberry and strawberry."

"Strawberry for us both please," I said and she nodded before prancing away.

"How did you know I wanted that?" he grinned with his fine ass.

His hair was freshly faded, and his beard and mustache were perfectly trimmed. He wore his usual get up also. He had on an army green crew neck, with the collar of his tan polo sticking out the top, and the bottom hanging out. His jeans were black, and he sported army green low top air force on his feet. He was always fresh and always smelled good as hell.

"I knew you wanted that because you said you loved the one from Qdoba. I'm sure the one here is better though," I laughed.

"Nah, Qdoba's is fire. You're tripping, baby girl," he smiled. "But I wanted to talk to you about some important shit. So I recently got a pretty big umm, let's call it a promotion. That means a lot of things are gonna change about my life."

"Like what?"

"Like where I live, how I move, and mainly the hours I put in," he answered.

"So?"

"So I'm moving out of my condo in a couple weeks to somewhere safer, and that means so are you."

"What? What about school and—"

"Jersey, we're still gonna be in Wilmington, chill. I'm just saying that we're moving in together but not in my current place."

"You didn't ask me if I wanted to move in," I half smiled.

"I don't think I need to. Let's see, you're my girl, you're having my baby, and I need to make sure you're good at all times, especially with this umm… promotion," he used air quotes when saying promotion.

"I know, I'm fine with it."

"But Jersey, you know what it is that I do, and shit gets very dangerous at times. You think you'll be down to ride with me? Or what?"

"I don't think I have a choice," I rubbed my stomach.

"Nah, you have a choice. We can co-parent and you can be free to have your own life. I don't want you to choose that, but you can." He grabbed my hands into his, and caressed the backs of them with his thumb.

"You should be able to tell from our conversations and letters, that I would always choose you Kill. But what I won't deal with is infidelity. You being who you're about to be I'm guessing, may call for that occasionally but it's either me or them."

"You ain't even got to worry about that Jersey, that's not my style at all. I like to fuck just like every other nigga, but I don't make decisions and changes in my life unless I know I'm ready for them. I agreed to take on this new job per say, because I was sure I could handle it. I'm choosing to be with you exclusively because I know I'm at a place in my life where I can handle it. And ultimatums are sexy as fuck by the way," he smiled and kissed my wrist.

"So is being faithful. For some reason I believe everything you say," I cheesed.

"That's good, that means you trust me. Trust is the most important thing in a relationship."

"It is."

FORTY-THREE

# Kilexis

---

*B*ecause I accepted Axel's offer, he wired ten million dollars to my account immediately. I was skeptical at first, but he said it was to get me back on my feet. With that money, I purchased a 1.4-million-dollar home in Centreville. It was a two-story colonial style home, with a long ass driveway, 5,000 plus square feet, and five bedrooms and bathrooms. The shit was way more than I felt I needed right now, amenity wise, but I liked the safeness of the neighborhood. And who knows, Jersey and I may end up having a bunch of babies. If we did, we wouldn't have to move.

Although I had a lot of money in my possession, I was still frugal by nature. However, you get what you pay for so I would never go the cheap route, I just didn't spend unnecessarily. I've never been the type to spend money just because. Don't get me wrong, I like nice things too, but some niggas just spent money because it was sitting there in their faces.

Axel had pulled some strings to have my record expunged, so that they wouldn't be suspicious about me making large purchases and such. This nigga was really looking out for me, but I knew it was only for the good of the empire. I wasn't tripping though, because who didn't like a new house?

Since I paid in cash, I got the keys immediately and I couldn't wait to surprise Jersey with it. I knew she would have some questions about whose name it was in and shit with her paranoid ass, so I already had plans to have it in both of ours.

From the outside looking in, I'm sure our relationship seemed like a disaster waiting to happen, but I didn't see it that way. I was really feeling her, and I had no problem with her being the mother of my child. As a matter of fact, I can't see anyone else that I would prefer being the mother to my kid.

From the first night I laid eyes on her, I wanted her, but felt I wasn't meant for a relationship. It wasn't until I got to know her over the two nights we spent together, that I started to have feelings for her. I don't know what she did to me, or what I did to her, but it was like I couldn't get her out of my mind, and she couldn't get me off of hers. I hadn't genuinely liked a woman since Margo, so it was all new to me at the time, and I didn't quite know how to react.

Even before that, I knew I really liked her ass, because I was way too damn jealous upon hearing that Tommy wanted her, when I had never even spoken to the girl. It was also a sign when my brother let me know she was coming over with her friends, and my skin started to get hot. My pride wouldn't let me pursue her back at the club prior, but I had to throw that 'play it cool' shit out the window; especially after I got the pussy.

I smiled at the thought of my girl, as I pulled into an empty space in front of Kantwan's house.

"Nigga, I know you're happy you waited to get a car," Elijah coughed, referring to my car.

I used the money given to me by Axel to get a 2016 Denali. I had a brand new Porsche truck being shipped just for Jersey too, because her Nissan Maxima was a bucket for sure. If someone hit her it would definitely fold and kill her. She hated when I said that but it was the truth.

"You should've waited to light that blunt nigga, you know you can't smoke in my car," I frowned.

Ever since I found out I was having a kid, I had come up with certain rules and regulations. One of them was that I didn't want people smoking in the car I would have my kid in. I got a Lamborghini Gallardo, and that was the car the homies could smoke in. I needed a family whip, and a homie whip.

"My bad, I forgot you got rules and shit now," Elijah laughed and ashed the blunt.

I sprayed some air freshener, while he cackled, and then we got out of the car. I took a deep breath, because what I was about to ask my brother was important, and I needed him to respond the way I wanted.

"Aye, nigga!" Elijah hollered and beat on the door's window playfully.

"Nigga, you scared the shit out of me with yo' dumb ass," Kantwan sneered and snatched the door open.

"Y'all niggas fight like an old ass married couple," I chuckled and so did they.

"I ain't know you were coming over," Kantwan looked at me as we all sat down on the couch.

"Yeah, it was a spur of the moment type of thing, but look, I need to talk to you, bro," I smiled and nudged him.

"Aww shit, what?"

"So you know about that meeting with Axel I had a few weeks ago?"

"The one I been asking you about and you kept dancing around the shit?" He looked over at me.

"Yeah, well anyway, he asked me to… well, he gave me his empire," I said and Kantwan's eyes almost popped out of his head.

"You about to be running shit?"

"Yeah, I am."

"I knew that's what it was. Kilexis Camren don't belong on the bottom," Elijah chimed in.

"Damn bro, that's great but crazy as fuck. That's some hard ass work," Kantwan said.

"It is, but I can do it."

"I know you can. I don't doubt that for a second. I couldn't though and I wouldn't."

"So that means you ain't gon' get down with me?"

"Get down, like in the drug game? Man—"

"Man nothing, you can do this shit Kant, we got the same blood running through our fucking veins," I said.

"It'll be the three of us," Elijah added.

"This shit is crazy right now," Kantwan rubbed his eyes.

"What you scared?" I frowned.

"Nah, I ain't scared nigga, the fuck? I'm just like wow, I mean what am I gonna do?"

"You gon' put in work and get paid nigga. I'm gonna have this whole muthafuckin area down here on lock," I said. Kantwan stared at me for a couple moments, and then took a deep breath.

"I guess I should put in my two weeks at Costco then, huh?" he smiled, and I yanked him into a hug. He pushed me off and we chuckled.

"Yeah you should, because I have to show you a couple things to make sure you ain't out here getting fucked off," I said. "Meet me at my new house tomorrow morning at 9am for breakfast. They're furnishing it now, and I'll be going to it tonight with Jersey. You can bring Cheyla if you like, just so Jersey has someone to chill with while we discuss things."

"Okay, text me the address," Kantwan nodded.

"Alright, now let's go because I gotta go home and get dressed," Elijah stood up.

"Get dressed for what?" I looked up at him.

"I got a little date tonight with Ivy."

"What about her nigga? Jersey's brother?" Kantwan asked.

"Oh, that's a wrap! That nigga hasn't been home for weeks, and I wish I knew where he was so I could send his ass a thank you card," he said and we all burst into laughter.

"Damn, please tell me you didn't smash," I exhaled.

"Okay, I didn't smash."

"He did," Kantwan shook his head, wearing a grin.

I just hoped this shit didn't cause any rifts in my relationship, but I knew it would. It was only a matter of time before Jersey and I got into it over Elijah, Portland, and Ivy.

## That Night...

"Kill, where are we?" Jersey asked with her jaw on the floor.

"Let's get out," I smiled and climbed out of the car. I went around to her side, opened the door, and took her hand to help her out.

"This is beautiful, and huge!"

"I know, go take a look inside," I smirked before placing the key into the palm of her hand.

"This is y-yours?"

"It's our house, baby. It's already furnished, but we can have some movers get anything you want from your place on Harrison."

"Okay," she whispered and started towards the house.

I followed behind her, and when we walked into the foyer, her mouth fell open at the twelve-foot ceilings. She spun around slowly, taking in everything around her. We headed to the kitchen, and she looked all around at the cherry wood cabinetry, and top of the line appliances that I didn't even know how to use.

"A breakfast area, Kilexis," she beamed. She used my government so she must've been excited.

"Can't we just eat breakfast in the regular kitchen?"

"Yes, but why when we have a breakfast area."

"True."

We looked through the rest of the house, and after the breakfast area, I think her favorite spot was the Nanny suite. She ran down every vision she had for the baby, and where she wanted the things that we hadn't even bought yet.

"Come here," I said and pulled her over to me.

"Thank you for this Kill, I lo- thank you."

"What were you about to say?"

"I was gonna say that I thank you, what I just said," she lied.

I scooped her up, and then carried her to the bedroom, where she plopped down on the bed wearing a pretty smile.

"You look so happy, I like seeing your face like this," I smirked as I started to undress.

"It's because of you though. If I had to live in this house with anyone else, I wouldn't be this happy. I mean maybe if it was Cheyla, but that still wouldn't be as good."

I neared her while on the bed, and her small smile faded slowly. I could tell she didn't know what was to come, and it made me chuckle. I reached down to cut the lamp off, and then stood her up. Leaning her head back, I planted a kiss on her lips as I unzipped her little dress.

"Take your hair down," I demanded as I pushed her dress down her sexy frame.

She immediately reached up and pulled her hair tie off. Her long dark curls fell down, and I put my hand in it. Gripping her hair roughly, I leaned her head back and began kissing and sucking on her neck. My hand smoothed down her stomach, and right into her lace panties. I began toying with her clit, while making my mark on her neck.

"Kill," she moaned softly.

I pushed her down onto the bed, and just stared at her. I let my eyes scan her from head to toe, trying to figure out what I wanted to do first to her fine ass. I felt like I needed more hands than I had.

I neared her, and then pulled her panties down fairly quickly. I spread her legs open, and just stared for a moment before running my tongue along the length of it. She jerked at first, but then her body relaxed. I caressed her smooth thighs, while making sure they stayed wide open. As she dripped I caught every drop, and then closed my lips around her clit.

"Mmm, shit," she pursed her lips, and then stared down at me as I feasted on her. "Oh, oh my gosh, mmmm!" she cried out and exploded.

I stood up, and then laid down on my back after removing my boxers. She crawled over to me with a lustful smile, and then took my dick into her hand. She began sucking the head of it, getting it nice and sloppy the way I liked.

"Yes Jersey," I grunted.

She gradually took my entire dick into her mouth, and seeing her lips hit the base alone, almost made me nut. I rubbed her curly hair back, as she made love to my dick with her mouth. I then gripped her hair, and pushed her off gently.

"Sit on it, baby."

She mounted my rod, and slowly made her way down it. Every time we had sex it was always like the first time. I never got tired of sticking my dick in her, and I think that was a lot of problems niggas had, even myself in the past. I could never see myself getting tired of Jersey.

"Kiiilll," she whimpered as she rocked back and forth, and bounced up and down very slowly.

I gripped her ass cheeks, and squeezed them. I licked my lips at the sight of her petite round breasts, slightly bouncing. Running my hands up her stomach, I cupped her breasts before playing with her nipples.

"Damn," I said in a low town as I felt myself nearing my peak.

Her small hand graced my chest, as her face balled up, and her thighs pressed against my ribcage.

"Uuuhhh!" she cried out as she came.

I slowly brought her onto her back, and she wrapped her arms around my neck. I placed her legs in the nooks of my arm, and then slammed into her until I filled her up.

"Nothing will ever come between us, Kill," she whispered as we made love with our mouths.

FORTY-FOUR

## Tommy

One Week Later...

*I* was sitting on the couch, bouncing my leg impatiently, as I waited for Jersey to pick up. This was the fifth time I'd called her today, and she hadn't answered yet. I tried dropping by her crib, but she was never there for some reason. I hadn't seen her car anymore either, so I was confused. Her little friend wasn't around either. I knew because I contemplated kidnapping her to get Jersey's attention. It's like they vanished from the fucking Earth.

I still didn't know if Kill was out of jail either, and Kantwan's bitch ass had been ghost too. I drove by Costco, and the manager told me Kantwan was no longer an employee. I didn't know who else to go to, so I just decided to bug Jerseys hoe ass until she picked up. For some reason though, it would only ring once and then go to voicemail.

"The number you have dialed has a mailbox that is full. Please, hang u—"

"Fuck!" I shouted and slammed my phone into the coffee table. I closed my eyes and ran my hands over my face, because I was beyond frustrated. I'd filled her voicemail up with messages, and now I couldn't leave anymore.

Something was not right with me and I could feel it. It's like my brain had some strange shit going on with it. My whole life revolved around Jersey, and I was tired of it. I could barely sleep at night because I was always wondering what the hell she was doing, and if she was doing it with Kill. The only way I would be able to go to sleep, is when I would convince myself that he was still locked up, and because I didn't know if he was or not, it worked.

Jersey had me losing my fucking mind, and I was confused on why. A part of me felt like it was because she was with Kill. The two of them had completely seized my mind.

I'd always hated him and how he thought he was better than me. For as long as I've known him I've always obsessed over him. At first it was because I wanted to be his friend. When I saw that he didn't wanna be cool with me, I became determined to be better than him. I never beat him out of anything, whether it was a video game or women, I was always coming out on bottom. He stayed winning over me, and this right here was not something I could lose out on.

As I was about to call her again, the front door opened, and Sasha walked in looking all sad and shit, like she always did these days. She needed to spruce the fuck up and quit acting like her damn life was over. Shit ain't like I was stopping her from being with another nigga. As long as she paid my way until I found someone else to, we were good.

"Pick your fucking face up!" I spat and turned my attention back to my phone. She just shook her head and sifted through the stack of mail in her hand.

"You know since I work all damn day, the least you could do is collect the mail from outside. My debit card was just sitting out there, Tommy!"

"Aye, I do fucking work, aight? Don't come up in here starting no shit with me, Sasha! I ain't in the fucking mood, and you gon' end up regretting the shit!"

She just rolled her eyes, and took her jacket off. She took a deep breath, and placed the back of her hand against her forehead. She then power walked to the back, and slammed the bathroom door.

"Stupid bitch," I mumbled to myself.

I was so tired of her annoying ass, and I needed to move on A-fucking-SAP! Only reason I hadn't was because I needed a place to stay. Robbing niggas only got me through the day and nothing more, monetary wise. Instead of worrying about Jersey's ass, I needed to be worried about how to get some more bread.

I tried getting me another Sasha, but most of these bitches were broke. And the ones who did have money were too damn smart for me to take advantage of. So for now, I just had to keep robbing old ladies to stay in the latest gear, and let Sasha pay for all of my necessities.

I was about to call Jersey again, until the sound of retching stopped me in my tracks.

"I know this bitch ain't throwing up," I said aloud to myself. I rushed to the back and burst into the bathroom to see Sasha throwing up violently. "What the fuck is wrong with you!" I screamed. She was about to speak, but puke flowed from her mouth instead.

*WHAM!*

I backhanded her and she flew back onto the floor. I straddled her, and then placed my hands on her neck.

"No!" managed to escape her lips before I cut off her oxygen with my hands.

"I told you to get rid of it, didn't I?" I twisted my lips. This baby would ruin everything I was trying to have with Jersey; I knew it. If she saw I had a baby by another woman, she would continue to chase Kill. "I can't let you ruin this for me," I said to Sasha as I squeezed her neck. "Jersey won't accept this," I added. "I love her. I love her and not you nor this baby," I finally admitted aloud.

Sasha's wild movements soon slowed down, until her limbs became limp. I loosened my grip on her neck, and then tapped her face a few times. I smiled when I realized she was dead.

"I tried to warn you," I chuckled.

I climbed off of her, and began to drag her body from the bathroom by her feet.

*BOOM!*

"Put your hands in the air!" someone shouted.

I looked over my shoulder to see three policemen standing in the living room, pointing their guns at me. I stood up straight, and slowly lifted my hands in the air.

"Sorry officers, my umm girlfriend here fainted and I'm trying to get some help," I lied. One of the officers yanked me and cuffed me immediately. "Aye, where the fuck are you taking me? I didn't do anything!" I yelled as he took me out of the house.

One of the other officers made a call while standing over Sasha's lifeless body. I was thrown into a police car, and then the other two officers came out and got into the car with me. One got in the backseat with me, and the other was in the driver's seat. He started to drive, and I knew something wasn't right.

"Where the fuck are y'all taking me? Huh? Where am I going!!!" I kept hollering and kicking the seat until I felt a needle in my neck. "Wh-where the fuck are you..." I passed out slurring like a drunkard.

▭

*M*y eyes fluttered open, and a bright light was up above me. I let out a sigh of relief at the fact that killing Sasha and getting arrested was a dream. I still didn't recognize my surroundings though.

"You awake, princess?" I heard a familiar voice ask. I shut my eyes and then opened them again. I saw Kill standing in front of me smirking. I tried to get up, but realized I was cuffed.

"Nigga, what the fuck is this! Un-cuff me! Fight me like a real man!"

He laughed at me and lit his blunt. "I've beat your ass enough times, no need to do it again. Tonight you die."

"Kill man, we're better than this!" I cried out, realizing he had the upper hand.

"Nah, we were never cool. But you setting me up was the last straw. No, wait, you constantly bugging my girl was the last straw. What the fuck is wrong with you huh? Did you honestly think you could get away with blowing her up and threatening to rape her and shit? You dumber than I thought, Tommy," he scoffed. "I always knew you were a fucking idiot, but damn, you're down right retarded my nigga."

He was pissing me off, but I didn't wanna die.

"I'm sorry man, I just got the wrong impression after she let me fuck while you were in jail," I lied. I was hoping I could turn him against Jersey.

"You're not good enough to make her open her legs Tommy, and we both know that. You couldn't get close to her pussy even if you were a fresh pair of Victoria's Secret panties. You tried and tried, and no matter what you did, none of it worked. I got the pussy before you, and I got to claim it so you nor any other nigga will *ever* get to slide up in that," he half smiled. "Did you know she was having my baby?" he asked sarcastically.

My chest heaved up and down abruptly, as I tried to contain my anger.

"She was mine first!" I couldn't help myself. "I'm tired of you winning!" I screeched.

"That's the problem we have now, she was never yours and she'll never be yours."

My head was throbbing from being tranquilized and from my shouting.

"Please Kill," I started to sob.

"Quit that fucking crying, you bitch ass nigga. Fuck niggas like you make me sick to my fucking stomach. Say hi to devil, you bitch."

I opened my mouth to speak, but he slid the gun in and popped me. All I could think about was how I still never got the pussy. If I were to be brought back to life, I wouldn't change a thing. I craved Jersey all the way up until my last breath.

FORTY-FIVE

# Cheyla

---

"This is our first night out as an official couple," I said to Kantwan as I threw my arms over his shoulders.

"I know baby, and I hope you know that you're in this shit until the end with me."

"I wouldn't have it any other way."

We moved in closer to one another, and kissed for a few moments.

These past couple of weeks have been like fucking paradise. No pill or any drug could get me higher than I was when I was with Kantwan. I think I loved him but I wanted to wait and be sure, since it felt like it was too soon. As I mentioned before, I've never had a boyfriend and I didn't want to mistake certain feelings and signs for the wrong things. As Eric Bellinger said, *if you never had nobody else, how would you know you don't want nobody else?* I wanted to spend more time in the relationship before I starting shouting out I love you's, since I had nothing to compare it to.

"Come on," Kantwan took my hand into his, and I squeezed it. He walked me to his Mustang, and then opened the door for me.

We listened to Miguel on the way to the restaurant, and I was grooving the whole way. "Do You" had become our favorite song as of late, so we always made sure to listen to it before we made it to our destination.

We pulled up to Hotel Du Pont, and I was a little surprised because I knew the restaurant inside was expensive as hell.

"Here, babe?" I questioned to be sure.

"Yeah here, you don't like the Green Room?"

"I do but that place is a bit pricey, don't you think?"

"Don't worry about that Cheyla, just get your pretty ass out the car."

I did as I was told, and when he came around to my side, we locked hands before walking towards the hotel. It was a little cold out, so I nuzzled up to him and lightly kissed his cheek.

"Look at you, and you were acting like you didn't want a boyfriend," he smiled.

He looked nice tonight in a red V-neck sweater, with a white collared shirt under, black jeans, and red, black, and white Jordan Retro 3's.

"I'm glad I came to my senses," I responded and kissed his lips as we approached the restaurant. We kissed a few more times, and then realized the hostess was waiting on us. "I'm sorry," I blushed.

"No, it's totally fine," she giggled. "How many?"

"Just two please," Kantwan answered.

The hostess nodded her head and then led us through the restaurant to an empty table. She placed menus down for us, and then told us about tonight's specials before walking off.

Before we could get a word out, a male waiter came to our table. We ordered drinks from him, and then told him we needed a minute to decide on food.

"I've always heard about this place but I have never been." I reached across the table for his strong hands. His caramel complexion was so dark and beautiful.

"I've been here once, but it was like a year ago."

"Lucky you, were you rich then?"

"Nah, I've never been rich but I have a feeling I will be pretty comfortable soon."

"I know you, Kill, and Elijah are about to come up. I do kind of wish it wasn't something so dangerous though," I sighed.

"I know, me too, but I think we will be good. I gotta ride for my brother, you know that."

"Yeah I know. That's good though, most siblings these days are rivals."

"That's true, how is your brother doing?"

"He's doing the same shit he was doing before he got locked up. I mean, I hate for anyone to do illegal shit, but he's just not smart about it. I would be more comfortable if he was cleverer about what he was doing. Like with you, Kill, and Eli, I know y'all are gonna be dotting all of your i's and crossing all of your t's, but Sonny isn't like that," I complained.

"Damn, I know how you feel baby. That's the way I see my oldest brother Ka'Shea. He's so wild and reckless. I mean Kilexis is too, but Kilexis moves smarter and smoother. I feel like when Ka'Shea gets out, he's gon' either go right back, or get himself killed."

"I think the same about Sonny. He's all I have, because you know my mother is somewhere doing God knows what."

"I guess we just have to pray for them. But Cheyla, you know no matter what, I'm gonna always have your back baby."

"I know, and I appreciate you for helping me stay clean. I was tripping at first, but I feel better."

Kantwan was not playing about me leaving the pills alone. When I first stopped, I just knew I was gonna die without them, but over time I got better. I was happy that Jersey didn't find out about my little habit, because she would've been so disappointed in me. I loved her a lot, and when she became dismayed because of me, it made me feel horrible.

"I think it's because you're out of the club," we chuckled in unison.

"I'm gonna get work real soon, I promise."

Kantwan had purchased a house in Alapocas, about fifteen minutes away from his brother. He'd kept his old house still, because he said it had sentimental value. He moved me into the new house right away, for safety reasons he said. I think he just wanted me living with him, and I wasn't gonna complain.

"Don't worry about that right now. You just enrolled for school this coming fall, and you should focus on that. I may need you down the line."

"You're supposed to always need me."

"I do need you, you know that. But I meant your mind. You know women are smarter than men."

"We are!" I laughed.

"Yeah, so focus on getting good grades and making it to a university with Jersey. Then once you graduate, you can settle into a career and take over the bills," he grinned.

"I was with you until the last part. You know I don't pay bills baby," I pouted playfully.

"So what, we gon' spend all my money while you keep your money to yourself?"

"What's wrong with that?" I quizzed and we both chuckled.

"Sorry to interrupt, but are you guys ready?" the waiter inquired.

"Yes, can I have grilled 6-ounce fillet please?" I said.

"And I will have the same," Kantwan added.

"Alright, that should be out shortly." The waiter collected the menus.

"I like this," I smiled.

"Like what?"

"This, us being together and stuff," I admitted.

"Me too, and I told your ass a long time ago you would, but you were being stubborn."

"Well I'm happy that you got my ass in gear," I cheesed.

"Anytime, that's what I'm here for."

## FORTY-SIX

## Portland

---

*I* was still at Breesha's crib in Lynford, like I had been for a while. Truthfully I was scared to go home to Ivy, because I knew she was mad as fuck about Breesha answering my fucking phone. It'd been two weeks since that happened, and I hadn't spoken to Ivy since. She called my cell a couple times, but I just couldn't answer then.

She had my mom and sisters blowing me up too, and going the fuck off on me in my voicemail. I didn't feel like dealing with none of their asses, so they never got called back either.

Today I wanted to go see her, so hopefully she had calmed down by now. I'm thinking she had, because I hadn't heard from her.

I stood up from the table after scarfing down the breakfast that Breesha had cooked me. I met her sexy ass while I was in jail. She came to visit her brother one day, and she had the fattest ass and the biggest titties I had ever seen on such a small ass girl. I just couldn't pass her up, so I didn't. Breesha was cool but definitely not someone I wanted to marry. Ivy had my son, and ultimately she was my family.

"Where you going today?" Breesha asked.

"I'm gonna go home and see what's up with my baby moms."

"Really Portland? I thought you and her were done!" she pouted.

"Nah, we not done. She has my baby, we ain't gon' never be done. You knew what was up before I was even released Breesha, so quit that bullshit."

"I'm not gon' keep doing this with you Portland, I'm not. If you go, don't come back."

"I'm coming back, and when I do you better act like you know what's up and quit bitching. I told you that was my girl, and you said it was cool to play the side. You lucky I didn't knock your ass out for answering my fucking phone, Breesha."

"Whatever, just go Portland," she sniffled and plopped down in the kitchen chair.

"Aye, chill out Breesha, you know I love you and I wanna keep you in my life. If Ivy was not in the picture, we'd probably be married or some shit," I said in a low tone and kissed her lips.

"Really?"

"Really. I love yo' ass so fucking much, but I need you to get off my back. I got with you because it was fun and it gave me a break from all the bullshit with Ivy. How the fuck you gon' turn my Utopia into a damn nightmare like that?" I smiled.

"I'm your Utopia?"

"You know you are. Now if I'm not back tonight, I will see you in the morning and take you to breakfast, baby." I kissed her temple and then her lips.

"Okay, I love you."

"I love you too, and quit crying, baby. You're too pretty for that." I thumbed her tears and then planted a kiss on her lips again.

I stood up and then grabbed my keys before heading out of the door.

I made it to Ivy's and my apartment in about thirty minutes, because the freeway was packed wall to wall like it always fucking is. They needed to build a new fucking freeway for muthafuckas to use, because that shit was ridiculous.

I jogged up the three stairs to our door, and when I stuck my key in, it wouldn't turn. I pulled it out and made sure I was using the right one, before pushing it back in. I twisted it side to side and it wouldn't move. I twisted harder and the shit just bent.

*BAM! BAM! BAM!*

I beat on the door while trying to get my fucked up key out of the door.

"Ivy!" I shouted.

I finally heard the locks twisting, and the door came open. Ivy was standing there in some little shorts, and some kind of bra top. Her golden blond locks were pulled into a ponytail, and her blue eyes and light skin were vibrant as fuck. Damn, my bitch was bad.

"Can I help you?" she raised a brow and poked her hip out.

"Yeah, what the fuck is wrong with this lock? I broke my damn key!" I frowned as I inspected the key. I slipped into the apartment past her, and saw a whole bunch of black trash bags in the living room.

"Nothing is wrong with the locks Portland, I had them changed," she said before picking our son Donovan up, and sitting him in her lap.

"Oh, give me a key so I can have it copied."

"No, you're moving out," she pointed to the bags.

"Moving out? What the fuck is you talking about? This is my muthafuckin' crib!" I barked.

I didn't know what the hell she was yapping about, but I was not in the mood for her bullshit. I came home hoping to make up and get some pussy before hitting the streets.

"No, we put it in *my* name, remember? I need for you to get your shit that I so nicely packed for you, and take your ass back to that bitch you had answering your phone," she replied calmly.

"Ivy, it ain't what you think. Okay, yeah I fucked around but you lied to me. You told me all this shit about retail jobs when you were really out shaking your ass!"

"Portland, please. Don't try to use that as an excuse because after you found out, we talked and you were good. Try again, nigga," she waved me off and adjusted Donovan in her lap.

"So what you saying, huh?"

"I'm saying get your shit and get the fuck out. I'm done. I can't do this shit with you anymore. I tried, I really did because I loved you and because of our baby, but I have to put myself before you sometimes, and that's what I'm doing," she said as a tear rolled down her smooth vanilla cheek.

"Ivy, baby, that girl don't mean nothing to me. What you want me to do? I will never hurt you again baby, I promise," I knelt down in front of her and begged as more tears rushed down her face.

"No Portland, how many times have you promised not to cheat on me, huh? This is the seventh damn time that you've fucked around on me and I cannot do it anymore! This breakup is long overdue! And that bitch sure meant enough to you for you to be laid up with her for weeks, not even calling about your son!" she spat and wiped her wet face.

"Ivy, baby—"

"Get out, Portland! I'm done! Look in my eyes, understand that this is it. Please get your bags and go back wherever you were these past few weeks. I'm tired, I'm drained, and this relationship is not what I want anymore."

"Oh, so you don't love me? I forgave you for shaking your ass for money while I was locked up, but you can't forgive me for the way I chose to deal with my anger?" I scoffed and nodded.

"I shook my ass for money to make a living, that little money you had delivered to me monthly wasn't doing what I needed, and I'll be damned if my son goes hungry just to feed your fucking ego. Yes, I stripped and showed my body to niggas for cash. Get over it!"

"You were probably fucking for cash too."

"Don't even worry about what I did because you and I are over."

"You got another nigga, Ivy?" I sneered. She didn't respond, she just refused to make eye contact with me. "You let another nigga get my shit?" I barked again. No response. I couldn't help myself, I backhanded her so hard I thought her neck would snap. "You better not have fucked nobody else while I was gone," I gritted.

Blood dripped from her lip, and she promptly got up to go take Donovan to his room. A few moments later, she emerged from his room, with blood still dripping from her face.

"You need to go before I call your parole officer," she dabbed her lip that was leaking.

"Oh damn, like that? Fuck you, Ivy."

"Perfect, now please go," she began to sob.

I loved this girl despite all the shit I've done over the years. I cheated on her constantly, but I was a man and that's what we did. It shouldn't matter what I'm out there doing, as long as I'm not spending money on them hoes. I mean Breesha was someone I *did* love, but Ivy was the main and she needed to appreciate her spot.

"Baby—"

"Go, Portland! Just go! Damn! It is over! I don't want to be with you anymore!" she pointed to the door, crying hysterically.

"I'll be back to check on y'all next week." I shook my head, grabbed as many bags as I could, and then left back to Breesha's.

Ivy couldn't do shit without me, but while she thought she could, I was gonna live it up with my other bitch; make her 'wanna be strong now' ass miss me. I needed to look into who she was probably fucking, because me and that nigga were gonna have problems. But first, I wanted to cop some smoke from that Elijah cat. He had some straight fire.

# FORTY-SEVEN

# Kilexis

---

"I love this house, and this bed!" Jersey beamed and hugged one of the pillows.

I was starting to love waking up next to her ass every morning. I loved seeing the smile on her face, and checking to see if her belly had grown.

"Come here," I pulled her closer to me. I pressed my lips against her soft ones, and caressed her belly. She was four months now, but she still looked small. "You are so sexy," I said in a low tone, making her smile.

"Are you just saying that because I'm fat?"

"No I'm not, I really think that. You know I don't say shit I don't feel, ever. I honestly think you look sexy, especially when that hair is all over your head like that."

I roughed her hair up and she nudged me back. I sat up, and then stood to my feet to stretch.

"What are you doing today?" she asked.

"I'm just gonna run some errands and stuff, why you're gonna miss me?" I bit my lip.

"Yeah, I am. You know I get paranoid when you leave me," she half smiled.

"Why?"

"I don't want you to ever go away again, like when you got locked up. We need you here."

"I ain't never getting locked up again, I can promise you that."

"Don't make promises you can't keep."

"I never make promises I can't keep and you know that. I promised you that I'm gonna always be here for you, protect you, be good to you, and most importantly be honest."

"I know." She stood on her knees and let the sheet fall off of her naked body.

"Now I'm gonna need some of that before I get my day started," I licked my lips.

I pushed my boxers down, and then climbed back onto the bed. She draped her arms over my shoulders, and I lifted her up before bringing her down onto my dick.

"Damn," I mumbled because she was soaking like a muthafucka already.

"Uuuh, uuuh, aaah," she cried out as I moved her up and down slowly.

She frowned her face every time she hit the base of my dick, and she looked so pretty. I loved seeing her sex faces. I stared deeply into her eyes, as I stroked her insides with long smooth pumps.

"Kilexis, shit," she whimpered and ran her tongue across her top lip.

I pecked her lightly, but made sure not to interrupt my sequence. I started moving in a circular motion, still nice and slow, and she bit down on her lip so hard I thought blood would spill from it.

"Right there, oh my gosh!"

She threw her head back, and then brought it back up for me to suck her full lips. Her small nose wrinkled, and her body jerked as she gushed on me.

"Fuck," I grumbled and gripped her tighter. She adjusted her forearm around my neck, and when I made sure she was secure in my grasp, I began tearing it up.

"Oh, oh my gosh uuuh, uuuh, uuuh!" she yelled as I beat her shit out of the frame.

As soon as I felt her juices spill, I burst all inside of her. She trembled a little, and I delivered a few more slow thrusts. I finally slid her off of my dick, and then laid her down on the bed.

"I love you, Jersey," I said before planting a passionate kiss on her lips.

"You do?" She caressed my face.

"I do."

"I love you too, Kill."

After kissing her for a cool minute, I got up and went to take a shower. Once I was clean and dressed, I dipped out because I needed to check out this office building in Greenville. It was an area I wanted to use for meetings and such, because going to restaurants and shit was not safe. The place would cost me $300,000, but it was a small fee for a great investment in my book. There was no way I was gonna be holding meetings in my crib like Axel used to.

I made it to the building I was interested in, and I spotted the realtor standing outside of her Bentley in a heated conversation. I got out of my car, and then approached her slowly, not knowing if she needed a minute or two. I wasn't gonna let her take too long though, because time was money 'round here.

"Rick, Rick I have to go. Okay yes, I love you too babe, goodbye," she jammed her finger into her iPhone screen to hang it up, and then looked up at me smiling.

"Mr. Camren?" she questioned with a surprised expression, and then let her blue eyes scan my frame.

"Yes, nice to meet you Evie."

"Likewise," she licked her lips. "I'm sorry, I just didn't expect to be speaking to someone like... you."

"Someone like me?" I cocked my head, furrowed my brows, and slipped my hands into the pockets of my Gucci slacks.

"I don't mean to be forward, but someone so sexy. How old are you if you don't mind me asking?"

*Didn't she just tell Rick she loved him? Damn, hoes came in all kinds of tax brackets.*

"I'm twenty-two."

Evie had long dark hair, full lips, and ice blue eyes. She put me in the mind of Angelina Jolie, except she was way thicker. I wasn't too sure of her race, but she wasn't black.

"Nice, well if you will please follow me, I can show you around," she ran her tongue over her teeth.

I followed her into the building, and she showed me every nook and cranny of it. She made sure to bend over unnecessarily, and spend a lot of time explaining every detail of the place. Every time she would check to see if I was looking at her ass while bending over, I would pretend to be captivated by something in the other direction.

"Well, what do you think Mr. Camren?"

"I like it. You said it's three hundred G's?"

"G's?"

"Grand, you said it was three hundred grand?"

"Oh," she chuckled. "Yes, it's three hundred grand, Mr. Camren. I don't really know too much thug lingo."

"I see that."

"Maybe you could teach me a little," she ran her pointing finger down my arm, but before she could trail it any further, I gently removed her hand.

"I'll call you if I decide to purchase. Thanks."

"Oh, umm, okay. Please don't forget, Mr. Camren!" she called after me. I just put my hand up to say I'd heard her and okay.

After leaving the realtor, I ran into Margo coming out of a coffee shop with her son Gregory. Why was she even over here? Maybe one of her sugar daddies lived nearby.

"Kill! What the fuck!" she yelled, stopping me in my tracks.

"What's up?" I stuffed my hands into my pockets.

"Where have you been, baby? I heard you got out and I've been calling you for the longest with no answer," she said, and her voice trembled like she was about to cry.

"I've been busy," I replied and smiled at her son Gregory.

"Busy? Busy working or with a bitch?" she turned her lip up.

"Don't really matter Margo, what you want? I have shit to do."

"I want to talk and shit. I'm serious about us, Kill," she whined.

"How long are you gonna make me suffer while you mess around with other women! I'm losing my mind!"

"Oh, is that right?" I asked and then squinted my eyes because the sun was in them.

"Yeah, it is. While you were in jail, I was miserable."

"Oh yeah, when I got out, I saw how miserable you were kissing some dude in the parking lot of McDonald's," I grinned. I chuckled because her jaw almost hit the floor.

"Kill, he was just a friend helping me out, and I was only being nice be—"

"Save it," I put my hand up.

"Even if I didn't see you out with him, we would never be. We've been a wrap since you found yourself pregnant with him, and we will never go back to what we had."

"You won't even try!"

"You damn right I won't! You don't deserve for me to try! I been over you and this relationship for years Margo, and you need to follow in my footsteps."

"You're a piece of shit, Kilexis Camren. You know I love you and what I did was a mistake, yet you won't forgive me!" she sobbed.

"Get a grip, Margo." I shook my head and walked off in the direction of my car.

There was no need to mention Jersey, because like I said, Margo and I would never communicate again. Plus, that would start drama that was totally unnecessary. She needed to just kick rocks for real.

FORTY-EIGHT

# Elijah

---

*I*vy and I were leaving Penn Cinema on Madison Street. We'd just come from seeing that movie with Cassie, because that's what she chose. I didn't mind paying to see it because it was a primarily black cast which will always get my money. And I just wanted to spend time with her.

"Did you enjoy the movie?" I asked her.

"Yeah, I did," she replied somberly.

She told me everything that went down the day she put her baby daddy out, and although I was happy she was really done, I felt bad because I could see that she was hurt. I just wished that she would let me beat the niggas ass for putting his hands on her. She begged me not to because it would cause a rift with Jersey and shit. I agreed so I left it alone, for now. If he hits me for some weed again, I may just knock his ass out then.

"What's wrong, Ivy?" I quizzed.

"You should've seen Portland's mother's face when I dropped Donovan off to her. She was so disappointed in me for going on a date."

"So what, how is she gonna look at you sideways when her son is the one damn near living with another girl," I frowned at my words.

287

I didn't know Portland's mom, but if she should be disappointed in anybody it should be her son. He treated Ivy like she had a damn tail, and for someone to encourage her to stay, they had to be crazy.

"Jersey and Raleigh said they weren't surprised that I'd finally left Portland, and that they couldn't be mad at me, so that made me feel a little better."

"Well that's good. At least some people see the light."

"Yeah," she chuckled.

We made it to the parking lot, and I hit my alarm before opening the door for Ivy. Once I got in on my side, I blasted the heat and pulled out of the park.

"You're right though, I shouldn't feel guilty for coming out with you Eli. I shouldn't feel guilty for liking you either," she sighed and looked out of the window.

"Nah you shouldn't, and to be honest baby, you should've been moved on. I'm all for forgiveness and giving chances, but after a while you have to realize that this person is not gonna be what you need them to be," I explained.

"I know. I get that now. I just wanted to wait it out because I knew Portland could be a great guy."

"I'm sure he probably can, but you shouldn't have to deal with all his bullshit until he decides to grow the fuck up."

"I agree. You know you're the first guy to ever get my attention since I met him," she said as I pulled into the parking lot of Joe's Crab Shack. It was a seafood shack right around the corner from the theater.

"Oh yeah? Well I'm flattered." I put the car in park, and then shut the engine off. "So what does that mean, Ivy?" I turned to face her.

"It means that I want to see where this goes with you."

"See where it goes for real and no bullshit, right?"

"No bullshit at all. I really like you Eli, and I have for longer than I should have."

I was happy to hear that, but I was still gonna make sure she didn't have any strong feelings for Portland. I knew her love for him wouldn't be gon' just like that, but I was willing to work with her as long as she was finished forever. I've never been no sucker ass nigga though, so she damn sure wasn't about to play me.

"I've wanted your little ass for longer than I should have too."

I grabbed her hand and kissed the back of it. I leaned closer to her face, and when our lips touched, my dick immediately got hard. After sucking face for a couple moments, I pulled away to contain myself. Although I'd been fucking her non-stop, I still got excited just from the slightest touch.

"Damn, come on before I try and bend your ass over in the backseat," I chuckled and so did she.

We got out of the car, and I waited for her to make it to me before taking her hand into mine. I had a feeling Portland wasn't gonna let her go so easy, and that was fine with me. Bring it on nigga.

FORTY-NINE

# Jersey

"Make sure you do smooth strokes, Cheyla," I said to my best friend as she painted my toenails.

"Look bitch, you need to take your ass to the nail shop," she sucked her teeth.

"I haven't found one that I like in this area yet, so you're my best bet. If I could do it myself I would, but my belly is kind of in the way," I giggled. My belly wasn't big enough to be in the way, I just didn't feel like painting.

"Yeah, yeah, yeah, stay your ass off Yelp and just pick a fucking nail shop, because this is the last time I'm gonna help your ass with these stinky ass feet."

"My feet do not stink, bitch!" We laughed in unison.

"There, done." She fanned my toes with her hand, and then blew a little cold air onto them.

"Thank you best friend," I smiled and she rolled her eyes.

"You hungry? Let's find somewhere to eat over here, even though I know it's gonna be expensive as hell," she said.

"Okay, look some places up while my feet dry."

While Cheyla looked some places up, my phone started to ring. I looked down at the caller ID, and saw it was from my older sister Raleigh.

"Hello?"

"Jersey, get over to Dad's house right now!" she shouted.

"What happened?" I stood up and Cheyla's eyes followed me.

"Just please come, oh my gosh!" she yelled and cried.

"Okay." Thank God I now lived near where my dad was. "Cheyla, take me to my Dad's please."

"What happened, Jersey?"

"I don't know but come on." I pulled her up.

We left the home I shared with Kill, and then hopped into Cheyla's car. She sped to my Dad's house like a bat out of hell, and when I got there it was about four police cars and two ambulance trucks. My heart began beating fast, wondering what the hell was going on. I climbed out of the car as fast as I could, and rushed up the small incline.

"Raleigh, what happened?" I hollered when I spotted my sister. She was crying hysterically, and so were Hannah and Trixie, as two men appeared to be talking to them.

"What is going on!" I screamed to no one in particular. I then saw a policeman walk out with my mom in handcuffs. She had blood all over her clothes, and on the bottom of her chin. "Mom, what happened? Are you okay?"

"Jersey, I love you baby, and tell your brother I love him too. I just couldn't take it anymore," she sobbed.

"Ma, what are you talking about?"

I started to cry seeing them put her into the back of the police car. I was so confused and no one would tell me anything. Why is my fucking mother covered in blood and being arrested? All I could hear were policemen talking, Raleigh crying, and Cheyla trying to find out what was going on like me.

I looked towards the entrance of the Thouse, and saw E.M.T.'s wheeling a body out of the house. I rushed over to them, causing them to stop in their tracks.

"Please let me see," I begged. "This is my father's house."

They didn't say a word, so I took the opportunity to unzip the top of the bag. Raleigh and I made eye contact, before I slowly pulled the zipper down. I didn't even make it past my father's fore-head before I fainted, falling face forward to the ground.

# Become a VIP Reader!

_To join my mailing list text **SHVONNE** to **66866** and stay up to date! Also, join **Shvonne Latrice Reading Group** on Facebook!_